SLAVES OF HYPERION

MICHAEL G. THOMAS

First published in the United Kingdom in 2012 by Swordworks Books.

ISBN 978-1-906512-31-6

Typeset by Swordworks Books
Printed and bound in the UK & US
A catalogue record of this book is available from the British Library

Cover design by Swordworks Books
www.swordworks.co.uk

SLAVES OF HYPERION

MICHAEL G. THOMAS

CHAPTER ONE

The mineral rich jungle world of Hyperion was never fully colonised prior to the forming of the Alliance. Its great continents were abundant with wildlife, and it was frequently assailed by mighty storms that flooded entire islands. Few lived there before the Uprising and even fewer afterwards. It was the final stages of the Great Uprising that saw the Echidna Union commit one of its most heinous of crimes, the firebombing of the only major city, New Stanley.

The downfall of Hyperion

Spartan glanced down at his datapad and examined the face of their target, for what must have been the hundredth time. Chraige Attez was a major player in the Kerberos underground, and according to his file; in the last six months his group had been responsible for the capture and execution of at least ten officers in the new

5

Alliance. If the file was to be believed, he had been a close associate of Typhon and the Zealots that had done so much to bring death and destruction to the Confederacy. It was much more than that though, this man could be traced right back to the bombings on Prime prior to the War. There was a good chance he was part of the ring that called themselves brothers and included Typhon as their number. Video evidence placed him at the scene of the infamous barracks bombing in which nearly three hundred marines had been murdered. This man wasn't just a terrorist; he was one of the faces of the enemy that had been the catalyst to the entire Uprising. The War may now be long over, but there were still plenty of sympathisers and collaborators that needed to be brought to justice.

"We're passed the last tracking station, and from here in, we're low and fast!" said the pilot over the helmet-mounted communication systems worn by all those on board. Spartan thought back to the briefing prior to the start of the mission, the words of the Major Daniels, the commander of Alpha Squadron, Alliance Special Operations Group, still echoing in his head.

No mistakes, it has taken two years to finally track him down. If you find him, you'll kill or capture him. Don't come back without his head on a platter.

It was a simple brief, and Spartan could hardly disagree with his commander's sentiments, a man like Chraige Attez had no place in civilised society. The man had chosen this path himself, and Spartan would see to it that his life took a completely different path from this day onwards. He would no longer have the chance to spread his messages of hate and violence to the citizens of the fledgling Alliance.

"Hey, Spartan!" came a familiar female voice. He turned to see Teresa, his dark-haired Hispanic partner and now mother to their first child. Most expected her to leave after the birth of their son, but she had left him with her grandparents on Carthago. Marines with experience like her and Spartan were in great demand, and she wasn't going to be held back by a child. Not that either of them had much of a choice. With the victory at Terra Nova had come the end of the War and the dissolution of the Confederacy. The birth of the new Alliance had put great demands on the soldiers still left, and although they had both tried, neither had been given permission to forfeit their commissions in the Marine Corps. He remembered the choice they had been given, either they found somebody to look after the child, or they would have to put him up for adoption in the state sanctioned department. If he quit, then he would still be sent back to prison, even after all he had done for the Confederacy. Spartan had been furious, but they had talked about it, and Teresa's grandparents had been adamant at playing a major part in this. Spartan was privately happy at the whole affair; he got his family but on his own terms, and where it fitted around what he and Teresa were doing.

Once the boy was a little older, he told himself that things would change, but for now the Alliance needed him more, and the grandparents on Carthago could do a much better job than him. There were things he would want to teach the boy, how to fight, how to lead and how to do a great many things. That day would come.

"Yeah?" he replied through his throat mic as he turned his mind back on the mission and away from his new family.

"The new satellite scans are in, look," she said and handed over her own device that showed a live feed of their target. It was at night, but the thermal imaging clearly showed the position of the guards as well as a local police headquarters just a kilometre away. The site was an old police station that according to their intelligence was now being used by Chraige Attez and his family. It was tempting to simply bomb the place, but they had to be sure. News reports of random Alliance bombings of civilians would cause uproar if they got it wrong. Anything less subtle than a Special Forces raid, and the man would melt away, just as he had done for years.

"You sure we shouldn't have told them we are coming in? I don't think the local security force will be happy to learn we're dropping in on their jurisdiction."

Spartan shook his head.

"No way, you saw what happened two weeks ago. There are too many moles. This is no minor raid. Chraige Attez is one of the biggest players we know of with the Zealots. We wouldn't even know about him if we hadn't come down hard on the groups on Terra Nova. Each operation leads us further up the ladder and tells us more about them. A year ago, we knew almost nothing about them, just their demands and the fact that they seemed to hate anything about us. No, we get him, learn what he knows, and then use that to find whoever is left in the movement. We do that, and we can apologise for the intrusion later."

He looked out of the window and could just make out the dull black shapes of the other three Cobra light aircraft crewed by the 27th Special Tactics Squadron. The unit had been formed at the same time as Spartan's new unit for just these kinds of operations. The Cobra was much smaller than the craft he usually operated with but was ideal for special operations. Shaped like a large bug, they were equipped with four rotating engines that allowed the machine to take off and land vertically. On the small stubby wings fitted to each side were dual-linked servo controlled L48 rifles as well as Hydra unguided rockets. The Cobra aircraft was short-ranged and could only carry a maximum of eight passengers, but this was more than enough for this kind of mission. He could see the two pilots at the front of the craft from where he was strapped in, and both wore helmet-mounted night vision gear. The inside of the craft was only very lightly lit with a dull red glow; it was as though the craft was switched off. The co-pilot looked over his shoulder.

"Lieutenant, we're three-minutes out," he stated simply.

Spartan nodded to the man and turned back in his chair to look at the others. Sergeant Morato was his next in command, and the other six were all experienced men and women, a mixture of police, soldiers and marines that had trained together for months. His old unit was being rebuilt following heavy losses and damage in the War. For now these ad hoc special units had been created to tie up the many loose ends remaining since the Union surrender. Spartan wished for a moment that he had the people he had worked with back on Terra Nova, especially Gun and Khan, his two Biomech friends in the Jötnar. Still, perhaps their brand of violence wasn't ideal for this mission. He grinned to himself as he imagined what the two giants would do upon arriving at this compound. They were just as likely to bring down half the structure, as they were to actually capture Chraige Attez.

It's time! He tapped his throat mic, making sure it was active.

"Lieutenant Spartan here, the mission is a go. Remember, we go in hard and fast, and we're after one prisoner. Anybody else that gets in our way is collateral damage. Either bind them or shoot them, and then move on. We do not have the time to take anybody else back with us. Good hunting!"

He glanced back to Teresa who was already lifting her

visor so that she was completely enclosed. Each warrior in the Cobra was wearing the thickly armoured, but tight fighting Personal Defence Suits worn by all Confederate Marine Corps personnel. The PDS allowed them to operate in space or even underwater and contained their own air supplies, filtration and basic medical aid features. Unlike the gear he had worn though, their equipment was black, and they wore no insignia of any kind. His main weapon was his small calibre, triple barrelled XL52 Mk II assault rifle, one of the newest and most modern weapons in the Confederate arsenal. Large stocks had been recovered on Terra Nova, and all Special Forces and elite military units were being equipped with them.

"Sir, we are on final approach, sixty-seconds!" called out the co-pilot.

Spartan nodded at him and looked around once more at his team. They knew the plan and were all ready for what had to be done. He looked down to his XL52 rifle and checked the setting one last time. He'd spent some time on the range with the new weapon, but this was its first use with his unit. Unlike the L48 rifles they normally used, these weapons were actually miniaturised projectile accelerators that had multiple coils used as electromagnets in the configuration of a synchronous linear motor to accelerate magnetic projectile to ultra-high velocities. A selector on the side of the weapon allowed the firer to select two different power levels, a rapid firing low power mode and a single shot high-power mode that used the full power capacity of the weapon. A quick twist of the muzzle would activate the silent mode, a new modification on the Mark II that kept the projectile subsonic for covert operations. This selectable power made the weapon perfect for special operations forces where firepower was always at a premium. At least that's what they had been told. Spartan pulled down his visor like the rest of his unit and checked the details on the head-up display (HUD). The health indicators for each of his fighters were in the safe zone, and they were all ready for the raid.

"Remember, no prisoners. We're on the clock with this one."

The Cobra shook slightly as the engines swivelled to feather the landing. They were coming in fast and needed to make sure they didn't slow down until the very last second. Too slow, and they would be heard, making the operation even more dangerous for the team. Too fast, and they could crash or overshoot the target area.

"Ten seconds!" called the co-pilot, and at the same time he hit the red light in the crew area. It was the signal that they would be landing. Each of the warriors did a quick final check of their gear and braced themselves for the landing, thirty-two elite commandos, heavily armoured and carrying the best weapons in the Alliance. He spotted a yellow flash outside, but before he could respond, they were already on the ground. The side doors slid sideways, and he was out. His feet hit the firm ground, but he was ten metres away before he spotted the fire. It was the first Cobra that was tasked with dropping its team directly onto the roof.

"Keep moving!" he cried and pushed on until reaching the outer perimeter wall. When in cover, he looked back at the crashed cobra and was relieved to see all eight members of the team moving towards him. The last two cobras came in fast and disgorged their own forces alongside the next wall about a hundred metres further along the compound.

"Status?" he asked, but it was superfluous. No sooner had he asked the question than he could already see their positions on his HUD. It was fast, quick to read and immediately told him the unit was in position.

"Okay, plan B, we go through the walls. Proceed as planned," he stated clearly.

Like a well-oiled machine, two of the men attached devices to the wall. It took just seconds, and they backed off, turning from the wall.

"Fire in the hole!" shouted the one and with no further warning, a chunk of masonry was blown apart. The hole was at least three metres wide, plenty big enough for them to enter. Spartan stepped through first, and the rest of the two squads followed him. A number of floodlights filled the outer sections with a dull orange glow, and the building in the middle was lit from several internal lights. Dusts and debris filled the air, and for a second Spartan almost lost his way. He connected to the recons that were situated almost three kilometres away near the main powerplant replay station for the area.

"Cut the power, now!"

It took less than five seconds for every light in the compound to cut out as well as every structure, streetlight and power coupling in the block. With the lighting gone, the entire compound was now almost totally black. The team inched forward, their dark armoured suits melting them into their surroundings. They spread out with Spartan and his squad heading for the main door while the others moved to their own targets. As he moved forward, he quickly communicated with the pilot of the downed Cobra.

"What happened? Casualties?" he asked.

There was a short pause from the pilot before he replied.

"Mechanical failure, no casualties, Sir. She's set for detonation when we hit the air. I've already stripped the data and communication core."

Spartan nodded to himself at the quick and precise information. It was an unfortunate loss and meant the second squad was now unable to assault via the roof of the compound. Still, the teams had been practicing this operation for weeks, and the loss of a single squad wouldn't stop their mission. When they left the site, they would trigger the charges and destroy the crippled Cobra in its entirety. Nothing but charred metal and burnt out components would remain.

"Transfer your gear to Cobra Three and provide extraction fire support."

"Sir!" came back the reply.

He looked to the door that was now just a few metres away. It looked almost identical to the one they had worked on back in the mock-up of the compound erected on board the ANS Santa Cruz. The old warhorse had plenty of space for their training now that so few people were stationed there. It was odd compared to her days of carrying thousands of marines. He looked back to the barrier now facing them. The hinges and bolts were hidden from view by the close fitting metal outer skin; it was designed for security and had been reinforced recently. He lifted his hand to give the signal but spotted movement on one of the higher levels. His instinct told him of the danger, and he sidestepped just as a burst of gunfire ripped through the courtyard. The soldier behind him took three rounds in his chest armour and stumbled back, hitting the ground. He watched him fall and then looked up in the direction of the attacker.

Bastard!

Spartan lifted his rifle and took aim through the holographic sight to the enemy watching down to the courtyard. With the target in clear view, he pulled the trigger. With an almost silent whoosh the firearm sent a surge of power through the coils and accelerated a single metal slug to just below the speed of sound. It struck the man in the forehead and sent him flying back into the room he occupied. The gun itself was completely silent, and only the crack made by the projectile crashing through the air made any sound at all. Two more rounds were sat in the two other barrels, ready to be released at any moment. He looked back to the fallen man only to see one of his corporals lifting him to his feet. He nodded to Spartan.

"He's okay, the armour did its job."

Spartan smiled inwardly. The armour was good equipment, but the thought of losing these well-trained individuals was always a heavy burden to him. They hadn't even penetrated the main building, let alone spotted their hated enemy. Losing a man so early would be a heavy price for the mission. They were interrupted by an almost elated message from Sergeant Yobun.

"Sir, we're in!" he called out over the communications unit. The commander of the Third Troop was on the other side of the compound and performing the same mission as Spartan's team. Just seconds later, and Spartan could already see ammunition expenditure on his HUD. It meant they were in combat and firing their weapons.

Third Troop is in action already. Come on, we need to get in the fight, or they'll be on their own!

He turned to Corporal Lina Sovana to encourage her

to speed up, but she was already on the door and placing charges at key points. It was fast work, and Spartan allowed himself a moment's pleasure at the skill and precision exhibited by his team. Most had come straight from the Marine Corps like himself, but some, such as Corporal Sovana, were from the police Anti Terror Units; the elite tactical teams used to bust drug dealers and stamp down on organised crime. She looked to him, nodded and then stepped back.

"Blow it!" he ordered.

With a simple tap on the detonator device on her suit, the series of three charges ripped chunks from the wall. Spartan pushed forward to find their way still blocked by the scorched but still standing door. Through the holes he could see there was another layer of armour behind the first section. He looked back to the young woman.

"It's still up, Corporal. Bring down the wall!"

She needed no further encouragement and took up position along the wall just a few metres away. It was a procedure they had tested already in case of such an eventuality. There was always a chance the entry points would be reinforced, and there might even be deliberate diversions from the main ways inside. Corporal Sovana placed a new series of shaped charges and double-checked them before again stepping back. She looked to Spartan who gave her the nod.

"Fire in the hole!"

There was a mighty flash that the suit's visor instantly deadened, much like the way a welding mask might react to the arc of a welding torch. His thermal imaging picked out the signatures of two figures, both on the floor but already standing. One was carrying a weapon of some kind, which was all he needed to know. He stepped inside the breach and fired two short bursts at each figure. The triple-barrels fired one after the other, allowing a high rate of fire yet giving the weapon time to load the chambers, a round to the head and a round to the chest, just as he had practiced so many times before. It was classic double tapping, and then he was past them and inside the lower level of the old police compound. The first eight fighters of First Troop moved in behind him while the second team set up a perimeter in case anybody tried to escape. They frequently practiced working with the troop of sixteen so that they could operate as one unit or break down to smaller groups of either eight or four. It gave them the flexibility to operate in all kinds of situations.

"Stay frosty people, we have reports of up to a dozen tangos in here. Watch for wires and traps. I don't want to lose any one today."

"Sir!" called Sgt Seven Troky from outside the building, "We're picking up movement at the militia barracks. Looks like somebody spotted the explosions."

Spartan checked the overhead view from their circling reconnaissance drone. The barracks was far enough away that he reckoned they had at least ten, maybe fifteen minutes before they might be found. The wrecked Cobra was no longer burning and not obvious from the ground. He spotted the shapes of the other three Cobras as they took off and moved away. While they were on the ground, they were vulnerable to gunfire. They had another way out, and there was also the assumption they would need a larger vehicle to extract prisoners and potentially wounded.

"Update me on their progress," he ordered and continued his approach to the main staircase on the left wing of the building. At the bottom he waited for the rest of his unit to catch up and did another quick check on the aerial view, still no change. He scanned every possible hiding place while keeping his rifle up to his shoulder. His HUD overlaid the information from his firearm, as well as integrating infrared and thermal imaging to create a visual feed, that gave him a major edge over the enemy. The infrared gave him a monochromatic view of the interior while the thermal imaging showed him heat sources.

"Ground floor clear, moving up!" called out Sergeant Yobun.

Sergeant Morato tapped Spartan's shoulder. It was a simple signal, but that was all he needed to take the corner. He moved to the far left, his rifle pointing directly up the stairs and in the expected direction of the enemy. Teresa moved to his right and the others behind them in two short columns, as they had rehearsed so many times before.

"Stun grenade!" called Teresa.

On cue, a hexagonal stun grenade sailed passed them all and to the next level. It was smaller than the equipment used by conventional ground forces and designed to operate on impact. It took skill and timing to use it correctly and could be as much a danger to the team as it was to the enemy if not used properly. It disappeared from view and was followed by a dull crump. It was the signal they were waiting for.

"Move it!" barked Spartan.

Both columns rushed the stairs, each of them scanning for signs of the enemy. A man staggered into view, either confused by the attack or temporarily blinded by the grenade. Either way it didn't matter, he was struck by two short bursts fired by the unit. None stopped as they continued their steam roll through the building. Spartan moved along the corridor and approached the next flight of stairs, taking him to the main level above.

"Sergeant, secure this level," he said as dispassionately as he could.

But it wasn't easy having the mother of his child as his number two. Not that he would have it any other way. They had worked together since joining the Marine Corps, and there was no one else he trusted more to watch his back. Sergeant Morato nodded and gave hand signals to the other three in the split unit. They moved off onto the level to look for signs of the enemy. Spartan looked back to the staircase and checked his own half of the unit was ready.

"Intel has this as the primary level in the compound. Watch for friendlies. Second Troop is entering from the south side."

With that, he moved up with the rest of the group close beside him. The staircase widened to an open foyer type arrangement with a circular reception desk facing them. Spartan spotted movement and threw himself to the right side of the corridor, knocking down the two closest of his men. A loud burst of rifle fire clattered towards their now vacated position. The weapon was large calibre, possibly even a light machine gun, and tore finger-sized holes in the walls around them. It was archaic compared to the triple barrelled XL52 Mk II assault rifle he was carrying.

"Taking fire on the northern stairwell. We need flanking fire, now!" he said calmly over the suit's communication system.

"Roger," came back the calm response from the Sergeant Tsuki Yobun, the confident commander of the Second Troop. Unlike Spartan, this Sergeant was an old school NCO back from well before the uprising. He was much older and had the scars and experience to prove it.

Spartan looked back to the top of the staircase and realised the precarious situation they were in. He twisted the muzzle to deactivate the more stealth sub-sonic mode. In this situation, he needed firepower and penetration over quietness. Not that any noise he made mattered now, the terrorists own firearms roared in the stillness of the night air. He glanced over to the other three who were all looking up to the position of the enemy.

"Give me covering fire, now!"

There was no hesitation, and each lifted their weapons and blind fired towards the position of the enemy. A sporadic burst of defensive fire hit back, but it was wild, and the shooter must have been ducking to avoid fire. Spartan lifted his head briefly and aimed at the position he had last seen the man firing from. The reception desk was flat-fronted and cool on his display, much cooler than expected. He could pick up the sparks and flashes from their rifle rounds failing to penetrate the target. He fired a short burst and dropped back.

"Sir, he's dug in. If you ask me, that desk area has been armoured for a day like this. I'd say inch thick plate or some kind of composite," suggested Corporal Lina Sovana.

The others had dropped back down but were still firing short bursts to keep the man pinned down. He looked down to his rifle and selected the high-power mode. It reduced his rate of fire to no more than one shot every five seconds but would expend the capacitor's charge to propel all three projectiles at the same tame to incredible speeds. According to the instructors demonstrating the weapon, a single slug at that speed could penetrate through an engine block. Three rounds in close proximity would be devastating. He waited the few seconds for the indicator to show on his HUD that the weapon was charged and ready.

"Again!" he called out and the others lifted their weapons to add more fire. A short burst ripped back towards him from the defender and then stopped for a second. It was his chance. He stood up to the right so that he was pushed up to the wall and took aim at the point where the muzzle flashes had occurred. He dropped his aim down by a metre and squeezed the trigger. With a loud pulse of blue light and an almost bellowing scream, the rifle released its cargo of three magnetic projectiles at super-high velocities. It smashed through the desk as if it wasn't even there, through the man and continued on through half the building. The man himself was hurled backwards by the impact almost two metres before crashing into the wall, and dead well before he even touched the ground.

"Forward!" cried Spartan and the group of four were up off the stairs and surging onto the main level. According to their plans, the area was divided up into ten rooms with two staircases at each end and a long corridor running between the rooms. A number of individuals stumbled about but were instantly cut down by his team.

"Rooms one through four are clear!" called out the second team who had already cleared over a third of the floor.

Spartan started to worry about their intel. They had

been promised the head of their target in this compound. Drone recon indicated he had been present less than an hour ago.

Where is he? Spartan wondered.

He moved to the corridor and to a short distance ahead. At the far end of the hall, he spotted the second team as they did the same. Both sides lifted their fists to acknowledge the position of the other. It would be a tragedy if two elite teams caught each other in a deadly but mistaken crossfire. It was easily done, hence the weeks of training and rehearsals. There were doors just ahead and on each side. Spartan waved with his left hand for two of his unit to take up positions on the one side while one stayed behind him. He counted silently with his fingers.

Three...two...one!

Then he spun around and kicked the door hard. It opened more easily than expected, and he was inside. A man carrying an L48 carbine, the same weapon he had used on many occasions, was looking out of the window and turned to shout. Spartan fired at his chest; completely forgetting his weapon was still on high-power. The powerful blast threw the man headlong out of the window as the three magnetic slugs hit him with enough power to tear through a toughened concrete wall. The body disappeared in the courtyard below. One of the marines with him started to laugh at the bizarre scene.

"Stop it," snapped Spartan. He wasn't in the mood for

games.

At almost the same time, two men emerged from behind a set of metal cabinets and slammed a heavy wheeled trolley at the group. Spartan took the brunt of the impact and flew back to the wall. He landed hard and slid down to the floor. Alerts flashed up inside his armoured suit, and a burst of adrenalin was pumped directly into his bloodstream to keep him going.

"Lieutenant!" cried the nearest marine, but the second man struck him across the face with a metal bar that almost broke his neck. If it hadn't been for the reinforced neck armour, it would have killed him outright.

Corporal Lina Sovana rolled to the side and avoided being stuck. In seconds, half of the team were down, and the remaining two were caught up in a violent hand-to-hand struggle. From the ground, Spartan spotted the young Corporal punch one of the men before being jammed against the wall while the second hit her repeatedly with the bar. He used every ounce of effort left in his body and forced himself to his feet.

"Get off her!" he growled.

One man kept her pinned, pulled a handgun from a hidden holster, and placed it at point blank range in front of Lina's face. The other, a slightly taller man, turned to face Spartan with nothing but the bar in his hand.

"First we have Confed criminals, and now we have Alliance dogs. Don't you get bored serving the same master?" he said with contempt dripping from his voice.

Through the doorway appeared Teresa and one of her corporals. Both had their rifles aimed squarely at the man's chest. Spartan turned to her and spoke quitely, so only those on the commuications netork would hear him.

"On my signal, hit the guy next to Corporal Sovana. I'll take care of him."

Sergeant Morato said nothing, but Spartan could tell from her body language that she understood exactly what he wanted. The lights flickered on, presumably from the internal backup genertators. Spartan thought that was odd. Surely they could have put them on at any point, unless it was their plan all along. He opened his visor and looked into the eyes of his enemy.

"You know we aren't leaving without you, Chraige Attez!" he announced.

The man showed no surprise, and that unsettled Spartan more than the situation itself. Even worse, as the lights came on, so did a low pitched hum through his communciations system.

"What's the problem, Alliance filth? Having problems with your communications?" he laughed.

From inside the room, a bright yellow light filled the window as the external lights reactivated and bathed the courtyards with dull light. The sound of powerful engines announced the surprising arrival of a ground transport of some kind. The side doors of the room burst open to reveal another four armed men, each carrying Confederate military issue L48 carbines, presumably looted from murdered officers or soldiers.

They knew we were coming. This is a set up, he thought bitterly.

It was at that moment that Spartan knew they were in serious trouble. Chraige Attez was known for the murders of so many people, and in a matter of seconds, he and the rest of his team would share the same fate. He looked down, seaching for his weapon and spotted his rifle several metres away near the man holding the pistol to the Corporal's head. His training told him exactly what to do, but there was a moment's hesitation. If he surrendered, he would give up the entire team. They would certainly be ceremonially executed and their bodies dumped in the courtyard. Corporal Sovana was already dead, all he could do was try and save as many as he could.

Do it, do it now!

With one quick action, he slid his right hand down and grabbed at the close fitting thigh holster. His hand touched the hilt before Chraige Attez even spotted the movement. Even so, it wasn't fast enough. A loud report from the man pointing the gun at the young Corporal announced her death. Spartan spotted the single bullet penetrating her visor and into her skull but did his best to ignore the carnage and aimed at the man. With great precision, he emptied five rounds into his torso and head

before spinning around to point the weapon at Chraige
Attez's face. Sergeant Morato and two of her comrades
unleashed a hail of fire at the four other men and cleared
the room in seconds. It was violent and bloody work, but
they were safe for now.

"Clear!" she said simply and moved to the window
to check down in the courtyard. An eight-wheeler was
approaching, and she could make out the shapes of a
number of men on the back.

"Spartan, we've got company!"

He nodded and stepped forward towards his prisoner,
smashing the grip into his face. The impact almost
certainly broke his nose and sent blood streaming over his
chin. Sergeant Morato lifted her visor to reveal her face,
a look of anguish showing clearly as she glanced over to
their own fallen soldier. Spartan nodded in her direction.

"Grab her, we need to get out and fast!"

Two of the team grabbed the Corporal and Sergeant
Morato lifted Chraige Attez to his knees, the blood
still dripping from his face. Then they were out of the
door and heading back to the staircase. Sergeant Tsuki
Yobun saw them from the other end of the corridor and
signalled with his left arm for them to follow him. They'd
practiced dozens of scenarios, and luckily one without
communications gear was one of them. It didn't take long
for the fifteen to work their way down to the ground floor,
even with two of them carrying their wounded comrade.

As they approached the secondary entrance, one of them spotted movement and lifted his fist. All fifteen ducked down low and waited. Spartan moved forward and leaned around the doorframe to look outside. He could make out the shapes of the other two groups of Alliance warriors, each in cover and watching the streets leading to the compound.

Sgt Kawa Naori spotted him and indicated for Spartan and the others to stay where they were. She pulled a device from her suit and pointed it up high. Spartan watched as an object puffed out and flew up almost two hundred metres before giving a short but bright purple pulse.

Good thinking, Sergeant. It was the emergency contact flare. A special electro-visual device that sent a digital pulse and small coloured flash to indicate they needed immediate support. A Marine Corps landing craft was already inbound for the extraction, and the signal would task the crew to come in fast to assist. That was when Spartan saw movement off to the right. It was at least a dozen armed men, and they were positioning themselves near the outer wall of the compound. Spartan stepped out from the shelter of the building.

"Contact!" he cried and fired a long burst into the shapes near the wall. Two were killed instantly; the rest went to ground and proceeded to fire sporadically at those in the main building. Spartan looked back and gave the signal for his unit to fan out into the compound and to leave the safety of the building. It offered good protection, but they needed to evacuate and fast. Another five minutes, and the local cell members of Chraige Attez's forces would be on them. This area was known to house a number of sympathisers, and they might manage to kill their prize before they could escape to interrogate him.

One of the windows smashed on the upper floor, and a man blasted down indiscriminately at them. Spartan ran to the first wall where the others were taking shelter and spun round to check for enemies. On the visor HUD he picked out at least six men, all armed and firing. They must have been in hiding, waiting for their chance to strike. Several rounds struck nearby, and Spartan was acutely aware they were using the L48 carbines, a weapon easily capable of punching through even their toughed PDS body armour. He took aim, taking out two as a burst of fire forced him to shelter amongst the rubble of the partially collapsed wall.

"Lieutenant, vehicle is here!" shouted one of the corporals, but he couldn't quite make out who it was at this range. Spartan pulled himself from cover and hoped the return fire from his own team would be enough to occupy those in the building while he checked the new arrival. He looked through part of the damaged section from the explosives they had used and could see the eight-wheel vehicle as it disgorged at least a dozen men. They looked similar to the Zealot warriors he had fought on so many other planets and warzones.

Where the hell have they been hiding?

"Put fire on them, and do not let them get away from the vehicle!" he ordered. His team were all excellent shots and in seconds had stalled the Zealot reinforcements, pushing them back into the cover of the lightly armoured vehicle. Spartan could make out the head of one of the men on the other side of the vehicle. He selected the high-power mode and grinned to himself as the three projectiles smashed through the vehicle, slamming the man to the ground. Muzzle flashes lit up from multiple directions, and the walled compound was starting to look less like their escape route and more like a prison.

"Sir, watch out!" called out Sergeant Morato who was busy trying to suppress those on the highest floor of the building. Chunks of masonry blasted from the walls as both sides exchanged fire. Corporal Jenkins was hit in the leg. Soon after, another burst of L48 carbine fire shattered Sergeant Tsuki Yobun's rifle, but incredibly the shredded round managed to avoid penetrating his armoured suit.

"Keep them busy. Help is on the way!"

Spartan flicked the weapon back to normal firing mode and held down the trigger. With all three barrels active and firing in sequence, the rate of fire was astounding. He had read the gun could almost hit fifteen hundred rounds a minute, so far the weapon almost sounded like a chainsaw. He was tempted to order a retreat back inside, but once there they might never get back out. A familiar screaming caught his attention. It was a Marine Corps landing craft; one of the heavily armoured assault vessels used to land troops and light vehicles directly into battle. A series of loud crumps hammered around the eight-wheeled troop carrier as almost thirty magnetic projectiles slammed around the vehicle, each fired from the door-gunners on the flanks of the vessel.

Good timing, people, he said happily to himself.

The large craft came down so fast it almost looked like a crash landing. As soon as it hit the ground, the four side doors slid open ready for access. The door-gunners continued their suppressing fire against the enemy in the open and also in the building. Spartan lifted his hand, indicating for them to board the landing craft. It took less than a minute for them all to make it inside without taking further casualties. Spartan counted them in. Once satisfied the entire team, along with their prisoner, was inside, he climbed in. The door slid shut just in time to deflect two projectiles that would have struck him.

"Hold on, we're getting out of here!" said the pilot over the sound system.

With a roar, the craft lifted up, and Spartan felt twice his weight as it accelerated into the sky. He looked over to Teresa and two of the other men who were busy checking the body of their fallen comrade.

"How is she?" he asked painfully, but he was aware she

had little to no chance of surviving. Teresa looked back at him with a bloodied face and shook her head.

"Not good. She's alive, but barely."

Spartan lowered his eyes and looked back to the small side window and the compound that was already quickly disappearing into the distance. He held onto one of the many grab handles and squeezed it tightly.

Somebody screwed us over. Somebody that knew we were going in. I'll find them, and damn help them when I do!

CHAPTER TWO

The early years of the Alliance saw the retirement for many of the most famous ships of the War. While some ships were simply too badly damaged to be economically repaired, others such as those that fought for the Echidna Union were best scrapped to remove their shame from the annals. The Santa Cruz was one of the few ships to emerge from the war with her honour intact and useful role remaining. She was changed from a heavy marine transport into a mobile base for Alliance Special Operations Groups, more commonly known as SOGs.

Ships of the Alliance

Spartan, Teresa and Sergeant Tsuki Yobun waited patiently outside the medical bay on board ANS Santa Cruz. They'd been there for almost an hour now as the surgeons did their work. It wasn't the waiting that was frustrating Spartan thought, not even the fact that he might have lost a good and dedicated warrior. No, it was the fact that somebody had let Chraige Attez and his Zealot friends know they were coming that hurt the most. Kerberos had suffered greatly at the hands of the Zealots and their Church of Echidna friends. By the time the rebels had fought the Union forces to a standstill, a large portion of the population had already been shipped away. It was one of the many problems still remaining for the fledgling Alliance, to find those hundreds of thousands of missing citizens. Some were known to have been used as slave labour, and in the early months of the War, a large percentage had been used to create the most savage and violent of biomechanical creatures.

"Spartan, are you okay?" asked Teresa.

He looked to her and nodded calmly.

"I'm good. I'd like to know which bastard turned us in though. They nearly blew the raid."

Sergeant Tsuki Yobun rubbed his chin as he thought. He looked as if he had experienced an epiphany as he waited.

"Lieutenant. If they knew we were coming, why did Chraige Attez stay there? Surely he could have just left the place, maybe even desert it and leave traps or charges for us."

Spartan said nothing at first, but he had to admit the Sergeant had a point. A sound from further along the hall marked the approach of a small group of marines. They wore the same uniforms they always had, but Spartan recognised the patches as being from the newly created Alliance. As the two men approached, the figure of Major Daniels followed them. He walked up to Spartan who saluted smartly along with his two comrades.

"At ease," were the first words Daniels spoke before he turned slightly and pointed at the door.

"Is there any news on your Corporal?"

Spartan shook his head.

"A nasty business, but you did what had to be done. The rest of your team made it out alive though. As I said in the briefing, he had friends in the local militia. We weren't sure whom, if any, we could trust. For your peace of mind, recon drones show four trucks of local militia arrived sixty seconds after you got out of there. If you'd surrendered your forces, you and your team would be strapped down and being interrogated as we speak."

He looked to the door and nodded in its direction.

"Your Corporal in there may not live, but at least she has a chance. Better this than a few days of agony in their hands. You saw what they did to Shoutarou, not a pretty sight at all."

Spartan nodded in agreement, but he would much rather have not been forced to dwell on what had happened to that unfortunate soul. Luckily, the Major appeared agitated and started to move away.

"I will see you in the briefing. You've got ten minutes

before I start. Don't be late," he said firmly and marched away.

Sergeant Yobun looked through the observation window into the medlab but could see little of note. There were two layers of smoked windows plus a fabric screen that blocked most of the light. He turned around to face Spartan who still looked angry at the way the mission had ended.

"Lieutenant, you made a tough call, and it was the right one. We bagged the target, slotted anybody that got in our way, and completed the mission. Like the Major said, if we'd stayed or done anything differently, we would have been smoked."

Spartan did his best to look as though he agreed, but the issue with the Corporal wasn't going to be resolved quite that easily. The Sergeant sighed and twisted away from the other two.

"I'm needed down in the training hall. We're running the ship hostage scenario again, and they need another instructor. Fill me in on the briefing afterwards."

Spartan nodded but said no more. The Sergeant moved off down the corridor, leaving just Spartan and Teresa alone. They were silent, happy to say nothing while they waited for news. They didn't have long though before the Major's briefing started. Spartan knocked on the door, and it was quickly opened by one of the four medical orderlies on duty. The man looked at Spartan and shook his head.

"Sorry, Sir, no news. She's stable, and her injuries are healing. She might come out of the coma today, in a week or never. As soon as there's news, I'll be in touch. I promise."

Teresa reached out and held his forearm.

"Spartan, let's go. There's nothing we can do here, not yet."

He looked at her and back to the orderly. The man did his best to smile at Spartan, trying to reassure him she was in the best possible place.

"Trust me, Sir. I will let you know immediately."

* * *

The briefing room on board the ANS Santa Cruz hadn't really changed much since the end of the War. The damage sustained in the final battle around Terra Nova had been patched up, and most of the crew had moved on. Some had quit the military, others were taking well deserved breaks with others just needed posting somewhere else. Like many of the survivors of the War, the old warhorse had been pressed back into surface until the new generation of ships could replace her. Only her designation and insignia had changed from the old CCS to the new style. Gone were her thousands of marines, and instead was this mixture of experts that had been tracking down the people and technology behind the War.

Major Daniels entered the room and took up his position at the front. He had aged considerably in the months and eventually years it had taken to win back the Confederacy from the Echidna Union and its allies. Although young, his hair was already greying prematurely, and his face betrayed a tiredness that only prolonged combat and exposure to tragedy could replicate.

"Be seated," he stated simply.

The hundred or so people sat down in their seats and watched patiently. Spartan glanced at them and allowed himself a small smile. This was being treated like a military briefing even though over half of the people there were actually civilians that had been seconded to the ad-hoc unit for the last six months. Service in the Confederate Marine Corps had definitely instilled an attitude into Daniels.

"Thank you for attending this briefing. As you are no doubt aware, the conference on Terra Nova will be the first to take place since the peace accords thirteen months ago. A great deal has happened since then, the founding of the Alliance, the disbanding of colonial militia, and the resettling of many of our lost colonies. The threat of the Union has vanished since we vanquished their Core and control systems, but their supporters still exist. There are terrorist cells on every colony, and be in no doubt, they will keep on fighting as long as just one of them remains. Typhon died on Terra Nova, and his legions surrendered, but what of his brothers, the so-called Sons of the League?

No trace has been found of them, and of the ten legions of Biomechs Typhon boasted of. Only four were found."

He paused for a few seconds, letting that information sink in. It would, of course, be of no surprise to the men and women of this particular unit. After all, they put themselves in danger everyday to continue the fight against the enemy. Major Daniels nodded as he watched them.

"But that isn't why we are here. The brothers of Typhon and the missing Biomechs are just one of the many issues left for the Alliance to deal with. For the last six months, you have been involved in seven operations, each one risky, but each bringing us closer to understanding those behind the War. Now we are starting to understand how they were able to infiltrate our forces. It didn't take place over months or years, not even decades. The rot started after the Great War itself. That is why we must show eternal vigilance and ensure this can never happen again. There are many of our enemies still out there, and work by people such as yourselves is bringing us closer to a better future."

He noticed Spartan in the group and nodded politely; a movement that was barely discernible to all but the most eagle-eyed of observers. He then looked to the rest of the hall and continued.

"I have gathered you here because you are to participate in a summit of the best scientists, soldiers and politicians to plan the future of the Alliance military. You will have a complete free rein to voice your opinions on your experience with this unit and also on operations in the War. Obviously, you will not discuss the operations themselves or your roles in them, but you can use this information to help others understand what works, what doesn't and what you think would help in the future. This short meeting may provide useful additional information prior to your arrival, especially since we have new intelligence and data from our last three operations."

He turned to a man in a suit, somebody Spartan didn't recognise. With a few quiet words, the man took his place on the podium and then pressed a button. A detailed image of Terra Nova appeared; the planet rotating like a marble orb.

"Thank you, Major. As the official research delegate from Kerberos, I would like to thank those of you that helped free my world from near annihilation. Even now, we are still finding the bodies of those mutilated and savaged during the occupation. It is this tragedy that has inspired a new generation of scientists and researchers like myself to ensure we build a strong, dependable and long-term future. The Confederacy was weak, and many paid the ultimate price. All of us have a duty to ensure it never happens again."

He turned and looked at the image of Terra Nova for a few seconds. The planet represented many things to those who had suffered in the War. The planet was the official capital of the entire Confederacy and had also been at the centre of enemy operations. It was also the site where the War had been decided. There were many with a great distrust of the planet and its people, who mainly seemed to have avoided the hardship faced by planets such as Prime, Kerberos and Carthago. He inhaled slowly and continued.

"I asked the Major for this meeting before we reach the conference because I have a few important observations I wanted to share with those of you travelling from Kerberos. The first is my thanks for your previous and continuing efforts to protect my homeworld. The second is my research that I think you will find interesting. When the Union left our planet, they gave us a legacy of destruction. But there is also something else they left behind."

He lifted a small leather case and placed it on the table beside him. With a gentle click the case opened up, and he removed what looked like a small metallic idol. He lifted it to show everybody.

"This was recovered from one of the shuttles brought down as they tried to escape during our own little insurrection. I know some of you have already seen this amongst the objects taken from captured or killed Zealots."

The screen changed to show a detailed image of the object. It was one of the common relics of Echidna. An item often carried by supporters of the religion and almost every member of the militant wing known as the Zealots. The shape was a bizarre mixture of a serpent fused with the classic shape of the mother goddess. Part monotheistic and part pagan, it mixed the essence of multiple religions together. As he held the artefact up, he moved a small computer device next to the relic for them to see. A number of indicators lit up, and it emitted a tone.

"As you can see, these are no simple metal devices. They give off a level of coded radiation that is astounding. So far, we have found no dangerous side effects, but, and this is a big but, they have one very important characteristic in common. They match the radiation patterns found at the destroyed research station in the Anomaly. We've been seeing these icons for decades now, but we didn't pay any attention until the martyrdoms on Kerberos. Now that we're looking, we're finding more of them. Or more specifically, your teams are finding more of them."

The mention of the Anomaly took Spartan right back to the last days of the War when the Confederate Fleet, outnumbered and desperate, had fought its last battle; a battle against the new Union of colonies run by the Church of Echidna hierarchy. The remnants of the Confederacy had fought battle after battle against the Zealots extremists and the biomechanical monsters they had been creating in secret.

He looked at the object and recalled seeing the symbols often tattooed, and sometimes even burned into the flesh of the Zealots with the same half woman and half serpent image. Even now, he couldn't believe that a mere handful had used the bridge provided by the Anomaly to travel to Terra Nova where they had landed and destroyed the Core. One swift assault, and the brains behind the uprising had been knocked out. It was a shocking and bloody end to the War, and one that still shook the Confederacy itself to her knees. It seemed like years had passed since then, yet it was only thirteen months ago, and so much had changed. He looked back to the man who was still talking.

"What does this mean? We do not yet know, but you can be assured that the best scientists on Kerberos are working on this, and I intend on presenting my findings at the conference. There is a definite link between the Zealots, their religion, the icons and the Anomaly, and I do not believe for one second that they have gone away."

With a polite nod, the man stepped down, and the Major moved back to his previous position.

"Based on the new intelligence on these artefacts, as well as the placement for three more Biomech research stations, we are now starting to make some progress. Interrogation of the Zealot commanders confirms there is a something more to the Church than we thought. Some of you may have heard mention of a Judgement Day, something I think almost all religions seem to share."

A few of those in the audience laughed nervously at the mention of the concept. Spartan noticed a few doing their best to avoid the response. It was hardly surprising. There were followers of a hundred different religions in the new Alliance, and many shared a fear of the concept of a judgement day.

"Well, it is clear to us that adherents of the Church of Echidna are expecting theirs to arrive very soon. In fact, the most common timeframe we're hearing is in the next six years."

He waited at the last comment and let it sink in to the soldiers, marines and civilians. They represented only a small cross-section of society, yet even they seemed unsurprised at his words.

"I see you have heard this before, and some of you probably from the dying curses of Zealot terrorists. What if I told you that every indication from the last two months suggests something is going to happen? That the surviving Zealots are working on something, in secret, that will make the uprising seem like nothing more than a diversion?"

The last part really caught Spartan's imagination. One thing he couldn't argue with was that the War had concentrated the minds of all involved in one thing, victory. If somebody wanted a diversion, they couldn't have done a better job.

"Once I have finished my briefing to the Alliance Security Council, I will see what else our forces have managed to uncover. But I want you all to know that this kind of intelligence wouldn't have been possible without the intervention by units such as yours. Units that have recovered schematics, Biomech plans and even brought in leaders like the criminal Chraige Attez," he explained, without looking directly at any of the handful in the room that had taken part in the mission.

Spartan knew full well who had done what, but it was in nobody's interest to draw attention to any of them, even in this close circle of friends.

"We will be picking up another group of scientists from the temporary research site at the Anomaly in seven hours. After that, we'll take the short trip through the bridge and rendezvous with the other representatives for the conference. We will be there for sometime, and I expect you to speak your minds. Let it not be said that you had ideas but didn't mention them, when it might have helped. Each of you has knowledge and experience since the War that will be critical in shaping our future. As members of the Alliance Special Operations Group, your advice will be invaluable. Thank you."

Major Daniels received a polite but slightly reserved applause as he stepped away from the podium and rejoined his security detail. A communications offer rushed up towards him to speak, and Spartan tried to understand what was happening. It was evidently important as the body language of the Major transformed in seconds. Teresa moved closer to Spartan and would have spoken but was cut off and interrupted by Sergeant Lovett, one of Spartan's marines from the end of the War, who rushed towards him with the same urgency as the communications officer.

"Lovett? I thought you left an hour ago on the shuttle. Aren't you transferring home for two weeks?" asked Spartan in surprise.

Lovett shook his head. His face betraying a bitterness that Spartan had seen so many times before. He reached out and placed his hand on his friend's shoulder.

"What is it?" he asked, almost dreading to hear the words.

Lovett's eyes were red, and it was clear some terrible tragedy must have just taken place. He leaned in towards his two friends and shook his head.

"I was waiting on the shuttle when an instant communication arrived for me from High Command. It was about the Atlantic Star."

Teresa looked to Spartan with a quizzical look on her face. From what Lovett had said, she assumed she should know something about this ship, but it was a complete unknown to her. Spartan looked equally confused.

"The Atlantic Star? Sounds like a passenger ship. What about it?"

Lovett nodded at his suggestion and took a few deep gulps of air before continuing.

"My fiancée was on the Atlantic Star, heading to

Orthrus. The ship was hijacked three hours ago. It's on the newsfeeds already, over a thousand dead."

"What? By Zealots?" asked Teresa.

"No way of knowing, but they detonated the engines an hour later. The ship's gone, no survivors. A rescue drone has been sent to assess the situation, but it looks like they didn't even give them a chance to leave the ship."

"Bastards!" snapped Spartan. "I don't get it. I thought the last Core controlled ships had surrendered at Carthago? What were they doing at Orthrus?"

Lovett shook his head in disagreement.

"Not all of them, no way. But they never made it to Orthrus. If they had gone that far, the planetary defence force would have stopped them in seconds."

He stopped and looked at the rest of the people in the room who were already dispersing. A few could see he was upset, but they were doing their best to pretend they hadn't noticed. He looked back to Spartan.

"No, this was while they were taking on fuel at the unmanned supply station orbiting Hyperion. There was no air cover. She was a private liner. The last transmission said a Zealot boarding party were on board. Next thing we hear, the engines are detonating. There wasn't even time to issue a mayday."

Spartan didn't know what to say, but Teresa, being more sensitive to people, moved closer and held him close. They'd spent months working alongside each other fighting for the Confederacy in its darkest hour. Even now, they still struggled against the remnants of the Zealots and their shrinking pool of supporters. He spotted movement and realised it was Major Daniels.

"Lieutenant," he said and then looked at other two, "Sergeants," he said in a rush and looked back towards Spartan.

"You and your NCOs in my quarters in ten minutes. We have urgent things to discuss. There have been developments."

Spartan nodded and saluted, and then the Major was gone. He looked back to Teresa and Lovett. Teresa raised an eyebrow in question; Lovett on the other hand seemed completely disinterested.

"Come with me, this looks important. I bet it concerns the Atlantic Star."

With that single mention of the passenger ship, Lovett snapped out of his trance. He grabbed Spartan as he made for the door.

"What is it?" he asked.

Spartan pulled his hand off his shoulder.

"Not here, come on, we will find out soon enough."

Sergeant Lovett was still standing there when Spartan and Teresa left the briefing room. He watched them go before realising he was supposed to be with them. He shook his head and did his best to throw the thoughts from his mind and chased after them.

* * *

Spartan and his two Sergeants waited outside the door of the Major's quarters for what seemed like an age. As always, there were two Alliance guards, both ex-marines, stood either side of the door. Unlike the other guards on the ship, they used standard issue L48 carbines. It was standard practice for those on ships to use special low velocity weapons that didn't risk the innards or skin of the ship. These guards were the last defence for the commander, although safety concerns were secondary compared to protecting the commander of such a critical military unit. The guard to the left nodded to himself and then looked to Spartan.

"You can go in."

He tapped the coded panel on the door, and with an almost discernible hiss, it slid open. Spartan stepped inside, followed closely by his Sergeants. Inside the room, the Major stood looking at a model of a ship on the computer display. The door shut behind them, and the three stood smartly to attention. Major Daniels turned from the model, a grim expression pervading his face.

"At ease."

He looked to Sergeant Lovett first and did his best to look sympathetic.

"I've heard the news and I'm sorry, very sorry. The Atlantic Star was due to bring a number of important people to Orthrus to assist in the rebuilding. The loss will be felt deeply."

He turned to the model and pointed to the engines.

"I don't know if you heard, but no hostages were taken. Contrary to the news reports, the attackers simply smashed a tug into the engines and a second into the propulsion powerplant. She went critical in seconds."

He turned back to the three and indicated for them to sit down. Spartan was no great fan of doing this, but the sombre occasion demanded it. Once comfortable, the Major tapped a button that removed the ship model and instead showed a map of the Alpha Centauri star system. Spartan had seen the map many times before but had never shown it much interest. Until the discovery of the Anomaly, the journey time between the two halves of the Confederacy had taken almost a year.

"Alpha Centauri," he said slowly while tracing the paths of the planets with his left hand.

Unlike Proxima Centauri, it was a binary star system with a complex arrangement of planets and their many stars. With thirteen planets, of which only six had been colonised, it was still the oldest part of the Confederacy. The planets were much better developed than their equivalents in Proxima Centauri and considered by many to be the old, more conservative colonies.

"While we were busy fighting the Union, most of these colonies managed to avoid the Uprising. They infiltrated high levels of military and political life years before the War. If you recall, once the fighting started, they initiated a blackout. Only one fleet of ships made it through to us before the Union were able to clamp down."

Spartan looked to Teresa as he tried to work out what the Major was getting at.

We know all of this, why doesn't he get to the point?

Teresa smiled uncomfortably but changed her expression as the Major turned to look at her. The short pause worried her, but he hadn't noticed and instead looked to Spartan.

"I know none of this is news. Since the fighting on Terra Nova, we have received the formal surrender of all remaining Union forces. Political posts and positions of military command have been scrutinised, and we're making progress. Without the Core, their ships, communications and Biomech support killed them overnight. This disturbing news about the Atlantic Star is a worry though. As I said in the briefing earlier, there are still plenty of Zealots left out there, and some have the support of the locals. We still don't know how they were able to obtain the technology, equipment or knowledge to cause so much trouble, and I suspect there may be more to come. If one ship has been lost at Hyperion, it means they still have some ships."

He tapped the screen and zoomed in on the green planet.

"High Command suspect the Zealots may have been operating from a hidden base on some of the uninhabited worlds here. It's been low priority with the peace keeping operations most of our ground troops are now involved with."

He paused and waited for the three to speak. Spartan looked a little confused before realising the Major wanted their opinions. He cleared his throat before starting.

"Well, Sir, this entire sector was infiltrated far deeper than Proxima ever was. They could have been running the entire operation from Terra Nova itself from the start."

The Major looked unconvinced by his reply.

"It is possible, of course, but how were they able to come almost from nowhere in this sector? We have never understood how the Zealots became so powerful and so quickly. It is as if they were elsewhere for months, perhaps years before. Maybe there is something out there we've not discovered yet? A missing link, as you will."

Teresa lifted her head slightly, implying she had something to add. The Major nodded towards her.

"We know where the Zealots were. They've been underground for a long time. We've seen how these movements form and expand. The power behind them, the reason why we lost so early on, was that they had access to massive numbers of Biomechs and ships."

Major Daniels nodded in agreement. "Like on Prometheus?"

"Exactly, Sir. That complex was kept hidden for years, and they had the capacity to create multiple generations of biomechanicals for the war effort. One other site could easily have done the same in Alpha Centauri. Unless they just transported them through the Anomaly."

He switched the device off and sat down.

"Anyway, this is all conjecture. I have discussed this at depth with High Command, and they have already decided that our sister ship, the Santa Maria, is being fitted out for a special mission to conduct a systematic sweep of every moon around the inner worlds, including Hyperion. They will be taking an escort, as well as enough troops and supplies to eliminate enemy ground forces, if and when they are located. The new government is being pushed to hunt down anybody associated with this recent outrage, and it looks like it will coincide with a major hunt in this sector. The operation could take months, and that's why I called you three in."

Spartan knew what was coming, and he wasn't surprised.

"Lieutenant, they have everything they need, but they do have a need for a replacement reconnaissance troop."

Spartan was about to speak, but the Major lifted his hand.

"No, before you say anything, it will not be you. This mission is important, but the rebuilding of the Alliance military is even more important. There is talk of shrinking the size of the fleet and relying more on local troops for combat operations. You have more experience than most of the senior command there, especially when it comes to operations against the Zealots and the Biomechs. I've a list of seven people already that want to speak with you about the fighting on Terra Nova itself."

Spartan shook his head angrily.

"But, Sir, this is admin and politics, and you know what I'm like at both. My reports are already on file. They know what I think, and they know the problems we suffered with local forces and commanders. Surely my expertise is better needed on the Santa Maria mission."

Major Daniels stood up, indicating the discussion was coming to an end.

"I'm sorry, Lieutenant. My hands are tied. Your knowledge and experience is required at Terra Nova. You will select the best reconnaissance team available, and it is my recommendation that Sergeant Morato is considered to lead it. I will, of course, leave the decision to you."

He stood smartly to attention, and the three stood to face him. Spartan saluted and turned for the door. Major Daniels was already at his computer model of the system before they even left the room. Spartan nodded to the guards as he stepped out into the corridor and looked back at Lovett and Teresa.

Dammit, so I stay for meetings and discussions on Terra Nova while my two best NCOs get to finish off the enemy once and for all?

CHAPTER THREE

The fall of Terra Nova marked a major shift in the path of the Zealots and their devotion to the Church of Echidna. With the Core destroyed and the Union torn apart, many returned home. Most were bitter and many blamed the new Alliance for their troubles. The first decades after the Uprising saw many feuds and reprisals occur throughout the old Confederacy. It was a hard and violent time but if it were not for the events at Hyperion the old troubles could easily have reignited.

Origins of the Zealots

Spartan looked out of the observation window and towards the shape of the planet below. The rotating of this part of the ship meant he had but a small period of time to watch before the planet moved from view. Those not used to it could become sick and disorientated but not him. Spartan had served on multiple ships with artificial gravity, and although they all left him with a sick feeling in his stomach, nothing caused as much pain as that blue green orb below.

Terra Nova, I never planned on coming back.

He thought back to his last visit and the violence of their landing. It had been the final act of the War, and a terrible full frontal assault on the planet itself. So many had died on both sides. Even the Jötnar, his implacable allies, had lost scores of warriors in that last, desperate rush to end the War. It reminded him of his Biomech friends, the Jötnar who had sided with the Confederacy and proven to be some of the most stubborn and trustworthy warriors they had access to. He had not seen them in months and was actually starting to miss his friends.

Still, I'll get to meet Khan on Terra Nova. That should be interesting.

He smiled inwardly at the thought of the outspoken Jötnar warrior on the planet. He was even less politic than Ko'mandor Gun, their enigmatic leader and could be guaranteed to cause a scene. That was something Spartan was quite looking forward to seeing.

"The next shuttle to the conference will leave in seventeen minutes. Please make your way to the landing bay," said a calm voice over the ship's speaker system.

Spartan glanced once more at the shape of Terra Nova as it whisked by and then walked away towards what many of them affectionately called the spiral. The people were waiting patiently as the rotating part of the ship moved along the central core. A number of long metal ladders ran the width of the section and appeared to move slowly around the core. A crewmember grabbed the metal and lifted himself up. He looked up and followed two more as they moved towards the rotating central core. Of course, in reality, the spokes and the rotating section were actually moving around the motionless central spindle. As they moved closer to the top, the spinning section appeared to slow down. It was all an illusion, however, as this part of the ship rotated at a complete three revolutions per minute. It was enough to create the same level of gravity as experienced back on Earth but was only used on the main habitation parts of the ship.

"Sir, good luck with the conference," said the burly sergeant waiting to help those climbing onto the spiral wheel.

Spartan pulled up a few rungs before looking back.

"Thanks, I can't wait."

He continued to move along the ladder and quickly noticed the change in gravity. Each rung made him feel lighter as he moved towards the central core. He'd seen many a marine feel sickness at this point, and vomiting in low or near zero gravity was a sight he would have happily forgotten. A few more seconds, and he reached the central section. He pulled himself onto the platform and waited for a moment as he relished the feeling of weightlessness. The spokes extended out around him to the rim of the rotating section. He turned back to the cylindrical section and pulled himself along the tube-shaped structure. It didn't take long for him to move through to the next part of the ship where the transport hangars were located. A young sergeant signalled to him from one of the larger craft.

"Sir, this is yours."

Spartan nodded and continued to pull himself towards the vessel. It was a slow and complex procedure to transfer from the rotating section to the stationary parts of the ship, and usually only carried out when absolutely necessary. During combat operations, marines would often be stationed in the annex quarters, a number of zero-gee rooms in the next compartment over from the landing bay. It allowed them to transfer to landing craft and transports in seconds rather than minutes. He pulled himself inside the vessel and towards a seat near the port side window. Like the other dozen people already inside, he quickly fitted his harness. The last thing anybody wanted was somebody floating about when they hit the atmosphere and the gravitational pull of Terra Nova.

"Departure in four minutes, please check your harnesses and stow any loose items," came the automated voice that he'd heard so many times in the past.

Spartan didn't need to check. He'd done this so many

times already. What he didn't like was the dress uniform he'd been forced to wear. Though most of the depleted Marine Corps units were now disbanded or amalgamated, they had yet to receive any kind of new dress uniform. Even Spartan's Vanguard unit had been unable to survive in anything like its original form. After substantial equipment losses and casualties, the survivors were now being used to train recruits on Prime and Terra Nova in order to raise more recruits for the elite unit. With major combat operations now over, most of the heavy exo-armour had been returned to the military stores for maintenance with just a handful retained on each of the Marine Transports. He'd been told that the unit was to be reformed with more manpower and equipment, but for now the unit had been placed as inactive, pending rebuilding. Since the formation of the ASOG units he'd been out of touch though.

Would rather be with them right now, he thought.

He had been forced to use his Marine Corps dress uniform until something more appropriate was designed for the ASOGs, assuming the unit didn't change again after the Defence Committee had finished making their decisions. Apparently, this was all part of the peace dividend.

Cuts more like.

The door shut and Spartan was now stuck on the transport. He looked about and noted the points of escape as well as the emergency gear and weapon cabinets. Each of the transports had subtle differences, and like any man with experience in the military, he wanted to be sure of his surroundings in case of an emergency.

He thought wryly. *How many times have I landed in one of these things, and there hasn't been a problem?*

* * *

The area selected as the VIP landing zone made Spartan feel uneasy. It was the exact same place he and his comrades had landed during the fighting, and he was finding it hard to suppress the feelings he had felt when landing under fire the last time. Back then the world had seemed alien, foreign, and almost exotic. Now the place was nothing more than a lavish reminder of the losses they had suffered. His transports circled the Palace as though they were looking for a sniper or some other miscreant before it dropped down and fired its landing rockets. From his view through the window, he could see the long colonnade surrounded by waterworks and crowds of people. His eye was drawn to follow the path up to the main building itself. Upon seeing the front, he almost choked.

The Palace was one of the most famous monuments in the old Confederacy. A mark of lavish expenditure that stood Terra Nova out as being different to any other part of the Confederacy, even Prime. Larger than anything ever seen on Earth, it had been the seat of the Confederacy for the last three hundred and forty years and included the Council Chambers, as well as multiple barracks for the city-based armed forces. As his transport settled onto the ground, he noted the ceremonial guards, the infamous Terra Nova Guards Brigade. He was aware of their long lineage back to when they had still been the City Militia Battalion. Apparently, Biomechs massacred most of their six thousand troops in the months before Spartan and his forces had arrived. He wondered if these were survivors, or if they were all new recruits to a reformed unit.

Looks like I'll find out soon enough.

The side doors hissed open, and four of the soldiers positioned themselves as an honour guard. Spartan stepped out first and took the salute of the first man. He watched him carefully; curious to establish what exactly had happened in the last months with the unit. The soldier in front of him wore the ancient uniform with scarlet tunic and a curiously antiquated glaive in one hand. Tucked neatly on his side was one of the newest L52a light carbines. Spartan had only seen one so far, and a pang of envy washed over him as he realised the static defence force on Terra Nova was receiving equipment before his own forces, even though his were in action almost weekly. He thought about asking a question, but his gaze was drawn to a slightly overweight officer walking towards him. The man's epaulets brought him quickly to attention, and he raised his hand quickly to a smart salute.

"Lieutenant Spartan, welcome to Terra Nova. I am Major-General Jack Aitken," said the senior officer with no hint of a smile.

His uniform was beautifully presented, and he carried nothing more than an army issue pistol on his belt. Spartan had met people like this career officer before, and it usually ended with an argument and him in some kind of trouble. He decided to try a little tact.

"Sir. It is nice to be here," he said firmly.

The General looked at the transport and back at Spartan.

"Yes, I presume this is a more preferable greeting to the one you received on your last visit?"

Spartan tried to understand exactly what the officer was thinking, but the man's cold expression gave nothing away. Like many of the senior officers he knew, this one was an expert at keeping his thoughts and feelings to himself. Some people thought the Biomechs were cold and calculating, but they were nothing compared to the senior commanders he had encountered. He was reminded of the incompetence he had encountered with local generals on Euryale and Prime. He just hoped this commander was cut from a different cloth. He looked at the General and the subtle indicators on his uniform and face. There was a scar on his left cheek, but it was well covered up. That told Spartan either he had suffered a major injury in the past, or he might belong to one of the infamous fraternities on the older colonies. Still, the number of medals on the man's chest suggested he had seen a long record of service with presumably some experience of combat.

"You know how it is, Sir. Landing under fire is never a good experience for a marine...or soldier." He added the last part, remembering how the distinction between marine and soldier had caused enough arguments back when he had been a raw recruit.

"Quite," was his curt response, but this time Spartan was sure he detected more than a sense of annoyance, perhaps even of disgust.

Great, what have I done this time?

The General indicated for him to walk with him, and the two men moved away from the transport and to the main path. On each side were the beautifully cared colonnades, worked on by master craftsmen over many decades. As they moved towards the Palace, he glanced briefly over his shoulder and to the skyline. He recalled the sight of the burning Yorkdale, the Confederate heavy transport that had been used by the Jötnar. They had landed hard, but their numbers had been what was needed to get inside the Palace.

It took several minutes for them to reach the main steps that led up to the great arched entrance. This had been one of the bloodiest parts of the battle. Spartan looked around and spotted the odd sign of damage and repair work. The General noticed.

"You recognise some of your handiwork, then?" he asked unapologetically.

"Sir?" answered Spartan in surprise.

"Yes, sadly the Brigade was never able to help in such a way as yourself. You see, while you were planet hopping, we were surrounded and disarmed by the biomechanical monsters. Do you know what happened to most of my men?"

Spartan shrugged. He honestly had no idea.

"Me either. The last I heard was that nearly three thousand had been shipped away to work at other sites. They have not been seen or heard from since."

Spartan was shocked at the revelation. He had no idea the forced relocation had occurred on Terra Nova, and certainly not to this level.

"I thought the Biomechs had fought an action against the Brigade prior to our arrival?" he asked.

The General shook his head.

"No, the political coup was absolute, and any military units that refused orders from high command were forced into the camps. We were ordered to assist, and my men refused."

Spartan nodded; gladdened to hear the unit had not sided with the vile and callous enemy. It often surprised him with the speed in which supposedly good and honourable people would change their allegiance and loyalties when something they valued was threatened.

"I had no idea. Why didn't you fight back? Didn't you have the largest military unit on the planet?"

The General glared at him, and Spartan knew he had struck a nerve. For some reason, he had a knack for insulting or upsetting those in authority, even when he was making an effort to not do so.

"The planet was overrun, and the militia already infiltrated before we knew what was happening," he said solemnly and stepped closer to the main door.

Another dozen guards stood to attention, each proudly carrying their ceremonial glaives and one in the centre with the standard. It was a bizarre sight to Spartan, who had managed to miss most of the pageantry associated with the military due to his rapid training and deployment during the conflict. The General stopped near the standard bearer and looked at it for a moment. It was made of silk and moved gently in the very light breeze. Just like those of a bygone age, this one contained the names of the famous battles the unit had been involved in. Spartan was surprised to see there were signs of damage and repair. As well as the symbols of many battles, it also included the names of famous individuals plus iconography of Terra Nova. It was as much a work of art as it was a battle standard.

Surely they wouldn't have carried that into battle?

Spartan was familiar with the idea of symbols and standards, but the idea of these lightly armoured soldiers was alien to him. They wore bright colours and displayed their flag openly. It would make them easy to spot and therefore easy to kill. The General touched one of the repaired holes and turned back to Spartan.

"What would you have done, Spartan? The Biomechs outnumbered my troops three to one, and all we knew was that we had lost contact with Alpha Centauri, and that our government was executing any that resisted. One flank company, the one that carried this standard, marched on this Palace."

He pointed to one of the few holes on the ground that had not been filled in.

"See this mark, Lieutenant? This is where the company stood, and this is where they fell. Only two men survived that day, and it is their individual courage that saved this standard from the Biomech monsters."

Spartan could now understand the bitterness the old General felt. He had been denied a death in battle unlike that which most of the warriors of the last few years had faced. He'd tried to do the right thing, but the glory was not his or his unit's. Instead, most had been killed or sent away, probably to work on mines or to be used in the early stages of Biomech development. He remembered the ships with so many people in storage, the vats on Prometheus, and the great factories that produced the creatures the enemy had used so effectively. He nodded in acknowledgement to the General; now well aware he had overstepped the mark and decided discretion was the better part of valour.

"The Biomechs were a terror. I saw many good men, just like yours that paid the price, some in the fighting and others in the processing plants. We've dealt with those now, and the only Biomech facilities still standing are those for the synthetics. At least that is something."

Major-General Aitken looked at him but said no more. It was the mention of the Biomechs and the facilities that seemed to hurt him the most. Spartan made a mental note to do a little digging later on with regards to what had happened in the many months before the discovery of the Anomaly. The commander turned to the entrance and marched forward. Spartan was forced to double-step quickly to join him, and they moved inside the massive structure. Inside, it was a totally different world to the last time he had been there. Large displays from scores of corporations littered the place, as did the banners and insignia of the new Alliance. It looked more like a corporate event than the sombre seat of power that it actually was.

"As you can see, Lieutenant, it has become something of a circus."

"Sir," he answered quickly.

Spartan scanned the open space and noted the majority of those there were businessmen and women in smart suits. They could, of course, be politicians, but was there really much difference between them? A captain and his aide approached the General and spoke quietly. Spartan noticed both wore the uniforms of the same unit, which intrigued him.

The unit must have been reformed.

The Captain moved away. The General indicated towards Spartan's military issue datapad on his belt. It slid out easily, and Spartan held it out but was a little unsure as to what the General wanted.

"I have your itinerary here. You'll note the Defence Committee is chairing a meeting on the future of the combined ground forces. Major Daniels has indicated he would like you to represent the ASOG and Vanguard units."

With a simple flick of the General's wrist, he transferred the file from one datapad to the other. Spartan saluted and the General was gone. As quickly as that, Spartan found himself alone on Terra Nova and surrounded by a crowd of people he didn't recognise. He glanced at his device and checked the timetable. As the General had already said, there was the meeting of the Defence Committee, but that wasn't for another three hours. He looked back up and saw a number of soldiers in Regular Army uniforms, much like those worn by the soldiers on both sides on Prime. He walked towards them and one, a young corporal, noticed him approaching. They stood smartly to attention, and Spartan returned the courtesy.

"Sir," asked the corporal, "Are you Lieutenant Spartan

of the Vanguards?"

Spartan looked at the man. He couldn't have been just out of his teens, yet his chest was emblazoned with medals. He looked at the others to find the same with each of them. The insignia on their dark grey uniforms was of a wolf. He didn't recognise the design but that was not surprising. The Army units were very large and followed different structures on every colony.

"Yes, I'm Lieutenant Spartan."

The young man smiled and extended his hand.

"Sir, I'm Corporal Broby Ramir of the 4th New Carlos Militia. Your unit protected our flank in the fighting back on Prime. I saw the assaults your marines held off, Sir. I just wanted to thank you."

Spartan sighed but this time of relief. It was rare for him to come across somebody with positive news for a change. The fighting at New Carlos had been a vicious mixture of ranged firefights and urban combat. It had been the first battle where they had made major use of the Combat Engineer Armour, the early version of what was known as Vanguard armour.

"Thank you, Corporal. That was a nasty business back on Prime. How is your unit?"

The Corporal smiled and indicated to his comrades around him.

"We're all that's left of our platoon, Sir. The rest were killed, wounded or retired since we pushed back the Union forces."

Spartan nodded.

"I see, you're not in militia uniforms now, though."

"No, Sir, after you left, the remaining units were combined into the New Carlos 1st Brigade, but we've kept the insignia of the old 4th."

Spartan understood why old soldiers like him were being sent to the summit, but these were rankers. They had experience of combat undoubtedly, but were they what was needed to make major decisions?

"What are you doing at this summit? I can't imagine you volunteered."

The Corporal smiled.

"No, Sir, we're here on an exchange programme. When the ships left with delegates from Prime, there was a call for six volunteers to visit Terra Nova. We're joining the Guards for six months, and they are doing the same back on Prime."

A woman, a private, in her early twenties with short curly hair joined in.

"That's not a bad idea. A little more mixing of units, and we might not have had this kind of trouble to start with, if you ask me, Sir."

All of their attention was pulled away from their discussion and towards some kind of commotion further inside the building. Spartan looked past the scores of people until he found what he assumed was the cause.

A number of people were running to a growing throng around one of the side entrances. A series of loud shouts followed, and then one of the soldiers staggered out of the group and collapsed to the floor.

"What the hell is going on?" asked one of the soldiers.

"I don't know," replied Spartan.

But he didn't like what was happening. Arguments and fighting usually escalated, and there were plenty of soldiers and weapons to be found in this place. He looked at the group and jabbed his finger in the direction of the sound.

"Follow me, it's time we broke this up."

He moved off at a jog and ducked in and out of those that got in his way. The nearer he came to the scuffle the more people he met until eventually he was forced to push through at a walking pace.

"Out of my way!" he snapped, his patience now starting to wear thin. A number of the civilians moved, and he and his group of young soldiers were able to approach the man on the floor. He seemed fine and tried to push back into the throng before Spartan grabbed him. He was almost the same height as Spartan but much lighter build and wore the uniform of a naval cadet. Spartan glared at him, his eyes almost squinting from the set of lights running along the wall.

"What's going on?" he demanded.

The man looked to Spartan and shook his head angrily.

"Get off me, man, they're here again, the animals! Get

off me!" he roared and struck Spartan in the face with the back of his hand. The impact caught Spartan by surprise and snapped his head around to the side. The attack may have been fast, but it wasn't enough for him to lose his grip. He held in tightly, pulling the man closer as he tried to get away.

"Do that again, and I'll have you up on charges!" he said calmly but with conviction.

The man lifted his hand once more, and Spartan delivered a powerful punch directly into the man's stomach. It was short and hard and knocked all the air out of the cadet's chest. He dropped to his knees and choked for air.

"Now, everybody clear this place!" he shouted.

This time the crowds moved back to reveal two Biomechs. Each of the monstrous creatures stood almost three metres tall and was heavily armoured in crude looking metal with the symbols of axes on their chests. The nearest looked to Spartan, but only part of its face was visible due to the armoured helm fitted tightly around his skull.

"Spartan!" it roared and then lurched forward, both of its arms raised high.

The young soldiers with Spartan fanned out, each adopting a balanced fighting stance, just as each had been taught back in basic training. The creature was already at Spartan and swung its right arm around in an exaggerated hook. It swept towards Spartan who took one step forward and did the same. Their muscled arms crashed together with a dull thud into a lock. Those around them watched in confusion and surprise at the odd turn of events.

"Khan, you crazy bastard!" laughed Spartan with genuine pleasure.

Khan started to laugh with the low rumble that all the Jötnar shared. These synthetic creatures were in fact the most recent models of Biomechs that the Zealots and their allies had created. Unlike the early designs, they were possibly entirely artificial and had been created in the factories back on Prometheus. It was hard to tell how much of them was made from harvested human material and how much was completely synthetic. They were sentient though, and Spartan was under no illusions that they represented a subspecies of humanity that deserved respect for what they had done. Khan turned to one of his comrades, a Jötnar warrior Spartan had never seen before.

"This is Osk," he said in much better English than in their last encounter.

Spartan looked at the Jötnar and scratched his forehead. "There's something different, what is it?"

Khan laughed even louder and much to the annoyance of the crowd who were starting to become frustrated at the noise. Spartan turned and looked at any that were coming too close. It was then that he spotted his comrades from New Carlos. He waved them over and each moved slowly, suspicious of the three-metre tall monsters.

"These are fellow warriors from Centauri Prime. They fought hard and in hand-to-hand combat during the battle for New Carlos."

Khan nodded to all of them and placed his hand across his chest.

"If Spartan speaks for you, then you have my respect. He told us of New Carlos. A difficult battle."

There appeared to be genuine warmth in the tone of Khan, and Spartan worried his friend may have changed more than he realised. He did see the look in his eye and detected the dark humour that seemed to lie at the bottom of every Jötnar's soul. He turned back to Osk and tilted his head towards the creature.

"Osk, the first female Jötnar," he explained.

"Female? How did this happen? I thought all Jötnar were male?"

Khan nodded at his question. It was a fair point, as the Jötnar had been created male with no ability to generate further offspring. From what the military scientists had explained, it was probably just a simple way of keeping their experiment under control with a limited lifespan and no ability to create further generations without their help. Khan gave a lopsided grin from his immense jaw at Spartan's confusion.

"Anderson, he said for our species to live we will need differences."

The female soldier with curly hair was listening to

the conversation with great interest. At the last part she seemed desperate to add her own views.

"It makes sense to us. The Jötnar are all based on a standard design with little variation. Even with male and female in the species, there will never be enough variation to avoid defects and interbreeding problems."

Spartan recalled the arguments after the fall of Terra Nova and the factories and equipment that had been used to create the Biomechs. The factories had been badly damaged, but there were also the implications of a race of beings that could be manufactured at will. Some humans rejected their place in society, and others were fearful the factories could produce untold millions of monsters that could enslave humanity. Then there were the liberals who worried about the Jötnar themselves. By controlling their reproduction, humanity maintained a yoke over them, and one that could consign their race to servitude or extinction. Only their war record, and the promises made by the Confederate High Command and the President himself had stopped a new war breaking out in the last weeks of the war.

Jötnar fighting the Confederacy, glad we avoided that one!

Spartan thought back to the last months after the fall of Terra Nova. There had been many reprisals, especially against collaborators but also against Biomechs in general. He had seen papers suggesting over half the population had been wiped out in the three months of purges and violence. The Jötnar considered the Biomechs their untamed brothers and had proven extremely capable in taming them and bringing them under their control. The Biomechs had quickly turned from confused and helpless creatures into violent monsters by their tormentors. He recalled the emergency briefings about a possible war between the crippled Confederacy and the Jötnar and their Biomech brothers. A deal had been forged that guaranteed the right to life for all the Biomechs and the choice to be rehoused with the Jötnar, a choice almost all took. Part of the deal was that the Jötnar would be granted control of any lost unprogrammed Biomechs.

The two Jötnar were busy talking about their comrades and Spartan listened with interest. The last he had heard from Gun, the leader of the Jötnar, was that they had been working with Commander Anderson on a variety of medical issues. He was confused though at how the female Jötnar had arisen.

"I thought the military forbade the creation of any more Jötnar or Biomechs of any kind? In fact, I'm pretty sure it was one of the demands of most of the colonies that it was to form part of the Alliance Constitution as well as granting limited right to the Jötnar?"

Khan nodded feverishly.

"Yes, but Anderson found two Biomech transport ships near Euryale, all with dormant and partly constructed synthetics on board. He had a choice, finish them or kill them. Gun said birth, or the deal with the Alliance was off. He used them to make random changes."

Khan grinned at him with a sly look and leaned in to speak quietly.

"One change wasn't though. Anderson let us alter the sequence so they were all born female. Osk was the first."

Spartan was shocked, both at the idea the Biomechs might now be able to reproduce but also that Anderson had gone along with such a plan. It wasn't that he disagreed, but he knew the Alliance and the Senate would probably have him court-martialled for what he had done. He looked at Osk and then to Khan.

"How many females do you have now? Can they reproduce?"

Khan grinned once more.

"Two ships, each with more than a thousand Biomechs. Almost half are expecting offspring already. First new Jötnar is due in a few months. We have a lot of females now, and they are taking their time choosing mates."

"They?"

"Well, there are lots of Jötnar and not many females to go around."

He looked around to Osk.

"They can be very...picky!"

Spartan stepped up to the female and looked at her. She looked very similar in build to Khan, and the only indications of her change of sex being a slightly larger chest and less harsh facial expression. He extended his arm in a sign of friendship. She sidestepped and pulled on his arm, instantly catapulting Spartan forward and to the ground. He landed hard but kept moving. He jumped up and kicked her in the back of the knee before she could turn. It was hard enough for her to lose balance but not enough to cause major damage. As she staggered, Spartan jumped up and forced his arm around her neck. The two crashed to the ground to the laughter of Khan. Two of the Terra Nova Guards jumped in to break it up, but Khan stepped in their path.

"No, leave them!" he roared.

Osk lay on her front with Spartan on top and doing his best to pin the much stronger Jötnar down. Apart from her name, he could see very little difference between the two of them. He pushed down harder and felt her twist. In seconds, he rolled off her to find the Jötnar pinning him to the floor. Her fist came hurtling to his face, and only months of experience of combat gave him the reflexes and muscle memory to avoid the strike. He used all the strength in his upper body and neck to head butt her in the mouth before she rolled off. Spartan lifted himself up and shook off the dust. Osk did the same and faced him with two trickles of blood running down her face.

"You want some more?" said Spartan as he spat a mouthful of blood to the floor.

She stopped and turned to Khan.

"Gun was right. He is good," she said with satisfaction before marching up to Spartan and swinging her arm much like Khan had done at first. Spartan twisted his left forearm to block it and stopped it just short of his chest. It was a strike although it was a mark of friendship. He looked at her bloodied face and friendly, if somewhat contorted smile. He knew the humour of the Jötnar and brought his right hand over to grasp hers.

"Osk, nice to meet you," he said as pleasantly as he could.

She nodded to him and stepped back to the side of Khan.

Spartan rubbed his face with the back of his hand and noted the blood, more annoying as the blood and dirt was on his dress uniform.

There is a reason I usually stay with my fatigues!

Khan called over to him and the soldiers.

"You, and your friends. You have time for drink?"

Spartan turned to the soldiers who looked confused.

"Well?" he asked.

"A drink with you and your Jötnar friends? Hell yes!" laughed the Corporal.

Spartan nodded, pleased that at least he could spend some time with soldiers and fighters rather than the myriad of politicians and businessmen that seemed to be lurking throughout the building.

"What about the rest of you?" he asked the other

soldiers.

A chorus of acknowledgements confirmed that the small band of soldiers would head to the nearest bar. Spartan gave Khan a friendly punch, and the group moved off down the main hallway, to the astonishment of the assembled patrons.

CHAPTER FOUR

Following the Union defeat at Terra Nova the 1st Jötnar Battalion transferred to the fire world of Prometheus. As their birthplace, it was also the only part of the Confederacy that was relatively unpopulated. As part of their agreement to fight in the War, they were guaranteed freedoms and rights, but many citizens resented the Biomechs playing any part in civilised society. A solution to the Jötnar Question may have been war, had it not been answered by scientists and the unexpected events at Hyperion.

The 1st Jötnar Battalion

The circular Senate House was probably the most elaborate and exquisitely detailed structure Spartan had ever sat inside. According to the information he had read on the flight down to the surface, this part of the Palace had been rebuilt in marble a generation before the Great

War of over fifty years ago, and had housed the Council for centuries. It had always been the seat of power for the planet and ultimately for the Confederacy. Scores of lavish marble sculptures adorned alcoves in the wall. The seating was on multiple levels, apparently in imitation of ancient designs back on Old Earth. Old paintings of important officials were shown on almost every flat service. It was evidently a solemn place, and the atmosphere of seriousness pervaded the room to the extent that Spartan could almost feel a chill down his spine.

Impressive, Teresa would love this place.

Spartan's eye was drawn from the room and its decorations to the centre of the chambers. On a large pedestal stood a massive sculpture of the spaceship Terra Nova, the original colony ship from which the planet had taken its name. Spartan had heard of the tales of the vessel but had never seen a model of it before. This one was almost five metres long, and it showed signs of repair that may have been due to violence or simple decay. Most of the ship seemed to be taken up by massive fuel cells, perhaps more than three quarters of its size. There were a few other key differences between this model and the ships he was familiar with. For one thing, it looked like the ship was unarmed. No vessel of that size would travel through space in his time without at least basic point defence and small calibre weapons. The ship would be at risk from pirates, raiders and kidnappers. There was also no form of rotating habitation ring like on the ships he was used to; in fact, the passenger section looked no different to the cargo holds on modern ships. He was confused for a moment before remembering what he had heard about the early voyages, and the time they had taken to travel long distances.

Of course, the first settlers to Terra Nova were frozen. If they'd made the journey the way they travelled now, they would have been dying of old age.

At least he was pretty sure that was how the first ship made the massive journey of about four light years centuries ago when they had arrived in orbit. There were so many myths and rumours surrounding the founding of each colony, and Terra Nova was no different to the rest. In many ways, the capital of the Confederacy had built up such a mythology that many believed the planet had been colonised for thousands of years, rather than the official three hundred and thirty years taught throughout the colonies. The sound of voices drew him back to what was probably the most boring meeting he had ever attended.

"Let me ensure I understand this new proposal correctly," announced a bitter sounding Marshal Arryne Youtler.

He was the current Supreme Commander of the Army, and from what Spartan could tell, a bitter rival of the Marine Corps and Navy. This was Spartan's fourth visit to the Chamber in the last week, and he was starting to be bored with the tedium of the discussion. Hours of wasted time, and he had not been asked a single question. He tried to think of something else, but the raised tone of the man's voice snapped him out of his daze.

"You have ignored my recommendation on splitting up the remains of the heavily depleted Marine Corps, and instead want to destroy the regular Army and use the resources saved to create battalions of weekend warriors? You understand this will reduce the overall quality of our armed forces, as well as increase the time it will take for us to be ready for major combat operations?"

Defence Secretary Howalt Sones stood up to address the question. In the room sat a panel of almost a hundred other personnel. Most there were senior military officers, but there were a small number of representatives from each of the heavily depleted branches of the armed forces. The Navy, Marines and Army were all there as well as senior commanders of the planets' own militia forces plus those from the civilian branches of the military.

"Yes, we must make cuts, Marshal, but not quite in the way you imply. It is not our intention to slash and burn the military, nor do we intend on leaving our current forces as they are."

The Army commander tried to keep speaking, but the Defence Secretary remained standing.

"Because of the incredible sacrifices taken by our armed forces, we have many units that are now unable to function."

He paused for a moment while checking some number before continuing.

"Army units in Proxima Centauri are operating at less than thirty percent. Marine forces have been amalgamated to provide just two functioning expeditionary forces. Don't even get me started on the Naval losses that are, quite frankly, astounding. In our current state, we are now incapable of maintaining any kind of major operation without a complete mobilisation of able-bodied citizens. Of course that is without looking at the asset stripping of Alpha Centauri by the Union during the occupation. It is not just the Army that needs reform," he explained as he lifted up a thin book and waved to the rest of the assembled men and women.

"Our military has become fractured and competitive. The Army vies for control of the colonies, while the Marines carry the mobility provided by the fleet but lack the heavy equipment and armour for sustained operations. While the Army retains the loyalty of its home planet, it suffers when stationed off world. The opposite is true of the Marines, who can be relied upon by the central command, but do not carry the same authority as the Army on many worlds."

He paused and took a sip of water before continuing.

"Now, these proposed changes to the military will create a new force that is flexible, more capable and loyal to the Alliance, not individual colonies or planets. I think you'll agree that the old idea of territorial forces has created a split that created more problems than it solved. At the same time, we have to reconcile the budget with the money now needed to rebuild following this war."

He sat down, and simultaneously half the members in the Chamber stood to argue. The discussion had been ongoing for hours now, and as far as Spartan could tell, this new paper was in its seventh revision; still they argued as if they had never seen it before. The Council Magistrate struck her hammer for the room to be silenced. Although she carried no actual power, it was her role to manage all meetings in the Chamber, and respect of her and her position was considered paramount.

"Perhaps we might hear the opinions of some of those further from the top? Maybe those that lack the weight of responsibilities carried by each of the honourable commanders?" she said in a stern but polite tone.

All but the Marshal returned to their seating, and it took a long, uncomfortable silence for the old army commander to finally be seated.

"Good," she said and then looked towards Spartan and the handful of junior officers.

"Would one of you like to speak of what you have seen and read so far?"

Spartan glanced to the men and women from the other services, but each appeared to be reluctant to speak their minds. Spartan could hardly blame them. They had each been sent to represent their respective branches of the military and would be expected to promote them at the expense of the others.

Well, if somebody is going to be unpopular and take the bullet, it might as well be me!

Spartan stood and nodded to the Magistrate.

"Sir, I would be happy to speak on behalf of those I have served with."

Compared to the rest of those assembled, Spartan looked very different. He was well built, muscular and tall. His face was slightly scarred, as were his arms, but they were luckily covered up by his hastily cleaned Marine Corps uniform. He was about to speak, but the Magistrate raised her hand first.

"Please state your name, unit and previous experience to the room, Lieutenant."

Spartan nodded and instantly felt uncomfortable with the formality.

"My name is Lieutenant Spartan, previous commander of the Vanguards unit of the Confederate Marine Corps. My previous experience was with the 5th Reconnaissance Battalion under Lieutenant Colonel Blake."

"Thank you, Lieutenant. I see from your military record that you joined the Corps at Prometheus as part of the deal arranged following a violent transgression. Perhaps you might enlighten us to your work prior to joining the military?"

Assholes, they can never just let it go, can they?

"I used to fight in the pit fighting circuit around Prometheus and its stations."

That seemed to get the attention of most of those present, and he could instantly feel them judging him over events they had no idea about. Would they care about the debts he got himself into, and that he'd been forced to work in the illegal world of underground pit fighting to pay back the money? Even the circumstances of his crime that resulted in his service were murky. He'd tried to do the right thing and been punished for it. He turned his attention back to his friends, the Corps and Teresa. He had good things in his life now and that calmed him, at least for a few seconds. He looked around the Chamber and noticed that all their eyes were on him, waiting for him to continue.

"I've fought in battle in space, aboard ships, on moons and on planets. I've seen the courage of all parts of the Confederate military, and I can say, without a doubt, we have some of the best men and women we could ever hope for."

He looked to the Defence Secretary and nodded towards him.

"I have the greatest respect for my family, the Marine Corps, but I do agree with the Defence Secretary. The divisions and rivalries weaken us. It is not the people or the equipment that's at fault. I've been in combat where more time has been spent arguing about jurisdiction and authority than has been spent in battle. I've also seen good soldiers that have been turned against loyalists simply down to the ambitions of regional commanders with political authority," he explained with a clarity that surprised most of the civilians present.

Now that he had spoken, one of the Navy junior offices indicated he would like to have his say. The Magistrate nodded to him and gave him the floor.

"Lieutenant Jerry Sonelsm, Sir. Just back from Kerberos. I served aboard CCS Crusader in the War. Since the surrender, I've served on two cruisers and seen action against Zealot holdouts and pirates around Prometheus."

The Magistrate nodded at his introduction.

"Your service aboard Crusader, what did it tell you with regards to our military posture and organisation?"

He nodded in acknowledgement but then glanced to the highest-ranking Naval commander there, Rear Admiral William Churchill, the only naval senior officer that had fought in the war and come out alive. The Lieutenant looked nervous as he spoke.

"Crusader was a tough posting, Sir. We fought many battles, and every marine and sailor I served with did their duty. I see no difference between the ships, crews or sailors on either side of the Spacebridge. I've had a good career in the Navy, but I saw treachery from politicians, not from the military. Maybe some things could be improved, but I think what we have works. We did win after all, Sir."

He sat back down, and the Admiral indicated he would like to add something. He stood but didn't bother to introduce himself. He was already well known.

"I respect the comments from the honourable citizens I see before me. My own forces were already on their way to Proxima Centauri when we were ambushed. My force was powerful, very powerful in fact. Even so, my vessels were infiltrated by the artificial intelligence implants we are all now familiar with. After we escaped and joined up with Admiral Jarvis in the Proxima Sector, I was able to experience first hand the debacle of the Confederacy. Petty differences between colonies were settled by the use of local militias and often Regular Army units as well. The Marine Corps I doubt were any more loyal than any other force, but they were independent, due mainly to them being based in space and not in colonies. It was a potent mix and resulted in the Zealots and their allies being able to turn colonial aspirations into a movement that coalesced into the Echidna Union. This was helped at every stage by ambitious politicians with authority in the military."

He looked at each of the figures in the room and stopped at Spartan.

"I would like to know what Lieutenant Spartan thinks of the proposed changes to the structure of the military, and in particular the merging of assets."

He stepped back down, and the Magistrate stood and invited Spartan to continue. One of the local governors tried to interrupt but was waved down by the Magistrate, much to Spartan's amusement. As he stood ready to speak, he thought of the words spoken by Admiral Churchill. He'd never really spent any time around the man, but his reputation in the fleet was well known. He took a few deep breaths and continued.

"Well, from what I have seen so far, I would say I agree that our armed forces need a chain of command that begins at the top, with the Alliance and the defence staff. A structure that encourages the things we want and not division and infighting. Since the founding of the new Alliance, we've already experienced changes, good changes. We now have a strong central leadership and reduced local control. Political office has been split from those military commands, and I am already seeing the benefits of this. It would sadden me to see the names and institutions change, but I can see the merits of merging the Army and Marine Corps into a single fighting unit. The mobility of the Marines, the strength of the Army, and it all backed up with the muscle of the Navy. Regional part-time soldiers will provide a sturdy backup with the numbers if required. I assume they won't be armed, apart from when on training or being deployed?"

Marshal Arryne Youtler stood to answer his question and was left to speak. He looked angry, and Spartan assumed the implication that soldiers had played a part in the uprising was a personal affront to him and his organisation.

"Yes, Lieutenant," the Marshal started as he stared at Spartan. He'd seen this kind of look before, usually just before he ended up in the brig on some one-way assignment on a backwater world.

Yes, Lieutenant, my ass. Here it comes.

"The proposal here is to create a large body of part-timers with basic skills and knowledge but no permanent infrastructure or equipment. You understand this means they will be useless until actually posted to combat units. In the case of a major threat, they could be annihilated before they can even be given a weapon. I cannot disagree more on this course of action."

Admiral Churchill gestured he wanted to speak, and the Marshall indicated he could follow from his point.

"That is true, but we must remember that large numbers of militiamen with access to heavy equipment were part of the problem to start with. I must concur with the Lieutenant here. The short-term power of the military must be professional and one hundred percent accountable to the Alliance High Command, under the auspices of the elected Consuls acting on behalf of the new Senate."

He sat back down, and the hostility in the room was now evident. Spartan had been invited to provide experience from the lower end of the scale, but it was apparent that this discussion was actually just a brawl between those at the top of the military, each vying for power. One of the senators, a middle-aged woman with greying hair, stood to speak. As with other more prominent members of the Senate, she failed to introduce herself. Presumably her reputation was well known but not to Spartan.

"The Senate appreciates all that you have shown us, and I thank those of you that have made a long journey to assist. The final vote on the proposed changes to the military structure will take place in the next three days. Implementation will be rapid, no matter what decision is made. We have a confusing system at present with substantial duplication of resources and capabilities. Before I call for a recess, I would like to mention one question put forward by Consul Hamis to the Senate. It is a minor detail, but if our ground forces are combined, what is the proposed name to be?"

Spartan knew right away that this point, probably more than any other, would cause massive trouble between those present. No man or woman would want to see an end to their traditions, and even worse would be for them to be ridden roughshod by one of their competitors. He was certainly familiar with Consul Hamis. He had been the Leader of the House back on Kerberos, and for the last days of the Confederacy had been the Acting President of the remaining colonies. Now the Doctor was one of the two most power people in the Alliance. The new position of Consul replaced the impotent figurehead of President and gave each half of the Alliance a strong individual that could veto the power of the other.

Politics, I thought they wanted my input. Instead, they spend their time arguing. Nothing changes.

The Senator remained standing, even though the rest of the Chamber was busy talking, some even shouting. She lifted her hands, and the Magistrate was forced to shout to force them to quieten down.

"We will have a recess of one hour and then examine the proposals on shipping, weapons procurement and ship dispersal," said the Magistrate before looking back at the Senator.

"Was there something you wished to add?"

The Senator nodded towards Spartan.

"I would like to speak with the Lieutenant after the meeting, that is all."

The Magistrate nodded and brought down her small hammer.

"Meeting adjourned."

* * *

Spartan waited outside the side entrance to the new Senate Chamber. He'd been stood there for almost fifteen minutes and was becoming impatient. One by one, those inside came out. Some had chatted with him, but most moved passed him quickly, doing their best to avoid eye contact. The door opened once more, but this time it was Rear Admiral Churchill. He stopped and shook Spartan's hand.

"Lieutenant, it is good to see a familiar face again. I'm pretty sure you have the same contempt for this kind of horse-trading as I do. You heard the news on the Crusader, then?"

Spartan shook his head.

"No, Sir, not since the recovery of the bodies."

The Admiral nodded at the mention of the casualties. It was almost as though he had forgotten, or perhaps he was merely trying to forget what had happened to them. He paused solemnly before continuing.

"Yes, that was a terrible time, but it's not what I meant. You're probably aware the Alliance is in the early stages of planning the next series of ships to replace our losses in the war? There are very few ships left in the fleet that are not needing major repair, rebuilding or even scrapping. There are also a lot of people out of work following the collapse of much of the private sector economy. One of the largest Alliance projects is a series of substantial public schemes to repair infrastructure and employ displaced citizens. Military numbers might be going down, but the bases, shipyards and ships will all be improved as part of these civic programmes."

He noticed Spartan appeared to be surprised at the news.

"I know, it seems odd to be doing this when we are still talking about the planning stages. Don't forget, the civilian government has mouths to feed and citizens to placate. The shipyards themselves need thousands of people to get them back into shape, and people with something to do is the highest priority. As for the ships, right now they're at the preliminary stages. But to get back to my original point, one thing I do know is they are going to be naming new ships and classes after our losses in the war. Crusader is at the top of the list and will be back, and rumour has it, so will the Admiral."

"The Admiral? As in Jarvis?" he asked in surprise.

"Indeed, the very same. She may have died in the last hours of the War, but her name will live on in the Navy. She won't be forgotten, Spartan."

He smiled and started to move away but turned back to him with a thoughtful look on his face.

"Listen, you've had plenty of experience on our ships. I'm meeting the planners for a short discussion on the new ships' ideas tomorrow. Interested in coming along? You've defended them and boarded them. Your insight could be useful and might give them ideas their researchers haven't come up with yet."

Spartan nodded but then remembered he already had plans for the next day and then even more meetings at the

Chamber.

"Sir, I have a prior engagement with the Jötnar and at least three more sessions here, perhaps another time?"

"Jötnar? They're here?" he asked with a mischievous smile. "I can't imagine that would make them very popular. Well, the comments of the Jötnar would be equally important. I will be working with the planners and designers for the next two weeks. Pop down when you and your comrades have a moment. If you can persuade them to come along as well, I would appreciate it. Changes are simple at this stage, but give it another six months, and we'll be stuck to the designs."

Spartan looked a little confused at all of what the Admiral was telling him.

"Admiral, I don't understand. How can we plan or design anything when we have no idea of what our future military will even look like?" he said before realising the door was open, and the female senator was stood just two metres away.

"Admiral," she said politely and looked to Spartan. There were only the three of them present as she continued.

"Lieutenant Spartan, it amuses me that you think this discussion was anything more than a showpiece. The decision was made almost three months ago. This is a mere formality and a face-saving opportunity for those with personal disagreements, mainly in the infantry. The vote in three days will ratify the work that has already started."

Spartan looked to the Admiral who was unperplexed at her comments. The Senator continued to speak with a serious and direct tone towards Spartan.

"But that isn't what I wanted to speak to you about."

She turned to the Admiral who was busy nodding in agreement.

"Yes, I expect little to change from now till the vote," he said, confirming what the Senator had just said.

"I am heading to the engineering department for the preliminary naval design briefing. If you and your comrades could be there tomorrow to provide additional input, I would appreciate it."

Spartan saluted to the Admiral who then turned and moved away along the corridor to leave him with the Senator. As he marched away, a pair of marine guards appeared from a nearby alcove and took up position behind him. Both wore their dress uniforms, but Spartan could tell they were wearing light armour beneath the slightly oversized uniforms.

They're armed for trouble, I wonder if we're expecting any?

His attention was brought back into focus by the Senator who was waiting patiently for him to turn back to face her.

"We haven't been properly introduced, Spartan. I am Senator Maria Hobbs and the primary representative of Euryale colony."

"Hobbs?" asked Spartan, doing his best not to spit out the name of the Confederate officer who had done so much to discredit him. She was one of the reasons they had lost so many people, and also one of the traitors that had met their death on this very planet. He hoped to the Gods this senator wasn't related to her.

"No, I am not related to the Marine Corps officer. I am well aware of her reputation and of her relationship towards you and your unit. She was a disgrace to the Corps and to the Confederacy. My only regret was that she didn't meet with an accident when she was on Euryale."

Spartan sighed in relief, that was one less thing for him to worry about. He remembered Euryale. It had been a bloody fight both on the ground and in space. It was the event that had nearly cost him his career when after the main fighting. He had left his unit to rescue the Jötnar that were trapped on an enemy ship. It had proven to be the right decision, but Hobbs had ensured he suffered for it. The Senator watched him thinking and seemed almost amused.

"Yes, she was certainly your nemesis, but I assure you, that is a mere coincidence," she explained with a smile.

Spartan relaxed at her comments. It was clear the woman had nothing to do with the other Hobbs. If nothing else, she had a pleasant manner, something the other officer never had, even when things went her way.

"You are probably unaware that I am running the Select

Committee for the Biomechs. The term may be unpopular amongst those with experience of the Jötnar, but it is the catchall for all synthetics. The mutated beasts seen on Prime or the synthetic constructions on Prometheus have been lumped into the same category. Now, I know you have substantial experience with them all, especially their leader, Gun."

Spartan smiled at her.

"That is an understatement. They joined us during the breakout on Prometheus early in the War. Gun is a close friend and an honourable man. His people might not be the same as us, but they did their bit. They never chose this life, but we have a responsibility for them now."

Senator Hobbs was a little surprised at the intensity and warmth Spartan had for the creatures. Few in the Centauri Alliance saw them as any more than pet Biomechs that could just as easily turn on them, as help them.

"I appreciate that a man of your experience and expertise is in great demand during this summit. You already have multiple meetings lined up, but if you could look over a report concerning the Jötnar, it would help me greatly. I don't need you to attend our meetings, but any input you could offer would prove invaluable, and it will be of help to the Jötnar. I'm sure you are aware they have many enemies and critics in every part of the Alliance."

Spartan shook his head.

"I would have thought that here, on Terra Nova itself,

that the people would know better. They bled and died not far from here to end the War. A war they never started."

She said nothing but looked at him. Spartan considered turning away, but deep down he was worried about his friends and the racism he continued to encounter towards them.

Maybe she can help them.

"Okay, no problem, I would be happy to help. What area are you working on, specifically?"

"Welfare, mainly. But you'll see in the report that the Senate has a great many concerns about all of the artificial life we have seen in the last few years. Few trust the Jötnar, and most want the Biomechs wiped out. I would add that I am not one of them. I am a firm believer in the right to exist for all sentient beings in our juvenile Alliance."

Spartan was a little taken back at the thought of annihilating the species. It was abhorrent, even to him. Especially as he knew deep down that most citizens saw little, if any, difference between those that fought for the Union and those now known as the Jötnar. If it ever came to something like that, he knew he would be forced to side with the Jötnar. He could never allow their arbitrary extermination.

"I see, well, please send it to my account, and I will be in touch."

The Senator nodded in appreciation and walked away. Spartan called out before she vanished from view.

"Senator Maria Hobbs!" he called.

She turned back to look at him.

"Is the Select Committee going to renege on the promises made to the Jötnar?" he asked, but he knew in his heart that they were all politicians and businessmen. If it were convenient, they would quite happily turn their backs on those that had helped win the War for them.

The Senator tapped her datapad and lowered it back to her belt. Spartan's own datapad beeped, as a file arrived, presumably the report from the Senator.

"Read the report, Lieutenant. It's all in there."

And with that short comment, she was gone. Spartan stood still and felt he was in the middle of a firefight. He was nothing but a lowly lieutenant, yet since his arrival, he'd been bombarded with arguments, requests and schedules from all manner of people. He would much rather have been back on the Santa Cruz and working with the ASOG teams. He quickly checked the time and assessed how long he had to get to the Admiral. He could make it to Khan, but he wouldn't have long.

Screw this! I'm not going anywhere till I've had a drink.

He glanced down to his datapad device and brought up a map of the immediate area. The bar he intended on meeting Khan at was just a few more minutes away. He turned back to the door and heard somebody approaching.

I'm out of here!

He moved away in the direction of the Senator as

quickly as he could without being too obvious. Once away from the Chamber, he slowed down and allowed himself to take in the splendour and beauty of the great hallways and corridors. The floors were all marble and artwork, dating back hundreds, perhaps thousands of years ago, filled any large space. He rounded a corner to find a large open space with a lavish red-carpeted staircase moving to the next level. What really made him stop dead in his tracks was a large metal sculpture of ancient design of a man. He walked around to look at it in awe of the detail but also of the simplicity. It was old metal, probably bronze due to the green patination and depicted a naked man, protected by nothing more than a large round shield and helmet. In his right hand was a long spear, perhaps three metres long, and pointing up the staircase. He circled the figure until he stopped at the front and noticed a simple plaque at the base that read *MOLON LABE*.

What the hell is that?

One of the Terra Nova Guards spotted him and walked over to stand to his right.

"Lieutenant?" asked the man.

Spartan looked over to the immaculately dressed soldier. "Yes?" he replied.

"The plaque. It reads Molon labe. In English it means 'Come and take them'.

Spartan looked back to the plaque but failed to see how the odd shapes could even represent the sounds, let alone the words of the phrase. He looked back to the soldier to see him smiling. He almost said something he would regret but noted the friendliness in the man's face.

"It is Ancient Greek, that's what the researcher tell me anyway," he explained.

Spartan smiled. The man was being polite after all.

"This is one of the oldest relics from Old Earth. It is of a man called Leonidas who led his people in a last stand against a million soldiers of the Persian Empire. The phrase is his response of defiance to the demands of the enemy to surrender their arms. His small force of just three hundred warriors fought them for days before being killed."

Spartan looked back to the figure. His body was sculptured like an athlete, and he was obviously a warrior of skill and prowess. He was sure the helmet was of a design he had seen before. Without looking away, he continued to speak with the soldier.

"These people, do we know what they called themselves?"

"Of course, Lieutenant. They're called Lacedaemonians after their territory in Greece, but most people named them after their city of Sparta. That's why we still know them as the Spartans."

With that last comment, he almost choked.

CHAPTER FIVE

After the robotic mules of the Marine Corps came a whole array of machines intended to reduce the number of military personnel. First were the supply drones, then the reconnaissance vehicles and then spacecraft. There were short-lived attempts to use Union prisoners in non-combat roles but sabotage and non-compliance made them even less useful than keeping than doing the work with machines. With the severe manpower shortages, the Alliance would become more and more reliant upon the synthetic citizens and machines it detested so much.

History of Slave Labour

With a final burst of its lateral manoeuvring thrusters, the Alliance Marine Corps heavy transport ANS Santa Maria moved into its orbital holding pattern. The massive warship contained two rotating cylindrical sections that simulated Earth's gravity. Large internal storage hangars carried landing shuttles and utility craft for military and civilian operations. The ship carried light gun batteries that were mounted on the rotating cylindrical sections. These were kinetic railguns capable of smashing through any current armour. A veteran of the Uprising in Proxima Centauri, the ship still bore a number of scars from the fighting at the Anomaly Spacebridge and in orbit around Terra Nova.

General Rivers watched their progress from the CIC (Combat Information Centre) situated in the heart of the great ship. As one of the few surviving senior commanders from the War, he was the Alliance's most experienced tactician. He was a hero to those on Kerberos and the other liberated colonies in Proxima Centauri.

"General, we're picking up no traces of the Atlantic Star. No fuel spills, no debris and certainly no distress beacons of any kind. She must have burned up in the atmosphere," suggested Captain George Cornwall.

He was the tall, grey haired commander of the Santa Maria, and it was his first combat mission in his new post. He'd transferred to the ship, following her recent refit at Prometheus, along with the rest of the replacement crew. Though far less experienced that an old warhorse like the General, he had served as a heavy cruiser captain under Rear Admiral Churchill during the War and was known to be a bold commander and a rising star in the Alliance Navy.

General Rivers glared at the viewscreen, as if by looking harder, he could force a sign of the ship to appear. It wasn't just that a vessel had vanished. It was the implication that the enemy could annihilate such a large civilian ship when they were broken and beaten. Even worse, they had done it out here, in the vicinity of one of the most unpleasant planets in the Alliance. He looked back to the Captain.

"Maybe, maybe not. Don't forget, Hyperion is well supported by moons, so we will have to scan every square inch of this place. What is the status of the automated supply post?"

The Captain took a few seconds as he checked the readings on the main screen.

"The supply post is showing as functioning, no security warnings or alerts. Computers are reporting the fuel supply is down thirteen percent, and the log shows the Atlantic Star took on supplies as expected."

General Rivers nodded and continued to monitor the situation.

So she definitely was here, and the only other information we have is her distress signal. Either she was destroyed, or she was taken somewhere else.

Captain Cornwall altered the view of the sector and zoomed out to show the planet and its moons. He pointed to the largest of the satellites.

"What if the signal was forged, and the ship simply hijacked and taken somewhere else? A well-trained crew could move the ship into orbit around one of the larger moons."

General Rivers looked at the map for a few seconds. It was true, the ship could have been moved, that didn't explain why though.

What is so special about the Atlantic Star? She had a large civilian crew and a number of specialists but no major hardware, supplies or equipment.

He walked towards the Captain and examined the moons once more.

"Captain, if you were running an insurgent operation in this area, why would you attack a civilian ship, and what would you do with it?"

The Captain rubbed his chin for a moment as he considered the possibilities.

"Well, there are only two reasons I can think of. The most likely is that they saw something they shouldn't have, or perhaps they would have detected something had they stayed any longer. The only other option would be that they needed the resources from the ship."

General Rivers nodded in agreement.

"Yes, my gut instinct tells me they are up to something in this region. I've seen how they work, and they are the masters at hiding facilities and operations right under our noses. Remember Prometheus?"

"Or Terra Nova," added the Captain.

Yes, that is true. An entire Artificial Intelligence Core that was based under the Palace of the Capital for decades. If they could hide that, what couldn't they hide?

"Captain, keep your crew at maximum readiness. We need to know what's going on here, and fast. I will brief our boarding parties, and they will be ready if and when you find something."

"Yes, General," he answered and the turned back to his crew.

He was needed to oversee the initial scouting procedures to be carried out in the sector. It took time to even prep the craft, let alone launch and send them to their destinations. The General watched as the Captain and his executive officer co-ordinated the large-scale operation. They were fast and efficient, and he was reminded of the quick thinking Admiral Jarvis back when they had planned and carried out operations in the War. Compared to those days, this operation seemed like a picnic. Even so, he knew what was at stake, and as always, preparation was paramount.

Satisfied that the operation was proceeding smooth, General Rivers nodded and then left the CIC and marched down the main corridor. His marine bodyguard followed him closely behind as they made quick progress. It took just a few minutes to reach the briefing room where a number of officers were waiting. As he entered, the assembled crowd stood smartly to attention. The ship was easily capable of carrying over a thousand fully armed men. For this operation the number had been slashed to just three companies of marines from the old 2nd Marine battalion, veteran soldiers that had served on the sister ship Bunker Hill. There were also a number of engineers plus a single ASOG Reconnaissance eight-man troop, commanded by none other than Lieutenant Spartan's wife, Sergeant Teresa Morato. He moved to his customary spot at the front of the briefing room and looked out to the group of no more than fifty people, indicating for them to sit.

"Marines, as you no doubt already know, we are now orbiting around the planet Hyperion, and our mission to discover the fate of the Atlantic Star is now underway. I know some of you may have known passengers on the ship, and I would remind you now that it is imperative you focus on the mission. The only way you can help them is to keep our plan running smoothly."

Teresa looked over to Sergeant Lovett and could see his face tightening up already. He saw her looking and did his best to smile back. She turned back to the General to see a three-dimensional model projected to his side, showing the planet. It looked much like Earth from space but slightly greener and with far less definition to the large land masses.

"Hyperion is a large forest world. It has higher gravity than you're used to and a thicker atmosphere. You will need breathing gear and lighter loads than normal. It is a world richly abundant with plant life and contains an almost impenetrable atmosphere, thicker than any other inhabited planet in the Alliance. There is a good possibility we will need to send drones to the moons but no immediate requirement to land ground forces. There is also a strong likelihood we might need to send units to the moons around us."

The large number of moons flashed on the moving model, drawing attention to them.

"You have all been trained to operate on low or zero-g objects, so keep it in mind. As for Hyperion, well, it is a mist-covered pea soup of a planet. Comms are difficult, and orbital scanning is nigh on impossible. If we want to scout the planet, we will need to drop recon birds into the lower atmosphere."

The model changed to the layout of the ship and the complement of marines on board.

"First and Second Company will prepare for planet fall within the next hour. Third Company and the Engineers will be held in reserve. Any questions?"

Teresa didn't bother looking around and simply thrust her hand up. The General nodded in her direction.

"Sir. What are we expecting to find?" she asked.

General Rivers nodded and tapped several buttons to zoom in to the planet's surface.

"That is a dammed good question. In short, we have no idea. Maybe nothing. Alternatively, we could end up with a Zealot training facility, underground factories or simply a black market trading post. All we know is that Hyperion is the perfect place to hide something, and that we have no current trace of the ship."

He paused and saw another hand lifted up. It was a short black marine from the Third Company.

"General. What about the planet itself? How much do we know?"

"Yes, Hyperion is infamous in folklore for its unusual atmosphere and climate. There are no known hostile life forms on the planet, but in the last hundred years traders and scientists have left invasive species. I have reports on seventeen seeding operations by Confed Bio-Teams to seed the oceans and some of the landmasses with a variety of non-destructive species. According to my report here, they should present no obstacle to our operation. In answer to your question, son, I don't think there are any monsters down there!"

Laughter spread quickly through the hall, but he noticed at least some of it was nervous. The rumours of beasts on Hyperion were well documented and could be traced back to the first unmanned landers that explored parts of the planet. It was rich in life, but nothing had ever been confirmed to match some of the myths of the last generations. Hyperion had been named thus, due to being one of the closer planets to largest of the two stars, Alpha Centauri A, and showed as the brightest object in the sky of its close cousin Terra Nova. The system itself was a complex one that included the binary stars plus the large collection of thirteen planets spread between them.

General Rivers looked to his group of assembled officers and marines. He had given this kind of briefing many times before, but rarely had he found himself with so little to actually say. He'd never visited the planet and, and for some reason, he'd never wanted to although he couldn't understand why.

Hyperion, what secrets are you keeping from me?

As he considered the planet below, he smiled to himself at the bizarre notion of naming the planet for Hyperion, the lord of light, and the Titan of the east. The reality was that the planet was a dark, wet and mist-covered world. The exact opposite of what its name suggested. The noise started to quieten, and he changed the display back to the view from orbit.

"We might not be assaulting a city or boarding a battleship, but this planet could easily swallow up an entire battalion. Remember, a group of skilled enemy terrorists managed to board a modern liner and destroyed her with the apparent loss of fifteen hundred souls. We have a job to do here, and I expect nothing but utmost professionalism from every single one of you."

He was about to continue, but one of his aides approached and leaned forward to whisper in his ear.

"General, the ship's scanners are picking up something. Apparently, it is heading our way. The Captain wishes to see you in the CIC."

General Rivers turned back to the assembled marines.

"Good hunting!" he said finally and then turned, and immediately making for the door. One of his more junior commanders marched from the side to take his place. In that brief moment, Sergeant Lovett stepped closer to Teresa, a look of hope in his eyes.

"What was that? Do you think they found something already?" he asked.

Teresa shrugged.

"I have no idea. Focus on your job, Lovett. If we can do anything for them, we will. Got that?"

He nodded slowly, but Teresa could see his mind was elsewhere. Her thoughts wandered to the planet below, and she imagined a dozen scenarios based on the terrors she had experienced through the War. The last image before she looked back to the commanding officer was of the dreaded Biomechs looming out of a mist-shrouded jungle. Her spine shivered at the very thought.

* * *

General Rivers marched into the CIC as quickly as he had left it. He moved directly to the centre of the room where the Captain was stood and busily discussing something with his executive officer. He spotted the General's approached and turned to face him.

"Sorry for interrupting your briefing, General, but I thought you should see this."

The video feed magnified the small vessel so that it stretched out to several metres in length. General Rivers marched to the main screen and examined the craft in detail. For a moment it looked as if he was ignoring the Captain. The rest of the CIC was buzzing with activity as the two-dozen men and women managed the ship, the automated drones and monitored the planet below.

The ship's XO, Commander Petersburg, moved a dozen images of similar vessels up onto the adjacent display. General Rivers looked at him, but he was unfamiliar. He made it his job to know those that worked around him, but all he knew of the man was what he had read in the man's dossier. Though experienced, the man had served on the Confederate Navy in Alpha Centauri and managed to avoid a single battle in the War. There was no suggestion he had deliberately avoided combat, it happened to many a good officer, but it was still a clear mark on his record. As far as General Rivers was concerned, the man was an extremely efficient career officer, and that could be just what the ship needed right now, a measure of direction and discipline.

"Captain, it's a Centaur class lifeboat, and standard issue on most large civilian ships. Shall I use the tugs to bring it alongside us?"

General Rivers seemed intrigued by the vessel and

moved even closer to examine the marking and scorch marks on the hull before finally turning to face the man.

"That's no civilian ship. I've seen the same craft before but not in this sector."

Captain Cornwall moved to the General and looked back to the XO who simply shook his head in confusion. He turned back to the General who had seen the exchange between them.

"Where have you seen this?"

The General nodded. "You recall the fighting at the Titan Naval Station, right back at the start of the War?"

"Only by reputation, General, both myself and my XO were in Alpha Centauri at the time. We were going through our own problems at that point. Why? There would have been many craft like this one on almost any station or ship in the Confederacy."

General Rivers moved the image to one side and brought up a series of grainy images from the epic battle around Prime. It had been one of the most violent incidents in the first year of the War when the main station had been overrun and held hostage by the Zealots. He moved through the images until coming to the Battleship CCS Victorious.

"The ship the Zealots captured? Didn't Admiral Jarvis assist in crippling her?"

"Assist? No, she fought the Victorious in a long and bloody duel that resulted in her destruction. What I'm more interested in right now though is this."

The image changed to a different shot of the battleship as she was wracked with hundreds of flashes and sparks. They were the obvious signs of the death throes of a ship. He enlarged a shape near the stern of the ship to show a small craft, and it looked identical to the small transport that was approaching them.

"That my friends isn't a lifeboat, it's a standard T9 armoured transport, the same kind of boat we use for transporting marines. Yes, it is based on the model used as a large civilian lifeboat, but you'll notice the improved armour modifications here and here. Plus, look at the front. The armour has been roughly reinforced. This boat is used for transporting Biomechs, and I would put money on that lifeboat out there being used for the same job," he added and pointed his hand off to the main screen.

The XO put the two sets of images next to each other. Side by side they shared a number of similarities, but it was clear they were not identical.

"Okay, what do you suggest?" asked the Captain.

"I know somebody here that's got more experience with Biomechs than anybody else outside of Terra Nova. Get Sergeant Morato up here on the double."

The XO moved his eyes to check with the Captain before walking away to use his communications gear. The Captain looked back at the live video feed of the distant boat.

"Okay, General, I assume you have a plan?"

General Rivers simply smiled back.

"A simple one. We drop a squad of the Alliance's finest on her and search every corner."

The Captain inhaled through his nose as he tried to imagine the interior of the craft. He'd seen images from the War but as yet had never encountered the enemy at first hand, only ever the Union ships.

"And if we find Biomechs?" he asked.

General Rivers seemed to relax a little. His shoulder dropped a fraction and his breathing slowed. He looked directly at the Captain with a look of satisfaction.

"Then we do what we always have done. We board her, draw our weapons and make them forget they ever thought about causing us harm."

* * *

Five days had now passed on Terra Nova, and Spartan's brain felt as if it would explode. Meetings with everybody from civil rights groups, city architects and a dozen different military officials had filled his schedule. The only good thing was that he'd been able to spend some time checking the news and border reports to start getting a better picture of how things were in the Alliance. It was clear the damage to most of the colonies was massive. A Mixture of war, piracy and mass population relocation had left many moons and worlds stripped bare. The casualty figures were in the millions, and thousands were still unaccounted for. With the collapse of Confederate control on Carthago, the planet had gone through its own short uprising that resulted in Union soldiers using atomics on three cities. Only Terra Nova seemed to have escaped the mass damage, but even there at least one in ten of the population had vanished.

"Spartan, what has changed?" asked Khan with an unusually serious tone.

He took a long gulp from the glass and rubbed his forehead.

"What do you mean?"

Khan pulled his head back as if confused at Spartan's lack of understanding.

"Your vote, for the changes in military."

"Oh, I see," he replied, now understanding the question. He still found it intriguing that the Jötnar, a race of creatures with a sometimes childish curiosity, could be interested in administrative details. Spartan was convinced they were becoming more sophisticated with every passing month.

"Well, the vote passed easily, and the changes to the military will be phased in over three months. At the same time, they will start looking at replacement ships and equipment to cover our losses in the War."

Khan nodded, showing he was following the

conversation.

"Is this good?"

Spartan took another sip and considered the question.

Good point, my friend, is it good?

"Well, I agree with most of what they are trying to do. We definitely need to fix the problems in the military that made it so easy for us to fight each other. I'm not happy with the reductions in numbers or equipment, and I'm not really happy at the merger of the Army and Marines. There will be lots of arguments over this."

This part Khan seemed to understand well.

"Yes, warriors are a proud people. Removing the Army will not be popular, I think."

You've got that right, thought Spartan.

He recalled the arguments in the Senate just hours before the final vote. With one decision, the Confederate Army was disbanded. All militia units were officially struck off, even those with outstanding war records. In their place, a small number of part-time Marine Reserve units would be established. Each of these would train personnel with one session a month. Almost all the Regular Army units were to amalgamate with current Marine Corps units, and several extra units would be established. The end result was an enlarged Marine Corps with heavier equipment and more closely tied in with the Navy. Gone were the days of large Army formations stationed on planets. Local security was now the job of the local police and intelligence forces.

Don't I have something scheduled for later?

His thinking about the Marine Corps and the fleet reminded him of the Admiral and his promise. He brought up his notes on his datapad device and found the last message about visiting the ship designers with the Admiral. He'd managed to put it off for over a week, but any longer and there would be repercussions.

How long have I got? He wondered before groaning upon seeing he had less than two hours. *Damn, what can I add to a discussion on shipbuilding?*

An image formed in his mind of the Santa Cruz, the ship he had probably spent the most harrowing of his time on. The more he thought about the ship, the less he could remember any details he thought might be of use. What could he add when it came to engines, armour, cabins or facilities? He sighed at the thought of being stuck in a room where he was forced to talk about such things. A noise distracted him, and it took a few seconds to realise it was the Jötnar sat opposite him talking.

"Spartan?" she asked, evidently not the first time.

"Uh, yes?" he replied.

"Spartan, what do you think then?" asked Osk.

Spartan turned to see her showing him an image of a heavily modified L48 rifle of the type Spartan had used extensively in the War. The grip and stock were much larger than normal and seemingly altered for use by the oversized hands of the Jötnar. He had to force himself not to laugh at the completely different levels of conversation between the juvenile and the mature Jötnar. But it gave him a thought, and the more he considered it, the more he realised how they changed over time. Then he noticed her looking at him, waiting patiently for his response on what must be an important issue to her. He looked at the weapon for a few seconds, leaned back and looked at her.

"Very nice, I've not seen this version before, and L48 if I'm not mistaken, but heavily modified. Who's working on these weapons?"

Khan leaned over the counter with a large glass of a dark red liquid. He threw back a mouthful before speaking.

"Our own engineers," he said with obvious pride.

Spartan raised an eyebrow, both impressed and surprised to hear the Jötnar had come on so far that not only did they understand the use of the equipment, but that they were now actively involved in the manufacture and modification of weapons.

"Jötnar engineers and Jötnar females. Things are changing for your people."

"Indeed. Commander Anderson had negotiated much of the old site for our use. We've been very busy!" he replied and threw back half the contents of the glass.

Spartan's mind was rushing ahead as he imagined hundreds, perhaps thousands of these creatures, working away in the hot underground environment of Prometheus. Anderson must have pushed hard to allow them to use the space, especially as large parts of the complex were being used to manufacture Alliance equipment up to the size of small ships.

"What about the Alliance shipyards and factories?" he asked.

Khan looked confused at the question.

"Jötnar are working in them as well."

Spartan said nothing for a while as he sat there with the two Jötnar. The situation on Prometheus was confusing to him. It seemed the Jötnar had been allotted space on the planet as well as equipment and facilities. Perhaps as part payment, they were working with Commander Anderson and his Alliance engineers. The thought of the facilities brought back the report he said he would look at. It had been days ago, and so far he'd tried to read it several times before going to sleep. Unfortunately, at almost eleven hundred pages, it was just too much to digest along with everything else he had to deal with. He opened it up and skimmed through the table of contents. There were columns of unintelligible technical points, but one caught his eye. It was 'Biomech Internment Schedule'.

"Hey, Khan. What's happening with the Biomech camps on Prometheus?"

Khan looked back to him with an expressionless look.

"The old ones are locked up. Young ones are being trained by other Jötnar."

"Trained?" replied Spartan, now intrigued by the idea.

"Yes, trained. Some for warriors, others for work in factories, making food, helping Alliance build things."

Spartan looked back to the report and read a little further. There were many tables of figures with most outlining the numbers of surviving Biomechs and their internment camps throughout the Alliance. Prometheus was the home to over ten thousand, but other sites were holding just as many. A quick scan of all the ships, stations and colonies brought him to a staggering figure. He looked back to Khan.

"Do you know many Biomechs and Jötnar are left in the Alliance?"

Khan shrugged.

"No. When a Biomech understands Jötnar, they can join us. Then they are Jötnar, like me. Gun said we have more Jötnar on Prometheus than all the marines," he explained and then grinned to Spartan. "So says Ko'mandor Gun."

Spartan looked back to the document and read further. The bit that gave him a sick feeling was when he reached a section on the early Biomechs. Two new terms were being touted, and it concerned him. Rather than the universal and easily understood Biomech, they were now being known as mutations or experiments. Both implied something dangerous, and the recommendations in most cases were destruction or testing of the specimens. It was the easy language of those that treated the creatures with a casual disregard.

Bastards, he thought with disgust.

"Hey, you two want to go to this meeting with the Admiral? He wants to talk about ship designs."

To his surprise they both nodded furiously in agreement. He was a little confused and unsure as to what to say. If it were anybody else, he would have assumed they were joking, but humour was an art the Jötnar were still learning to use.

"Uh, okay. Finish your drinks and we'll head over there."

* * *

The Alliance Naval Architects Department was like no other place Spartan has visited before. The underground rail system had taken them on the short ten-minute journey to the complex deep inside the research and development wing of the Military Academy. Gone were the old fashioned marble buildings, to be replaced by stone and glass. Scores of uniformed personnel watched him as the decorated Lieutenant marched past with two Jötnar in tow. This particular part of the department consisted of a long, wide glass corridor with glass rooms off to each side. They walked briskly to a set of tall double doors at the far end. Once inside, he could see the size of the main foyer, with its dozens of personnel, computers and scale models of scores of different ship designs.

"Where now?" asked Khan who was becoming

impatient.

In the centre of the room was a circular desk manned by three women, each of them impeccably dressed in their new style dark blue Alliance uniforms. Spartan approached the desk and beckoned for the two Jötnar to follow. As he reached it, the nearest looked up at him and smiled before spotting the two creatures. Her smile turned quickly to discomfort. Khan started to laugh.

"Looks like she hasn't met my people before!"

Osk chortled in amusement at her discomfort, and Spartan was forced to interject before it got out of control.

"These are official representatives of our allies, the Jötnar. This is Captain Khan and this is Osk. I am Lieutenant..."

"Spartan?" she interrupted in a clipped and almost artificial voice. She smiled at him and touched her hair with her left hand.

"We've heard of your...reputation, Lieutenant. Perhaps you would like a refreshment?"

She stood to go and get him something, but Spartan lifted his hand to refuse.

"Thank you, but our time is limited. Can we see the Admiral?"

The young woman looked disappointed, as did her two comrades who both watched him with interest.

What the hell is going on in this place? He wondered.

She pressed several buttons on her computer system

while continuing to smile at him. It didn't take long before her face changed to evident disappointment.

"Oh, the Admiral would like to see you immediately in the simulation room."

Spartan raised an eyebrow.

"Which is where?"

The woman laughed nervously, but Spartan could see it was nothing but clumsy flirting. She lifted her left hand and pointed to a long glass entrance in a dark corner. Spartan nodded politely and made his way to the door.

"If I can help you with anything at all, please come and see me," she added as he moved away.

Spartan shook his head in amusement at the emphasis on the word 'anything'. He made it to the door only for a green beam to shine down and scan him and his two Jötnar comrades. It only took a few seconds, and with a low beep the doors opened to reveal blackness. Spartan stepped inside and the Jötnar followed closely behind. No sooner were they inside did the door hiss shut behind and the lights altered slightly. Spartan moved forward and through a generated black wall into a long room. Inside was a sunken space, almost like a small stage. Around it sat a dozen men and women. Some wore military uniforms, others lab coats, and two wore suits.

"Lieutenant, glad you could make it!" said Admiral Churchill with genuine pleasure.

The two men shook hands, and Spartan turned to

introduce the two Jötnar. The Admiral shook both of their hands, indicating for them to join him to a raised seating area overlooking the sunken stage area. Once sat down, he spoke in almost hushed tones.

"You might have already guessed that I didn't ask you here to just talk about ship modifications."

Spartan looked even more confused than the Jötnar at this comment. He moved back slightly in his seat before replying.

"Uh, well, I'm not quite sure what you mean, Admiral."

"Well, I have been commissioned by the Senate to come up with a new class of ship, a craft that will become a universal warship for use in all kinds of operations. The Navy is to have its capital ships slashed to a total of thirty. That is a fraction of the size we are used to. Instead of battleships, cruisers and transports, they want a more economical class that can engage other ships, land troops and reinforce ground operations."

Spartan was shocked at the number.

"Thirty ships? I thought we had a Navy of nearly three hundred ships?"

The Admiral nodded.

"Yes, but over half are due to be decommissioned due to age or damage, and that number also includes small vessels like destroyers and frigates. The smaller craft are not the issue; the plan is to rush a new vessel into production in the next twelve months to replace cruisers, marine transports and battleships. Any slower, and we'll be forced to rely on broken down and failing vessels. Nine ships are being decommissioned this very month. We need replacements and fast. If we build different classes, we'll face a major capability gap. I don't need the best, but I need as good as we can get at everything, and fast."

He looked at the three of them, and each looked as confused as the next.

"The basic recommendations have always been agreed by Navy High Command, a ship of about the size of an Achilles class cruiser with similar firepower. More powerful engines and the capacity to carries up to five hundred marines or a similar sized flight group. A flight deck to handle the landing craft when used for marines or gunboats, and fighters when configured for carrier operations."

Spartan looked both impressed and surprised at the information.

"That is, well, optimistic. Can you deliver that level of miniaturisation into a single ship in the time you have?"

"We have to. The design will be flexible so that each ship can simply alter its crew and craft on board depending on the mission. So some can be used as pure marine transports, like Santa Maria, while others will operate aircraft and perform as carriers."

"I assume they can do both with a smaller unit of marines and aircraft as well?"

"Exactly, you understand the plan, Lieutenant. Now, what I need is any advice you can offer as experienced ground troops. What worked and what didn't aboard the Santa Cruz? I already have information from scores of experienced Navy personnel, but now I have one of the Alliance's most respected marines and two of our best cousins, the vaunted warrior Jötnar."

"Yes!" roared Khan with undeniable pleasure.

Spartan looked at the Admiral and did his very best not to look too happy at being offered the chance to play a part in something so important. He looked at the holographic models being shown in the centre of the room and then to the Admiral.

"Okay, so what can I tell you?"

"Straight to the point, I like it. Tell me about Santa Maria and Santa Cruz. Then I want to hear about that old warhorse, the Yorkdale."

The mere mention of Khan's old military transport caught his ear and his attention. It didn't take long before the four of them were arguing away at the merits and failures of the ships and the units stationed on them.

CHAPTER SIX

The fighting that engulfed the Proxima System proved once and for all that the divisions in the Confederate Military were a major weakness. Marines, soldiers and militia fought each other while Union soldiers and their Zealot soldiers ran amok. It was the violent lessons learnt on the scores of battlefields in the war that paved the way for the new order, the Alliance Military with her modern fleets and well trained marines. The days of politicians leading colonial army militia into battle died with the end of the Proxima Emergency.

Reports of the Proxima Emergency

Sergeant Morato and her team waited patiently inside the Marine Corps landing craft. In the zero-g environment, they were forced to rely on the straps and clamps to stay still while the craft manoeuvred alongside the suspicious transport. The medium-sized vessel was the standard craft used to insert marines into battle and was big enough to land a large unit directly into battle. On this occasion, however, it was just a single marine platoon led by a young Lieutenant Harper and her eight-man ASOG reconnaissance troop. The name was something of a misnomer, as the recon part of the ASOG teams contained the best-trained and experienced members of the ASOG unit. As well as being expert fighters, they were required to be the best at survival techniques, infiltration and a host of other specialisations.

"Sergeant, your troop ready?" asked the Lieutenant, a slight tremble in his voice betraying his frayed nerves.

"No problem here. We go in first, and I'll give you the signal to follow. Remember, watch for friendlies. We don't want any accidents in there."

Teresa watched him nod in agreement before he turned back to the thirty marines in his platoon. With the significant downsizing of many units, it was only the most experienced and mentally stable that was left. So many had been granted long-term leave, and even more moved back to their home colonies to assist in the recovery effort. He gave them a quick pep talk, but it seemed they were all ready and competent. If they were anything like her, they just wanted to get on with the operation. Teresa did wonder why she hadn't feigned mental instability to get out of another tour, but it was just against her nature. She had fought hard to get where she was now, just like

Spartan.

I hate the waiting!

All of his men wore the dark grey PDS armoured suits as worn by marines for a good number of years now. Each of them was encased in close fitting armour and carried L48 carbines with the small-calibre box fitted. When in space-borne operations, it was critical for combat units to avoid large calibre weapons as they could easily penetrate the ship's armoured skin and depressurise an entire section. The optional modification gave them more ammunition, a higher rate of fire and a safer round. Teresa looked back to her own unit but said nothing; they knew what had to be done. She and Lovett had done this kind of thing a hundred times before. The other six were almost as experienced.

"Okay, make sure you keep your weapons on low mode. I don't want to get blown out into space, alright?" she said with a cheesy grin.

The other marines present thought she was being serious, but the rest of her unit knew a joke when they heard it. Unlike the marines, they were carrying the L52 Mark II Assault Carbines, much to the envy of the marines. These weapons could destroy large chunks of the transport if not handled correctly, but that wasn't a concern to Teresa. If these experienced men and women couldn't control their weapons, nobody could. They wore exactly the same armour as the marines with one simple exception; the grey paint had been interspersed with black tiger stripes. It was a minor detail, but it made the distinction between ASOG and marine very clear. A scraping sound indicated they had made contact with the target. The impact shook the marines inside, but it was nothing serious.

"Here we go. Remember, watch for friendlies!" said Teresa.

Almost in perfect synchronisation each of the ASOG fighters activated their visors. With a quick buzz, the fronts of their helmets clamped shut to encase them in an airtight suit. The PDS armour was proof against light small arms but not designed for complete protection against heavier weapons. Unlike the massive power assisted suits of the Vanguards, they were more a replacement for the earlier body armour and webbing carried by soldiers and then marines.

"Five seconds," said the co-pilot in a quiet voice over their suits' intercoms. The interior lighting had already switched to red, and they all clung to the rails in case of a sudden impact. Then came the final crunch. The external hatch slid open, and the automated coupler unit created a bonded vacuum seal between the two craft. It took seconds for the procedure to complete and was followed by the diamond-edged cutters that proceeded to take away the target's exterior hatch. Teresa watched the action from a live external feed taken by the landing craft. She could see the glowing metal where the cutter was busy at work but not much else.

What are we gonna find in there?

In answer there was a much louder clunk as a chunk of metal drifted against their own airlock, a slight hiss, and the interior hatch slid open. That was her signal and without hesitating, she pulled herself away from the wall and kicked. The weightless drifting was an odd sensation, and she was acutely aware that without contact to the walls, she had no control. Her head and arms entered the airlock first, and she failed to find the nearest rung. As soon as she made contact, she made four hard pulls and was inside the vessel. The rest of her unit followed. In less than thirty seconds, they were aboard and inside what appeared to be a large storage area. They spread out, each using one hand and their legs to manoeuvre around the floor, ceiling and walls while keeping the right arm free to handle their rifles.

"Talk to me, Sergeant, what have you got?" asked the impatient Lieutenant still waiting on the landing craft.

Teresa had already switched to thermal imaging and then infrared, but so far this section seemed empty. A quick glance at her team confirmed they had found the same.

"Nothing in the landing area, Sir. We're moving to the crew section."

She pulled herself along what looked like the ceiling to the next section. From the external shape the crew on the Santa Maria had sketched for her, they were about a quarter the way inside. The craft was easily double the size of the landing craft, and Teresa estimated it could carry about two hundred people or a large amount of cargo.

Corporal Smith, a veteran of the Euryale campaign, lifted his hand, the common signal for the team to stop. They all waited, completely motionless save for their breathing inside their suits.

"I've got readings in the habitation section," he explained over the suit's sound system.

Teresa checked her own data that was being collected from her comrade's suit. The networked integration was one of the new features of the PDS armour and being trialled by some of the ASOG troops scattered through the sector.

"Yeah, I see it. Looks like two-dozen tangos in the next section. Wait...one is moving."

On her HUD she could see the shape of the heat blooms as they were projected inside her visor. If she altered the power mode on her rifle, she would be able to blast through the separating wall and destroy the target. Unfortunately, a high-power blast would breach the hull, depressurize the craft, and kill whatever was in the room.

"They could be survivors from the Atlantic Star. Move on!"

Corporal Smith moved through the small connecting corridor and into the multi-room habitation area. It was laid out like most transports with lines of seats, but with the lack of power or lighting, it was hard to tell what was inside. Teresa entered the first section and moved alongside her Corporal. Both lifted their rifles and scanned the area. At the far end, about ten metres away, were five people. None appeared armed although it wasn't easy to tell by using the thermal and infrared overlay alone.

"Alliance Navy, who are you?" she asked.

Her thermal imaging sensor overloaded and quickly deactivated as the internal lights switched on and bathed the habitation area with light. At the same time, three more of her team arrived and spread out with their weapons at the ready. At the end of the space stood a bearded man with long robes and a beautifully detailed sash. On either side of him stood two creatures, much like the Biomechs she'd seen before. But these were different, smaller in stature and less animalistic in look. They carried firearms but of a pattern she was completely unfamiliar with. There was one thing they all had in common, the colour red. All five carried blood red symbols of a snake goddess emblazoned on their chests. Two of her men moved ahead only for a fifth guard to appear. He swung a mace type device that embedded in the man's shoulder. The armour managed to absorb the impact but still sent him spinning out of control. Teresa twisted slightly and placed the central figure in her sights.

"Hold your fire!" she barked.

The man lifted both his hands, but she couldn't tell if

they were the common sign of surrender or simply to get attention. Either way, his guards lowered their weapons a short distance, and the stray guard moved back to the side wall while two of Teresa's team pulled the wounded man back behind them.

"Greetings, soldiers. My name is Pontus, and I bring a message of peace and reconciliation on behalf of my brothers. I wish to speak with your Captain."

Corporal Smith looked to Teresa, and she could just about see his bemused expression through the smoked visor. He raised an eyebrow and looked back to the man. She didn't recognise the name Pontus, but these were clearly not Alliance citizens, and the symbols were very similar to the Echidna iconography she had seen so many times before.

"What do you want? Where is the Atlantic Star?" she demanded in a firm voice.

The man smiled and reached into his pocket. The ASOG troopers turned their aim directly to him, but Teresa lifted her hand to halt their eagerness. From the folds of his robe, he removed what appeared to be an identity chit. He smiled and pushed it away towards Teresa. In the zero-g environment it moved in a perfectly straight line but slow as if being draw by an invisible cord. It took nearly five seconds to reach her, a time that increased the tension ten-fold in the habitation area. She reached out and caught it, then pulled the chit up to her visor. She examined it carefully before looking back to him.

"I have large numbers of the survivors. A tragic accident, you might say. Now, bring me to your Captain so that we might discuss the issue."

Sergeant Morato nodded to her unit who moved in closer around the man. His guards lifted their weapons and directed them at her. The troopers stopped their movement forward, but kept the enemy in their sights. Pontus smiled at her.

"That is quite far enough. Now, I am waiting."

She looked at him for a few more seconds and finally contacting the Lieutenant.

"Sir, we've got a security chit from the crew on board the Atlantic Star. We also have guests."

There was a short crackle from the communications gear, and only a few of the words made it back to her. She changed the coding and tried again.

"Sir, I have a man here called Pontus. He says he is a brother, that's how Typhon described him and his comrades on Terra Nova. He says he wants to see the Captain. Oh, and apparently, he has survivors from the Atlantic Star."

Still there was no answer. She was about to make arrangements when two of the marines appeared along with Lieutenant Harper. Once next to her, he tapped a button and opened the visor of his helmet. Teresa shook her head angrily at the reckless stupidity of doing that.

The PDS suits lacked the sensors to check the immediate atmosphere, and he had little to no protection against biological agents. He looked to Pontus and back to her.

"Comms are non-functioning. Must be something to do with the interference from the atmosphere. Who is this?"

She maintained her aim on Pontus but leaned in close to him so Pontus and his guards would be unable to hear her. The Lieutenant looked just as much worried, as he was surprised, to see the man on the vessel.

"Sir, I think he might have some kind of relationship with Typhon and the Zealots. He describes himself as one of the brothers, and he's got a Biomech guard."

The young Lieutenant examined the man from a distance and was intrigued by his armoured bodyguards. With a hand gesture, he ordered his own men to take up flanking positions.

"What does he want, and why the hell is he here?"

"He said he's called Pontus, and he wants to talk with the Captain."

The Lieutenant shook his head at the suggestion.

"Does he now? Why would I even consider this offer? He might be carrying a weapon, or a bomb of some kind."

As they talked, the man stood silent, watching them both with a bemused expression on his face. He seemed to become more and more exasperated by their talking until he finally interrupted them.

"I can see that neither of you is in charge of this little endeavour. It is very simple. Either you bring me aboard your ship to meet with your Captain, or my pilot will detonate our engines. He looked to his left hand where he carried some kind of time device.

"I will give you thirty seconds to decide."

Teresa looked to the Lieutenant for a decision, but he seemed uncertain as to what he should do. He tried once again to contact the Santa Maria, but their communications had dropped from the odd lost data packet to disconnection. The system reported a total signal loss at a distance of more than a few metres.

"Sir, something is going on here. I recommend we leave this craft immediately."

Pontus shook his head.

"Twenty seconds. If anybody leaves this vessel, I will have the engines detonated. I have no wish to cause harm, merely to speak with your Captain. You may search me, and my guards will stay here during my visit. What do you say?"

* * *

General Rivers waited patiently in the briefing room. A dozen heavily armed guards stood nearby and outside were another three squads, all ready to jump in with a single word. He heard footsteps approaching and looked to his personal guards. They were ready for trouble. From the right hand door the familiar shape of Sergeant Teresa Morato appeared.

"Sir, he'll be here in less than a minute."

"Good," he replied, more relieved at the end of the waiting than anything else.

The lights in the room flickered and returned to normal.

"Is it just me, or are we experiencing more than the usual level of equipment failures and disruption right now?" he asked rhetorically. As if to answer his question, the figure of the ship's executive officer entered the room. He saluted quickly to the General before speaking excitedly.

"Sir, our ship-to-ship comms are still functioning. We cannot reach Alliance Fleet Headquarters though. The Captain is concerned that the transport may be carrying some kind of device. He is withdrawing the ship to high orbit and away from the craft, just in case."

"Good," replied the General.

But there was no more time, as four marine guards entered, closely followed by the flowing robes of the stranger, Pontus. He marched directly to the General and stopped in front of him. He held out his hand, but the General ignored his attempt at mock friendship.

"General Rivers, your reputation amongst my brothers is well known. It is an honour."

He chose to ignore the obvious slight and stepped next

to the executive officer.

"I presume you are the ship's second in command. What might your name be?"

General Rivers lifted his hand to stop the XO from speaking.

"Pontus, that is your name? I have questions for you."

He smiled at the words, his face betraying a cockiness and arrogance that sent a shiver down the General's spine. He stepped back and looked around at the almost completely empty briefing room. It had been stripped of anything of note apart from a small number of the old recruiting posters at the start of the War. One showed a burning city with dozens of civilian bodies littering the ground. The title read *Remember New Carlos*.

"On behalf of my brothers, I have a short statement to make," he explained.

General Rivers signalled to one of the marines who stepped beside him with a video recording unit. Pontus looked at it and to the General.

"Hyperion is ours and has been for nearly thirty years. A day of reckoning is coming, a day that will render you and your friends irrelevant. My master informs me that no ship may enter within half a million kilometres of this planet without facing severe consequences. You have already forfeit these ships, and what we do with your lives is another matter."

The General gave a short signal with his right hand,

and two marines leapt forward and grabbed the man, shackling him between them. He then marched close to him and pushed his face directly in front of the man's.

"How dare you threaten an Alliance ship! Tell me, who are you and what are you doing here? The War is over. The Echidna Union was destroyed, and your Zealot friends have vanished like the cowards we both know they really are."

The last line seemed to rankle Pontus more than anything else. His amusement changed to bitterness, and his tone altered to a higher pitch.

"You will unhand me and listen to my terms, or face the consequences. If you do not then..."

He was cut short by a quick uppercut from General Rivers that landed under his ribs. Pontus dropped to his knees, his chest heaving from the pain. As he lay there, General Rivers called over four marines from outside. They moved in and attached security poles to their enemy's arms and shoulders.

"Throw him in the brig."

They dragged him out through the door, and as he vanished, he could hear the man shouting as loudly as he could.

"You have ten minutes, General, then you will reap the consequences of your actions. Trust me, my brothers will make you and the crew of your ships suffer like never before."

He said something else, but by now he was too far away for anybody in the room to actually hear him anymore. The XO looked at the General with a confused expression on his face.

"What do you think he meant?" he asked.

The General scratched his chin and then made for the door.

"I don't know, but knowing our friends, it can't be good. We need to get to the Captain and fast, come on!"

It didn't take long for the two officers and their entourage to run the short distance between the two important parts of the ship. When they arrived in the CIC, it was clear something bad had happened. At least half of the computers were showing nothing but diagnostic screens, and two flashed on and off repeatedly. The mainscreen was functioning and showed an image of the small taskforce of five ships as it made slow progress in moving further from the small vessel.

"We need to get away from that craft and fast!" he snapped.

"It takes time to shift orbit," explained the Captain who was already busy discussing the problems with his chief engineer.

"Screw the orbit, just move us away from them, and fast!"

The internal alarms triggered, and there was only a brief warning to those on the ship before the engines triggered.

Any change in acceleration would act as an additional force on the ship and cause a variety of complications to those not strapped in. Even the rotating artificial gravity sections would be affected; the occupants would hit by multiple forces pulling in them. The alarms continued as the engines burned and pushed the heavy warship into a higher orbit. The four escorting cruisers were at different levels, and two were in a lower orbit as they oversaw the scanning of the planet's surface.

"Captain, I'm detecting an energy signature from the northern continent. It is something massive, Sir," said the tactical officer.

Captain Cornwall's gut instinct told him something was coming. He wished he had some kind of functional shield he could activate, but in this age, it was armour and defensive weapons. He glanced at the XO who was waiting for the command. All it took was a nod, and Commander Petersburg dove into his procedures.

"This is the XO. Battlestations, this is not a drill. All crew to your stations, prepare for battle!"

The familiar red lighting and low level siren echoed through every part of Santa Maria as the ship moved to a battle ready state. The crew were fast, very fast. Captain Cornwall watched as security and medical teams reported in, and the weapons crew activated the many weapon systems on board. Like most ships in the old Confederate fleet, she was equipped with different weapons for different situations. Her main guns were medium-calibre railguns that were fitted into the rotating sections of the ship. They were deadly against medium to large targets. For close defence, she had been retrofitted in the War with additional point defence systems. These were small-automated turrets with multi-barrelled Gatling guns. Though primitive compared to the railguns, they were cheap and easy to install and gave decent protection from missiles, rockets and other projectiles.

"What did he want anyway?" asked the Captain in the brief lull before whatever was about to happen.

"He wants to speak with you, or we will face the consequences. He said our ships were already forfeit, and all that was left to discuss was what to do with those on board."

Captain Cornwall considered his words as the rest of the deck crew went about their duties in preparing the ship.

"Did he now? Well, there's no way in damnation I am giving up our ships."

The General nodded in agreement, moved to a chair on the right, and started to pull on the straps. It was a requirement when in battle to put them on, and he had no desire to fly around the CIC and crash into people or equipment.

"Captain, all stations reported in. We're ready for battle," said the XO.

Captain Cornwall had strapped himself into his chair and checked the tactical disposition of his force on one of the smaller side displays. Two of the cruisers were already a good distance away, and the third was the same distance as his ship. What concerned him though was ANS Thunderer was still very low and moving away from Pontus' vessel more slowly that the others.

"What's the hold up with Thunderer?" he asked.

"Sir, emergency contact by the chief science officer on Thunderer. He says they are losing power to main systems. Something about an energy burst from the surface, Sir," said Lieutenant Nilsson from her communications desk. She was one of the many experienced officers from the destroyed battlecruiser Crusader that had found new homes throughout the fleet.

Proximity alarms sounded even louder than the battlestations alarm. The XO looked at the displays and back to the Captain while simultaneously lifting the microphone.

"This is the XO. Brace for impact!"

Captain Cornwall watched the mainscreen with dread as what looked like a green pulse of energy moved up from the surface and towards his ships. For a second, he thought it was heading for the Santa Maria, but instead it altered course by a few degrees and hurtled towards Thunderer.

"What the hell is that?" he demanded.

"Unknown, Sir. Its energy signature is off the charts," replied the tactical officer.

There was no more time for analysis. What happened next only took less than ten seconds, but to those on the bridge watching it appeared an eternity. First the energy pulse rushed towards Thunderer. The point defence systems did their work, and streams of projectiles ripped into the object, yet still it came. It collided towards the rear of the cruiser and flashed with intensity of a low yield nuclear device. With no air to carry a shockwave, there was no sound or blast inside the Santa Maria, but the damage was obvious. As the light flash quickly dissipated, it revealed the wreck of the cruiser, split into three by the blast of energy that was more powerful than any weapon they had seen before.

"Gods, what is that thing?" muttered the Captain.

The three large chunks of the cruiser drifted out of control, yet they remained in orbit. Each of the crew watched as small numbers of lifeboats tried to escape the carnage. Molten metal and debris littered their path and for every two boats that got away, one was trapped or destroyed by the field of rubble.

"Engines all ahead, get us out of here!" demanded the XO to the rest of the crew.

He seemed unscathed by the terrible event that had just occurred, but in reality he was just doing what he had trained to do for years. When trouble hit the ship, it was his job to operate on autopilot, and to ensure the safety of the ship and the crew, no matter what was happening around them. He was forced to shout several times to snap the crew out of their daze. Over the speakers was the sound of crackling and static on the open channel. At least three of the lifeboats called out in desperation before Lieutenant Nilsson cut the feed; there was little need to spread the terrible sound to anybody other than those that could help in some way.

"All crew accounted for, Captain, looks like just the one shot against Thunderer," explained the tactical officer.

The rumble of the engines increased as the Marine Transport pushed away from their current position with all the power that could be forced from the smaller engines. The large ship was equipped with powerful engines for long distance travel, but it took time to prepare and fire them up as well as a large number of internal procedures that must be carried out prior to them being activated.

"Is this what that bastard in the brig threatened?" he snapped, his rage almost uncontrollable.

"He didn't give specifics," said a resolute General Rivers who until now had kept quiet. His job was to command the overall operation and to plan the ground phase of any missions. The running of the ships was out of his jurisdiction and his knowledge.

"That was clearly a message, though. Can they hit us again?" he added.

The tactical officer already had three screens showing the weapon and pages of data from the attack. He looked over his shoulder for a brief moment.

"So far it seems to be a magnetically shielded fusion bomb. It must be controllable though and big, very big. At least the size of a shuttle and well armoured. Based on the rate of assent and its ability to track and hit a cruiser moving at speed, I suggest we need to leave orbit and fast. I cannot give you an accurate limit to its range."

Two of the displays shut off, and the rumble from the engines stopped. Captain Cornwall looked over to the status indicators to his right. They showed that two of the powerplants had shutdown, and a large number of systems were following.

"What in damnation is happening to my ship?" he demanded.

General Rivers looked at the screen and to the Captain.

"I think it's time we had a little chat with our guest, don't you?"

As if to emphases his point, the mainscreen flickered and went black. The few computer systems remaining showed garbage or corrupted data and imagery. Even more worrying was the fact that remaining power system was starting to overheat due to the heavy requirements now being placed on it. The Captain starting issuing orders via the computer system while simultaneously calling over to General Rivers.

"General, we've got problems here. Can you get down to the brig and negotiate something, anything? We can't afford to lose another ship out here."

General Rivers was already on his feet and holding one of the many side rails to stop him from falling. He tapped his communications unit and reached Sergeant Morato.

"Get your entire troop down to the brig. We have things to discuss with Mr Pontus."

He dragged himself to the door and looked back briefly at the confusion in the CIC. It reminded him of the worst moment in the middle of battles, especially some of the situations he and the Admiral had been involved in. The Captain was competent, but he was in no way a match for the old Admiral Jarvis. He sighed and dragged himself out into the corridor.

"Come with me, to the brig!" he said to his waiting guards.

CHAPTER SEVEN

The status of Earth reached its lowest point with the founding of the Centauri Alliance. With each colony now providing senators to the Terra Nova, the old worlds became less and less significant. With the first colonies established at Epsilon Eridani, Gliese 876 and Procyon the significance of Earth would not change until the great scouring, an event that made even the Great Uprising pale into insignificance.

The Decline of Earth

Pontus waited in his cell and listened with pleasure at the sound of the shouting and confusion aboard the Santa Maria. He'd expected no better than to be placed in the most secure part of the ship, and the shouting from some of the crew about the loss of a cruiser merely improved his mood. The cell itself was basic and protected by a strong, triple-bolted security system that was monitored by a central command station. The two marine guards stationed at his door wore their armoured suits and carried the by now well-known L48 rifles. He sneered at them as he remembered some of the more bloody encounters he faced in the last decade with men just like them.

Insects, worthless non-believers with nothing to commend them other than blind obedience to their parasitic capitalism. They even refuse the salvation of our holy mother, Echidna, she that is many.

He lowered his head reverently at the mere thought of his God and master.

By the time General Rivers and his entourage arrived, he was thoroughly enjoying himself. The Marine officer evidently wasn't wasting time as he ordered the door to be opened and marched right in to face him. Pontus was tempted to strike. It was probably the best opportunity he'd come across to remove this troublesome man, but he had his orders.

"General Rivers, how nice to see you. I trust you now understand the gravity of our meeting? I was not joking."

He spotted the movement of the man's arm, and his stomach muscles tenses up at the expected blow. He could have avoided it if he wanted, but it would have been futile. The General was surrounded by loyal guards, and all probably desperate to strike him down. No, he took the attack and dropped down to his knees and wheezed. They waited for him to recover and stand back up before any of them spoke. One marine leaned in and whispered into his ear. The General looked even angrier but resisted striking again.

"Ah, I see," he said with obvious relish. One of the marines took a step closer, but his Lieutenant grabbed his shoulder and pulled him off. Pontus smiled as though thanking him before continuing.

"By now you will understand that I was being entirely truthful with you. I have no interest in seeing your people suffer. Be under no illusions though, Echidna will not let your ships leave this system, and any further attempts to circumvent her will, will have severe consequences for the rest of your little fleet."

General Rivers shook his head angrily.

"Hyperion is an Alliance world and nothing to do with your group of terrorists. You will surrender your forces immediately, or we will be forced to direct tactical atomics onto the surface."

Pontus merely chortled at the suggestion. The General recognised the self-importance he had seen on other members of the cult and knew the man could not be reasoned with. He decided to try and learn as much as he could.

"Who are you, Pontus? What are you doing out here?"

Pontus nodded and scratched his cheek as he considered the questions.

"I am one of the Children of Echidna, like my brother Typhon. We serve her and await her coming."

He grinned at the obvious confusion in the face of the General.

"She needs workers to finish our great temple, and your war has provided workers in the thousands for us."

Alarms triggered inside the ship, and a marine ran inside the brig section with obvious terror on his face. A crewman carrying a mobile engineer's datapad, a large device that allowed remote access to certain management parts of the ship, followed him. The sound of what appeared to be gunfire came from a long distance inside the hull of the ship.

"Sir! We need to move you, now!" he said, grabbing the General. The General easily brushed the man's arm aside and looked back to the sneering face of Pontus. He stepped closer and pointed his right hand at his face.

"What do you want from us?"

Before he could speak, the marine tried to grab him again, but this time was stopped by a marine guard. The two started a rowdy disagreement while the General concentrated on the prisoner.

"Echidna needs labour, and the people on your remaining ships will be a useful asset. Stay in orbit, and wait for our transports to arrive to take you to the surface. My guards are coming for me. Refusal to let me leave, or any attempt to leave your current position, and your ships will meet the same as your first cruiser."

General Rivers' guard moved closer, but the Sergeant

of his guard unit leaned in and whispered.

"Sir, we have a major situation here. Machines in the secondary landing bay, looks like a boarding party of some kind. We need to get you out of here."

General Rivers looked to Pontus, but the Sergeant looked adamant.

"Sir, now!" he said as firmly as he dared.

The General stepped back and towards the door. A group of marines, all in their PDS armour and carrying carbines ran past him and took up positions at the end of the corridor. He was convinced he could hear the metallic clunk of machines moving, but it could easily have been his imagination. The engineer turned his device around to show him.

"Sir, look. They are remotely shutting down our systems, one by one. Weapons and propulsion are down. Life support and gravity will be next."

He looked back to the guards in the brig and nodded to the man at the security station.

"Release him," he ordered, turning to the other guards.

"You will put him in irons. He's coming with us to the secondary landing bay."

The marines and crew went about their business to release and shackle Pontus while General Rivers assessed the situation. He looked carefully at the systems failure on the engineer's equipment.

"I don't understand. Most of these systems are

hardwired. How are they gaining access and controlling them?"

The engineer shrugged.

"The only option is that they have something or someone on the inside. I have been locking down the subsystems one at a time and posting crew to manage them at each station. It takes time, but so far I've completely isolated the last remaining powerplant."

Pontus was now out of his cell, fitted with restraints and a locked collar attached to a metal rod.

"How long until you can lock down the entire ship?" he asked.

At least three hours, and that's assuming I can reach the main conduit here," he explained while pointing to the section of the ship.

Captain Carlos, commander of the First Company and four more of his marines arrived and ran to the doorway. He was a decorated veteran of Euryale and as loyal and experienced an officer as existed in the Corps.

"Sir, the Captain sent me to retrieve you and bring you back to the CIC before we lose control of the ship."

General Rivers shook his head and pointed to the map. It showed a bright green schematic of the ship and its primary systems. He tapped the primary conduit.

"No, either we regain control of our systems or we start falling into the atmosphere. This conduit is on the other side of the secondary landing bay, right?"

The engineer nodded.

"I thought so. Right, you all come with me, and get Pontus out at the front. If they want something to shoot at, they can have him."

He looked back to the engineer.

"Can you reach the CIC on that thing?"

The man shook his head furiously.

"No, Sir. After they breached the habitation seals, we lost all internal communications, and that includes data access to all networked and connected systems. That's why the Captain sent out engineering teams like us to restore and protect what's left."

"I see," he replied slowly.

He looked back at his men as he formulated a quick plan in his head. It seemed simple to him. Either they ejected the boarding party and restored their systems, or they let Pontus and his people leave to achieve the same. Either way, he was going to be there and if possible, he would make the man pay.

"Right, to the secondary landing bay, now!" he growled.

With that order, the first small group of marines pushed off ahead. They took the shackled Pontus with them and pushed him out to the front like a mine detector. About ten metres further back was the General and his personal guard unit. They made quick progress as they worked their way there. Unlike the main bays, this one was actually located in the retaining habitation ring. It was very difficult to actually land inside but perfect for the launch of small lifeboats. General Rivers assumed the only possible way of landing there successfully would be a forced entry with drones of some kind. The only surprising thing was that none of the compartments had explosively decompressed. They moved passed two crew, one was bleeding was a gash on the shoulder.

"What's happening back there?" asked one of his marines.

"Machines, in the habitation ring, and they're killing anybody they find. They...they are coming this way!" said the young woman, her voice trembling.

The marine looked up to the General, half expecting him to order a retreat. Instead, the veteran commander simply shook his head and nodded in the direction of the sound. All that changed was that he reached down and pulled out his Marine Corps issue pistol and pulled back the slide.

"We're ending this, now!"

The marine nodded, and with that the entire party continued on and towards the sounds of screaming and violence. General Rivers felt his pulse quickening and although he might hate to admit it, the thought of getting back into action made him feel alive again. It was only when he rounded the last bend to reach the double width access corridor, could he appreciate the carnage and violence the machines had caused. At least a dozen shredded bodies lay strewn about the floor. Heads and limbs had been torn off, and all that remained were three metal machines, like some monsters from ancient myth. Like mechanical spiders, the things were larger than a man but featured no discernible head. Their eight limbs were thicker than a man's legs, yet more fully articulated and ended in scythe shaped toes. At the sight of the marines and Pontus, they stopped and froze completely as if they had been switched off. The nearest of them was bathed in red blood, presumably one of its many victims.

"Let me leave, and they will come with me. Resist, and they will carry on their fine work aboard your ship. Your choice, General."

At the last words from Pontus, the three machines lifted up four of their eight legs and extended their razor sharp talons towards the General and his men.

"What the hell are these things?" cried one his men only to be berated by Captain Carlos. He leaned in towards the General.

"Sir, what do you want us to do?" he asked.

General Rivers looked to Pontus and then the blood splattered machines that waited for their order to continue on with their violent rampage. What he wanted to do was to lift his pistol and blast the things apart. His gut instinct reminded him of the failures on their ship and the hundreds of men and woman that had already died. He lifted his pistol and pointed it to the forehead of Pontus.

The man looked back, and his expression changed from surprise to amusement. Pontus could see the General was torn between what he should do, and either through malice or just simple amusement, he decided to play one final card.

"Oh, one last thing General. Either you or your Captain will accompany me to the surface. Now, release me!"

General Rivers glared at the man, his right hand twitching with desire to blast the hated enemy. The machines nearby moved towards the marines. It was very slow, almost creepy in nature, but they were drawing the confrontation to a head.

"You have sixty seconds to make your decision, General. Or my metal friends here will send a coded signal to our ground base to use our weapon against your pitiful little fleet.

The young engineer from the CIC spoke into his left ear.

"Sir, before I left, we detected additional signatures from the planet that matched the last weapon impact. It is likely they can do it again."

That wasn't the news he wanted to hear. Now he was stuck in a small space with a dozen armed marines, three robotic machines, and a psychotic terrorist facing him. Sparks from one of the malfunctioning display terminals on the wall snapped him out of it. With just seconds remaining, he needed to make a decision.

Do I let him this bastard go and let him take me with him? Or do I end this now, and put a bullet in his skull?

He looked at Pontus and tried to work out if the man was bluffing? Could he trust this man to keep his word, and was he prepared to die? The more he looked into the man's face the more he knew this man was happy to die. It might even be what he really wanted.

Bastard!

* * *

Spartan was in the greatest battle of his life. The area was more than a bit like that of a professional fighting ring, and its walls seemed to be carved out of solid rock. The only light came in through a narrow hole in the distant roof, bathing the floor in a pale blue sheen. A dozen bodies lay around him, and yet four more Biomech gladiators stepped in for him to fight. It seemed nothing he did would stop the unrelenting hordes of enemies.

"Die!" he roared and rushed forward to the nearest creature.

In his right hand he carried a great axe, and in his left a small metal buckler. He reached the first and smashed its weapon out of the way to leave the creature's head exposed. In a quick movement, he twisted his hip and brought down the axe with such force that the monster exploded in blood and gore that drenched him from head to toe. He pulled the weapon from its body to reveal nothing but a pool of blood and gore. A loud roar and buzz made look up to see a great black shape rushing for him. It made a terrible buzzing sound and stopped him in his tracks. He shook his head and shouted only for his voice to seem weak and muffled. He opened his eyes to the sight of the flashing light, and the buzzer on his video comms unit droning continually. For the briefest of moment, Spartan almost struck it with his fist.

He'd been in the middle of a dream, a violent reimagining of one of his gladiatorial contests back from before he had been a marine. The tone was loud, and the slowly increasing internal lights made him lift his hand to his face.

What the hell is going on now? Somebody forgot a meeting appointment?

He looked to his left and could see the blinking unit next to his bed. A bright red light flashed several times a second to remind him somebody wished to speak. He slid over the bed and lowered his feet to the floor. The coldness made him jump as shivers ran up through his muscles.

Here we go again.

Spartan tapped the button, and the black, featureless face of the unit changed to that of a naval officer. He rubbed his tired eyes and tried to focus.

"Lieutenant, Admiral Churchill here. I need you in the

Defence Committee room in fifteen minutes. We have a major situation developing."

Spartan shook his head, partly out of confusion and also in surprise. He was after all merely a low ranking officer. Strategy and operational planning were not something he was ever involved in. His brain went into overdrive as he considered the kind of problems that could occur on Terra Nova that might require his special skills. Perhaps somebody had been kidnapped, or a terrorist was threatening to blow up a building?

"What is it, Sir?" he asked, his voice still dreary.

"Not over the official channel. Fifteen minutes, Spartan, and don't be late. This is important!"

The signal cut out completely, leaving Spartan alone in his room and wondering what was going on. He looked about, noting it was still dark.

The time?

A quick glance to the clock on the wall showed it was only just past three o'clock in the morning. That might explain the dull ringing in his head. It was certainly more likely than the fact he'd taken a mace impact to the jaw while fighting in the arena. He slid out of bed and to the bathroom to get ready. After starting to wash his face, his brain started to wake up, and the gravity of what the Admiral had said worried him. He wiped his face and grabbed his combat fatigues and gear without even thinking. It took less than two minutes for him to leave the room and make his way to the elevators. Inside, a soldier from the Terra Nova Guards saluted. The decision may have been made to scrap the Army in its entirety, yet this one paradox remained in the capital.

"Where to, Sir?" asked the man.

"Defence Committee," he replied, much to the surprise of the soldier.

He paused, but upon seeing Spartan's expression, turned and pressed a button. It was a fast device and took him below the ground a substantial distance before slowing to a halt. The doors hissed open to reveal the main foyer and a number of high-ranking officials from the Navy and Marine Corps. There were also a significant number of politicians, but he recognised none of them. He stepped forward only to find Khan step from out of the crowd.

"Spartan, what's going on here?" he asked.

Spartan couldn't work out what was more surprising. The fact that he had been called to such an important meeting, or that Khan had also been brought there. He raised his eyebrows and shrugged.

"Beats me, come on, let's get in there, looks like they are starting."

They moved along with the others into the committee room, a place much like the room he had been in to look at ship designs. When they were all inside, the door shut and a high-pitched squeal reverberated through the room. Khan winced at the sound.

"What's that for?"

"Sensor sweeper, checking for bugs I would think."

The audience of no more than thirty people quietened down as Defence Secretary Howalt Sones stood up to speak. Spartan recognised him from the Senate's debates concerning the future of the Alliance military. His face was grave, and Spartan's stomach lurched at the feeling he was about to hear something very bad.

"Thank you for all coming so quickly. I will get directly to the point. A situation is brewing in the Hyperion Sector."

He pressed a button, and the centre of the room lit up with a model of the planet and its moons. Spartan's pulse, on the other hand, had already increased significantly. Teresa was on board the Santa Maria, and their mission was in that part of space as well.

Please tell me nothing has happened to her.

"I have important news concerning the recent deployment of the Hyperion Taskforce. This powerful group of ships and marines was sent to investigate the disappearance of the civilian liner, Atlantic Star. As you are undoubtedly aware, the force is substantial and consists of five capital ships, including four cruisers and the marine heavy transport ANS Santa Maria. As well as thousands of crew, these ships are carrying three full companies of marines plus a single ASOG. It is much more than a simple reconnaissance mission. They are operating under the command of General Rivers, a man whose reputation is known by you all. They have the ships, equipment and troops to search, investigate and if necessary, destroy any Zealot presence."

The model changed to one of the taskforce. The cruisers were substantial, but it was the bulk of the heavy transport that took up most of the space. A transport was a bit of a misnomer, as she was more an amphibious assault ship with the troops and firepower to get large numbers of warriors into and out of action in a short time. Defence Secretary Howalt Sones paused as though for effect and switched off the unit.

"As of fifty-two minutes ago, we have lost contact with the taskforce. The last messages received were that the force had spotted a small lifeboat. Less than a minute later, the signals from all five ships vanished. Navy engineers have already confirmed this cannot be caused by the destruction of one of the ships. Even with just seconds left our vessels eject black boxes and transmit distress signals. Something out there blocked their signals completely, and it has stayed that way."

Spartan almost vomited at the news. Hyperion was almost two weeks away using a ship with sufficient power and waiting at full readiness. Anything could have happened to them by now, and there was nothing that could be done for days. He lifted his hand to speak, but the Defence Secretary continued speaking.

"Our top scientists are working on this, but so far the list of options I have been given range from one of the many solar storms that can lash Hyperion through to sabotage, engine powerplant failure or mutiny. We will continue to monitor the situation, and I will inform you as and when the situation changes."

Spartan stood up, no longer willing to wait on protocol.

"Sir, there are thousands of men and women out there, we cannot just sit and…"

The Defence Secretary lifted his hands and spoke over him, using the volume of the sound amplification to drown him out.

"I appreciate your concern, Lieutenant, as does every man and woman here. I have convened an emergency meeting of the Senate to take place in six hours. In the meantime, I suggest you assist Admiral Churchill in his efforts to identify the possible solutions to this problem."

Spartan looked over to the Admiral and could see him looking right back, shaking his head slowly. He cast his head to the right as if indicating he wanted Spartan to look at something he was hiding. Then Spartan worked it out.

I see, he wants me to meet him, probably right after this meeting.

* * *

Captain George Cornwall couldn't believe what he was

hearing. He was already slumped into his chair, but the news that the General had been taken from the ship was almost impossible to believe. Just one hour earlier, the ship had been fine, and the only anomaly was the lifeboat moving towards them. Now they were trapped in orbit by the demands of a madman, a man that had an important hostage and a weapon capable of both disabling and destroying any vessel under his command. He sighed and looked around his CIC. All systems were now back online as well as the secondary powerplants.

"So let me get this straight?" he said to his XO.

"My marines have let the General be taken as a hostage in exchange for not destroying our ships? What are we supposed to do now?"

The XO turned to the marines, specifically Captain Carlos who had seen the General leave along with Pontus.

"Did the General give any indication as to what he was doing? Any kind of plan?"

Captain Carlos looked distinctly unimpressed with the questioning.

"He had seconds to make a decision. Kill Pontus and we all die, or he went to buy us some time. Pontus said he would be sending craft to take off the crew and bring them down to the surface. Any attempts to leave or refuse will meet the same fate as with Thunderer."

Captain Cornwall rubbed his glistening forehead, the fear and worry now very obvious on his brow. The marine officer could sympathise with him, but it was hardly as though they were left with a large number of options. The XO moved back to the Captain, but even he looked confused at the situation.

"Sir, our engineers have checked and checked again on their weapon. We cannot withstand even a single strike. Our armour is no thicker or more durable than that fitted to the cruisers. Our only advantage is our greater number of point defence turrets."

The Captain shook his head.

"Like they did anything with Thunderer."

He sat back and examined the disposition of the remaining four ships. He had something in mind, that much the XO could see, but what? The force was still powerful, and the marine complement on board Santa Maria gave them a fighting edge. Assuming a single one of them could actually find somebody or something to fight. The Captain looked back at them.

"What about these machines? Are they something we've seen before?"

The Marine officer shook his head.

"No, sir, this is something new. The technology is far from unique, but I've not seen that level of autonomous behaviour and speed in a combat ready piece of equipment. They were fast, accurate and followed Pontus' commands instantly. I would suggest a mental or a visual control system tied in directly to the man. It was something exceptional and deadly. The closest I've seen is with a pre-programmed sparring drone."

He looked back to the display and took one more deep breath before continuing.

"They don't have any craft in the area right now. We could attempt to split the fleet, different heights and speed. We might lose one ship, but it would maintain the attention of their weapon so that the others could escape."

The XO shook his head vehemently.

"What about their technology? They were able to jam our communications and shutdown our systems remotely. If we try and split up, what's to stop them doing the same?"

Captain Cornwall pointed to the display and the projected trajectories from the remaining ships. He tapped the shape of the Santa Maria and expanded out to show the increasing radius between the others.

"If we activate our long range engines to full burn, we can be out of the gravitational field of Hyperion in mere seconds. The others could do the same. The only other option I can see is we abandon the ships."

The door to the CIC opened and in walked Sergeant Morato and three of her ASOG troop. She approached the Marine Captain and saluted.

"Sir. We've cleared all access points from the breach, and there's nobody else on board. We found this during our sweep."

She held up a small metallic object about the size of

a man's fist. At least half of its surface resembled a shell with slightly recessed contours on its smooth finish. The other half was ribbed and heavily indented before it reached a broken inlet pipe of some kind. Burn damage had marked in the rougher side, and it was heavily scored. The XO took it and examined it carefully before passing it to the Captain.

"So?" he asked dismissively.

The Captain looked at it but only for a moment before looking back to the Sergeant.

"Well?" he asked though without the rudeness of the XO.

"It's a mobile communication node, like some of the gear we've found the Zealots using to communicate underground. I would guess somebody on board has been speaking with a person on the surface below or another ship."

Captain Cornwall looked devastated at the implication.

"That is a serious accusation, Sergeant, and you have very little evidence to back it up. Right now, I have more important things to worry about than finding the odd trinket and piece of scrap on my ship."

He turned to his right and nodded to the XO.

"Get us ready, we move out in five minutes. I don't want to give these bastards any more time than we have to."

The XO nodded in agreement and moved back to the

mainscreen. He picked up the microphone and proceeded to manage the men and women on the ship for a potential high-energy sprint from the planet.

"Tactical, I need a full time and velocity assessment of their weapon. How long do we have from warning to impact?"

"Sir," replied the man, turning back to his console.

"Captain!" exclaimed a desperate sounding Sergeant Morato. "If we have a mole on board, then they could tell Pontus of our intentions. So far he has kept every one of his..."

"Enough, Sergeant. Take your troop and station them near the landing bay. We may need you again should Pontus and his robotic friends attempt to board our ship again."

He moved to Captain Carlos of the First Company.

"Captain, get your men ready for potential action. I don't know what's coming, but three companies of marines could be quite a useful edge."

He saluted, making for the door as the Captain called out one last time.

"Oh, and make sure everybody is in zero-g gear. Just in case."

With the marines now gone, he turned back to see his crew moving about their business in the CIC. According to the diagnostic systems, the ship's power was up to almost eighty percent, and all the main stations were reporting in manually on the communications system. He recalled some of the stories from the Great War where some ship's had been forced to run on oral commands than computer systems. It was slow and manpower intensive but alleviated the problem of hacked or damaged computer equipment.

She's getting back to normal. All that remains is can I get her out of here before that bastard does something else!

CHAPTER EIGHT

With the creation of the new Alliance Military came a more professional and better-equipped fighting force. Gone were the days of militia, Army and Marine forces and instead the Navy and Marines would provide all the fighting power. The enlarged Marines were equipped with a mixture of weapons, but one lesson they had learned from the Proxima Emergency was the importance of close quarter training. Sergeant Spartan of the Vanguards had led the way, and never again would humanity's ground forces forget their skills with blades.

Edged weapons in the Emergency

The journey through the thick atmosphere did nothing to improve General Rivers' mood. The gloating Pontus and his entourage of machines and Zealots said nothing, but the look of amusement on the face on Pontus told him all he needed to know. He considered saying nothing, but it seemed they thought they'd already won. It was an opportunity. At least he hoped so.

"So, Pontus. You have me, what are you planning next?"

Pontus said nothing.

"That's it, then? You don't even have the guts to tell me your cunning plan?"

One of the Zealots leaned over and whispered into Pontus' ear. The two laughed, but again no one answered his question. General Rivers decided on a different tact.

"I'll have to speak with your master then as you're obviously incapable of answering even the most basic of questions. Just another lackey like Typhon."

The mention of Pontus' brother seemed to strike a nerve.

"You and your people can join the rest of your slaves. The ones that are left, anyway," spat Pontus.

The craft shook violently, and Rivers felt his side strike the sides of the small craft. It was a small vessel, much smaller than an Alliance shuttle.

Probably taken from one of our civilian ships. He thought angrily.

That was when he felt the backup pistol fitted into his jacket. He'd completely forgotten about it, as in the last year he'd had little opportunity to make use of it. He slid his right hand down and checked to ensure he wasn't mistaken. The hardened plastic of the small hilt confirmed that it was a P12 high velocity coil- pistol, a variant of the more powerful carbines and rifles used by the ASOG units. Pontus looked at him suspiciously, and for a moment he worried he'd been spotted.

"My people won't leave me behind you know? They will hunt your friends down, just like I've been doing, and kill each of you, one at a time."

Pontus shook his head slowly but said no more. But it had given him a window, and even this small group of fanatical Zealots hadn't noticed him slide his hand into the internal pocket of his jacket. He tapped the side and accidently pressed the high-power option. It buzzed and caught one of the men's attention.

"What was that?" asked Pontus.

The nearest Zealot shook his head and looked about before settling his eyes on the General.

"It must have been him."

Pontus struck the man across the face angrily.

"What? Why was he not searched? Do it now!"

General rivers knew this was it. He had one chance, and he took it. He grabbed the pistol grip, twisting his wrist so that he could point it at Pontus. The enemy spotted him and unclipped his safety belt just in time. The blast was deafening in the confines of the craft. The impact tore though the nearest Zealot but also punched through the separating wall and into the pilot, killing both instantly. Alarms blasted and the craft spun out of control, throwing anybody not strapped down around the interior of the vessel.

What the hell have you done! He thought with sickening amusement.

* * *

From space, the group of warships gave the impression they were idly orbiting the planet. The calm exterior hid the movement and procedures being carried out to ready the ships for what was to come. Marines fitted on their armour and checked their weapons while the crew double and triple-checked their systems while fitting on emergency gear and life-support equipment. Every one of them was ready for whatever terrible event might occur.

"Sir, all compartments report ready for full burn. Marines are equipped and ready for battle. Cruisers Bellerophon, Minotaur and Defence all report they are also ready to power up on your command," said the XO.

Captain Cornwall placed his chin in his hand and looked at the video feed of the planet below. His gut told him to fire the engines, but nagging doubts wracked his body at the previous loss of Thunderer. If they were able to hit Santa Maria, the losses would be catastrophic.

Indecision is the killer of ships. He remembered from decades ago during his academy days.

Even though he had made up his mind, he was still wracked by doubt. The object Sergeant Morato had shown him was suspicious, but he had neither the time nor resources to throw at it when faced with such a deadly danger on the planet. That reminded him. He looked back down to the surface of the mist-covered jungle world and tried to look through the haze to get some idea of what was there.

What are you doing down there?

He inhaled and tightened his belt on his commander's chair.

It's time.

The microphone was already in his hand, and the crew were sat, monitoring their data streams but also waiting for the order. The rotating sections on all four ships were still moving, even though all crew and marines were strapped in and waiting for the inevitable acceleration of the main engines being activated. When powered up, they would maintain a contact acceleration of the same order as Earth's gravity. The engines would then only cut prior to rotation and the reverse burn, but on this occasion the course was much shorter and designed to take them a day out from the deadly planet.

"This is the Captain, prepare for..." was as far as he got before alarms triggered.

As before, some of the systems shut down, but unlike the last time the internal communications remained active.

"Status report, all stations!" barked the XO.

Reports flooded in from each section, and as each one

arrived, it was obvious they had problems.

"Sir, engines are not responding, neither is navigation. Minotaur reports her engines are operational."

"Tell her to go. Everybody else, find out what the hell is going on!"

The fear in his voice was clear and did nothing to instil confidence in the shaken crew. They checked their stations, but there was little that could be done from the CIC, it would require small teams to trace the faults. Either way, his attention was diverted from the current problems by a shout from the tactical officer.

"Sir, the weapon signature on the planet has just activated."

"What?" cried Captain Cornwall, but in his heart he knew exactly what was about to happen.

"I'm picking up seven blooms, exactly the same as before."

Seven? What can we do against such power?

On the main screen a bright flash was all that remained of where ANS Minotaur had been as her powerful engines ignited. The great warship quickly accelerated and blasted out of orbit and away from the danger of the planet. The sight of the ship escaping the torment of the ground weapons sent a pang of relief through Captain Cornwall's body. He looked back to his CIC and was brought instantly back to the situation at hand. The XO was straining to lean over to speak to the tactical officer. Both of their voices were loud in desperation, not anger. He looked back towards him.

"Captain, we have two minutes until impact! We've got three ships with no power, and Bellerophon's life support has just cut out," said the XO.

Two minutes!

"Listen up!" he called out to his crew. "We have seconds to make a decision. If anybody has any kind of a plan, now is the time."

There was silence, just the sounds of alarms, and the continuous audio traffic from those stations still functioning and the other ships in orbit. Captain Cornwall looked to his XO to see nothing but his second in command shaking his head.

That's it then, all we can do is sit and take the punishment.

"Sir, I have the source of the weapons on the surface, and they are based in a hexagonal shape around this one point. We could go to the surface?" suggested the tactical officer.

"The engines are out. We can't manoeuvre, and this ship would burn up on re-entry."

The XO nodded at the suggestion.

"He's right, Sir. If we head to the boats, we could evacuate the ship and land as close as we can to the weapon sites."

The Captain looked as though he'd just woken up.

"Yes, we could then disable or destroy them, and

potentially find the source of the ship control or communication."

He looked over to the tactical officer. "How much time do we have?"

"Seventy-two seconds, Sir."

This is going to be close!

He nodded to the XO and pulled at his straps. Luckily, the artificial gravity was still operating, and that would speed up the escape.

"This is the XO, abandon ship! This is not a drill! Commence evacuation procedures. You have less than one minute to leave the ship. Landing zones are being sent to the nav units on all boats. I repeat. This is not a drill. Evacuate the ship!"

With that, he unstrapped himself and made for the nearest escape lifeboats. In case of emergencies there were pods and boats situated at key areas along the outer skin of the rotating section. While the pods were very small, the lifeboats could carry up to twenty people. By the time Lieutenant Nilsson, the ship's communication officer reached the nearest boat, she could already feel the reverberation through the metal plating of them ejecting from the ship. Their powerful retro-thrusters would blast the side of the hull as they moved away as quickly as possible. As she reached the door, she glanced back to see just three people left behind, and they were also moving for the door. The Captain and the XO were barking orders, and one marine guard was doing his best to manhandle them from the CIC towards the last lifeboat.

"Captain!" she shouted as loudly as she could.

He looked over to her, a look of disappointment on his brow.

"Get off the ship, Sir!" she added and turned and threw herself into the escape pod. The door hissed behind her and with just a three second warning, the unit unbuckled from the ship and fired its engines. Her breath was forced from her lungs as the brief moment of acceleration forced her into her seat. Two other crew were already inside, and all of them groaned at the feeling. Then as quickly as it had started, the engine cut and the pod used its micro-thrusters to manoeuvre. She pulled her head around and looked out through the auto-block glass porthole. It was very small, not much bigger than her head and triple plated for protection. She could see the Santa Maria as well as the other two cruisers that appeared complete dead in space. Scores of small shapes continued to blast away from the cruisers as well as a two larger landing craft that were following close behind her lifepod.

"Look!" said the young ensign sat opposite. He looked barely old enough to serve, and yet his face betrayed exposure to terrible events. She recognised him as one of the new replacements that had joined Santa Maria's crew at the same time as her. She watched his gaze and looked through the other porthole to see the glowing orbs of energy coming up from the surface. They must have been more than halfway to the ship now and showed no sign of slowing down or changing direction.

Gods no!

As she watched, even more life pods continued to eject from Bellerophon's hull. They were taking too long, probably due to the loss of power to their habitation unit. With little or no gravity, it would take them much longer to reach the boats. In the seconds it had taken her to watch the ship, the projectiles had reached a height of just a few kilometres from the ships. They were out of time. As the glowing orbs reached a thousand metres, the automated point-defence turrets opened fired. Thousands of metal shards were showered on the approaching objects, yet they seemed to achieve nothing, and the seven shapes slammed into the remaining taskforce.

"Come on, get out!" she shouted uncontrollably.

Bellerophon never stood a chance. The first orb struck her underside and towards the bow. With a bright flash, a chunk the size of a landing craft was blown off, and the bow of the ship tore off into space. The cruiser might have survived had the second not struck her centre. Fuel cells or ammunition must have been struck because the entire vessel vanished in a bright orange flare of energy that quickly dissipated to reveal large chunks of drifting debris. Lieutenant Nilsson turned away, unable to watch the rest of the assault upon the now defenceless and powerless ships.

* * *

Spartan paced outside Admiral Churchill's office with his patience now reaching breaking point. He considered booting open the door but was saved from the indignity by it opening from the inside. A marine guard beckoned for him to enter. Spartan needed no further encouragement and was inside and stood in front of the Admiral before he even had time to turn around.

"That will be all, Lieutenant," he said to the guard who saluted and stepped outside. Spartan tried to speak, but the Admiral lifted his hand for him to be silent.

"I know, Spartan, I know exactly what you are thinking and what you want. Hell, I agree with you, but not even I can force ships to be sent to the area for a rescue mission."

"But, Sir! You're an Admiral!" answered Spartan bitterly.

"Yes, I am, but even an Admiral has to work through the chain of command, and I have been given instruction that I am not to conduct ship-based operations without the express authorisation of the Defence Secretary."

Spartan tied to speak, but Admiral Churchill lifted his hand once more and walked to his personal computer unit. He turned the display around to face him. It showed the ANS Santa Cruz, one of his old ships in orbit. Spartan looked at the image for a few seconds. The shape brought back memories of the war, but also more recently, of the special operations he had been running. The Admiral turned back around but kept the image up on the screen.

"The Senate is doing what it does best, talking. At some point, it might be today, it might be next month, but eventually, they will send a force to investigate. Don't forget, we have lost a major civilian ship and now potentially a complete five-ship taskforce. They will just say, in fact they are already saying, we can't just throw another ship into the same situation. Right now, the assumption is still that the area is dangerous to enter due to the frequent solar flares. My opinion of that? It's all bullshit. You know as well as I do that our ships can stand a beating. Even the storms of Prometheus weren't enough to hold back Confed ships, not back in the day!"

He spotted Spartan desperately trying to speak and once more had to nod to let him finish first.

"Now, I want you to take a team of specialists, perhaps a few with the right kind of reputation to run an inspection of the Santa Cruz and kick her into shape. You will appreciate that a number of exchange platoons are currently settling in, and she's not expected back in the line for at least another six months. Major Daniels was supposed to be taking leave, but I have asked him to join you for a shakedown crew due to the current crisis. It is dangerous with us having no rapid reaction force. I have decided to post a number of training ships not far from here to help ready crews and troops for potential security issues. You run a series of readiness drills, you never know when the order might arise to leave orbit, and there are plenty of destinations that would be perfect for the training of these men and women."

Spartan could easily read between the lines of the somewhat distinctly unsubtle approach put forward by the Admiral. In his experience, it was often best to give politicians well-prepared solutions to problems. A ship with a team of the best people and equipment, and already waiting in orbit, would be a priority for use in any kind of reconnaissance or rescue operation.

"You're probably aware we are well down on our numbers right now. Most of our senior officers are on leave, retired on in training. The War really hit us hard, and it will be at least another nine months before we're back to anything like full strength. Our ships are spread thin and crew numbers are low. It is in my power to grant you a temporary promotion, and for this operation I think you're going to need it. As of twenty minutes ago you are now Captain Spartan, second in command of the 2nd Alliance Special Operations Group, with duties to help increase fleet readiness in case of emergencies."

He moved a file over to Spartan's datapad, and a low beep indicated the arrival of the high-level encoded material.

"That is authorisation for temporary transfer of noncommissioned Alliance military personnel for the training mission under the supervision of Major Daniels. Now, get moving, Spartan, and get boots on that ship...fast. When I am able, I will give the order for your deployment. I have already transferred the information on your new mission to the Major, and he will be in touch shortly."

* * *

Teresa had been lucky. Of the craft that had left the Santa Maria, hers had been the last and the most at risk when the enemy weapons struck the nearby cruisers. She'd seen one landing craft destroyed completely by a direct impact that scattered the craft in chunk of shattered metal. She could only hope and pray that the majority of the crew and marines had made it out before the end.

"You okay?" asked Sergeant Lovett.

It was odd, but since the devastation of the small fleet, he seemed to have awakened. It was as if the pain, desperation and tragedy had forced him out of his stupor and back to being the marine she was used to. She was well aware of his loss, but right now they had their own problems.

"Yeah, I'll live. Don't know about the rest of the marines though. We've just lost a lot of good people. Did you see what happened to the Santa Maria?"

Sergeant Lovett shook his head.

"No, last thing I saw was the cruisers getting hit. They were all blasting away with their turrets. You think she could have survived?"

Teresa looked at the window, but there was nothing but the flames of re-entry. She looked back to the number of computer screens, but all of them were showing the same image, digital distortion of the planet's thick atmosphere.

"Make sure you're strapped in, people. We're coming in to the marked landing zone, and we're coming in hot."

Sergeant Lovett looked surprised.

"What? Why the rush?"

With almost perfect timing, they broke through and to the cloudy skies of the planet. The landing craft bumped and buffeted through the thick air, and moisture hissed over the superheated exterior of the vessel. At the same time, the built-in countermeasures suite activated.

"What the hell, now what?" asked one of the marines further back in the craft.

Teresa checked her straps and looked up to the fixed weapon rack above her.

"It means we've been detected. If they have surface to air weapon systems, we can expect them any moment. Why do you think we came in so fast?"

A fast sequence of flashes rippled from the sides of the craft as it released scores of superheated flares to distract any head tracking weapon systems. Almost simultaneously, a dull crump shook the landing craft and threw one man against the ceiling.

"You heard the pilot, make sure you're strapped in. This is going to get ugly!" shouted Teresa.

On cue, part of the port armour plating ripped off to expose the side of the landing craft. Howling winds screamed in and sucked out anything not bolted or welded down. Teresa stretched out her arms and grabbed the rails above her for extra grip. Through the breach she could see yellow streaks of gunfire flashing around them.

"Will this never end!" she muttered under her breath.

More alarms sounded through the craft but were entirely pointless. Shells and bullets ripped into the flanks until holes started to appear in the metal. Teresa had been in crashes before, and she remembered the jokes she'd shared with Spartan about how few successful landings either of them had ever made. As far as she was concerned, any landing from space was usually destined to end with them being shot down. She looked about the cabin with a calm stoicism that would have done Spartan proud.

"Marines, remember your training. Keep your heads down and hands up. When we hit the ground, I want a fast dispersal. Get your arses out of here and establish a secure perimeter. Do not stay inside under any circumstances, or you're likely to find yourselves in the middle of a burning bird."

The men and women nodded to her, but she saw a few look past her and to the breach. It was understandable, but she knew that any marine not focused on the mission was a liability.

"Hey, Corporal! Yes, you! Get your eyes away from there and check your gear. We're landing soon."

The woman stared at Teresa for a little while longer, and as if she'd been struck about the head, woke up. She looked down to her right and went through her equipment checks. A crackle and a quiet voice in her helmet was the first contact she'd had off the boat since they'd left. She tapped a button to increase the volume.

"Sergeant Morato, report in," said the voice, but with the crackling and howling noise it was hard to identify, even with the noise reduction filters.

"This is Morato. I have one uninjured bird, setting down on the landing site. Who is this?" she answered.

"Excellent. Captain Carlos here. We've just landed three hundred metres north of the landing co-ordinates. The enemy strongpoint is somewhere within fifty kilometres from here. Watch yourselves, there are..." his voice was drowned out by the sounds of shouting and then it cut.

Always the damned same!

"Thirty seconds!" called out the pilot.

Teresa knew that the lack of information from the cockpit wasn't down to negligence. With the damage sustained and ground fire coming up at them, she had no doubts the two pilots were under immense strain just trying to get them on the ground safely. The readout in her helmet showed the current atmospheric pressure was with acceptable tolerances, but she couldn't remember off the top of her head what the air situation was on the ground. Her suit showed a ninety-seven percent level for now, and that was more than enough for a day's normal use.

"Brace!" shouted the pilot, but it was too little too late. The landing craft struck the ground harder than any landing Teresa had ever experienced. The initial impact would have broken her back had she not been encased in the protective PDS suit. The breach of the side of the hull ripped open and tore away to split the landing craft into two sections. She felt her body being thrown about and then it stopped. Internal sensors flashed on her suit to warn her about the pressure changes and a slight leak in her leg armour. It required no attention, as the suit was capable of projecting small amounts of adhesive to the damaged section. It was quickly fixed and would last for a number of hours.

"Okay, we're down, now it's time to get out!" she said and pulled the lever that maintained the seat locks. The belts snapped off, and she slid out of the seat and towards the ceiling of the landing craft. It hadn't even occurred to her she was upside down. Just in time, she lifted her hands and crashed heavily into the metalwork. Incredibly, nothing was hurt and she rolled over, looking about the craft. This section consisted of two-thirds of the cabin, and already a large part was filling with muddy water. Outside the craft were lines of thick trees, but they must have found one of the few reasonably open clearings. Even so, the ground was waterlogged and maybe a metre deep in places. Tree stumps and foliage made establishing who was where almost impossible. To make matters worse, a wisp of fog hung over the ground like a permanently running smoke generator.

"Sergeant!" called out a marine to her left.

She turned around and spotted a dozen marines already pulling gear from the wreckage and helping to pull the wounded from the twisted metal. She noticed four had stopped moving, and one was pinned to his seat with two snapped metal bars pushing through his chest. The sight of the body reminded her of Sergeant Lovett and his never-ending question to find his fiancée.

"Lovett!" she shouted, half-expecting to find his to be one of the bodies. She was pleasantly surprised to be replied by a hand tapping her shoulder.

"Here."

She looked around to see the familiar face of the Sergeant covered in mud. Scratch marks ran down his armour, yet there were no signs of major damage and more importantly, no signs of blood.

"Good. How many made it?" she asked, almost dreading to find the answer.

"Thirty-two came down, twenty-three made it out in one piece, including the two of us. The front section took one hell of a pounding in the landing."

She made to move forward to check, but he held her back.

"Trust me, it's a mess up there. Leave it to the medics. We need to protect what we have left."

Teresa wanted to see the damage, but the two of them had seen plenty of action and the consequences of that. There was nothing interesting or glorious about the smashed bodies of their friends and comrades. Either way, her interest was overridden by the sound of gunfire to the west of their position. She listened for a second, instantly recognising two distinct tones.

"They're ours!" she said firmly and looked to the marines who continued to drag equipment from the shattered remains of the landing craft. The gunfire from an L48 rifle had a very distinctive sound due to its large calibre ammunition and high velocity. Most of the sounds came from these with the odd thud from L52 Mark II Assault Carbines that were carried by the ASOG troops; the sounds from the coil weapons was unlike any other kind of firearm.

"Only ours, though?" asked Sergeant Lovett rhetorically.

The internal comms inside Sergeant Morato's suit crackled again, and the signal was able to burn through whatever had been causing the interference. This time it wasn't the Captain, It was the XO from the Santa Maria.

"Commander Petersburg here. All units rendezvous

at the second landing site. We are under attack and need immediate assistance. Hostiles are in the area. I repeat. Hostiles are overrunning our perimeter."

Crap! Teresa thought.

She, Lovett and another twenty-one marines and ASOG troopers wasn't much, but it was better than nothing. The last two were already out of the craft and carrying one of the destroyed landing craft's pintle-mounted machineguns. Luckily, the Marine Corps had the foresight to modify the weapons mount system so that the gun could be detached upon landing for such an eventuality. She was pleased to see her six troopers were all safe, but of the marines she could identify only half. All were junior ranks, mostly privates with the odd corporal thrown in.

"Okay, here's the plan. We'll form into two units, one under me, and the other under Sergeant Lovett, here," she explained while pointing to her old friend.

"Split up, half with each of us. Carry as much of the gear as you can. We need to get to the Commander and fast."

A series of quick acknowledgements greeted her followed by a flurry of activity. Each strapped on what they could, and half of the marines lifted up the salvaged containers in pairs. It took just seconds for them to be ready to move out from the vulnerable landing zone. Its only advantage was the open space that provided a killing ground for their firearms.

"Good, let's go!" called out Teresa.

The two groups of ASOG troopers moved out in front of the marines in four pairs. They moved fast and with their carbines held up to their shoulders. They trained for rapid deployment and were easily able to cover the ground quickly while protecting the unit. Behind them snaked the two columns of marines, half carrying equipment, and the other half checking the area for signs of the enemy. On her display in her PDS suit, Teresa identified the position of the Commander. It was almost four hundred metres from their position and through the thick jungle. They moved to the treeline, and as soon as she stepped inside, the available light cut in half. Her suit was equipped with light amplification imagery and easily adjusted.

"Watch your corners and expect trouble. There's something out here, and it ain't friendly."

* * *

Spartan entered the bar to find Khan and a dozen others of his contacts waiting for him. The regulars that had been inside must have left in the last hour as no other soul was waiting, other than a single barman handing out a continuous supply of glasses. He walked into the middle of the room and looked at each of them. Most were marines, men and women he'd served with, but a few were there by reputation alone. Khan had brought Osk plus another of his brethren that he'd not seen before. Major Daniels sat in the corner, flanked by two sergeants. To his surprise there were also two soldiers from the Terra Nova Guards, both decorated men in their late thirties.

"Captain," announced the Major, spotting Spartan's arrival.

Spartan approached him and saluted.

"Sir. Do you think you could have found anywhere a little less conspicuous?"

Daniels smiled at him. The two went back a long way, and although their first encounters had been more confrontational, they'd learnt to respect and trust each other. He pointed to the Terra Novans.

"I didn't have time to do much. The message from the Admiral got to me less than thirty minutes ago. The Santa Cruz already knows I am bringing a training crew with some of the finest and most specialised people in the Confederacy."

"Ahem," coughed one of the marines sarcastically.

Daniels smiled at the reminder.

"Yes, as I was saying, the most specialised people in the Alliance. I have your recommended PT instructors from the Marine Corps, tech specialists from Prometheus, and underground warfare experts from Carthago."

Even Spartan looked impressed as the Major pointed out each of the individuals. As he reached the tech specialist, he was sure he recognised a face.

"Kowalski? What are you doing here?"

An old friend of his and Teresa's, Kowalski had been working on Prometheus since before the final battle at Terra Nova. He was a marine and also one of the best hackers and computer experts in the military.

"Commander Anderson sent me and a team to request additional equipment and personnel for back on Prometheus. There are big changes happening there."

"Yeah, I heard. Who else did you bring?"

The door opened behind him and another four people entered, including the large hulk of a familiar looking Jötnar. He pushed passed the others and grabbed Spartan, pulling him close to his vast body.

"Spartan!" he growled in a voice that anybody else would think was that of a creature about to try and kill him. Unable to breathe, let alone speak, Spartan was forced to wait until he released his grip and stepped back.

"Gun? You're here with Kowalski?"

His old friend and leader of the Jötnar nodded.

"Not just me, I brought a whole squad of my brothers. Have you not heard? We have our own underground city on Prometheus. We called it the Arsenal."

Spartan grinned at the name.

"Why am I not surprised?" he said in amusement.

Major Daniels stood up and shook the hands of the recently arrived.

"Okay, time is of the essence. Remember, this is an

official training operation. The Jötnar are here to test the troops on the Santa Cruz for their Biomech combat drills, and the rest of you have your own duties. Under no circumstances imply we are there for any other reason. Understood?"

The assembled men, women and Jötnar nodded in agreement.

"Good, take separate shuttles. I will see you all in due course aboard the old girl. Good luck to you all."

One of the marine instructors opened the door and stepped out, the rest followed in ones and twos. Gun approached Khan, Osk and Spartan and leaned in close.

"I have things I want to talk to you all about, when we're up there," he said, his hand pointing to the ceiling.

"Is this good or bad things you want to talk about?" asked Spartan.

Gun grinned, and Spartan instantly recognised it as one of those grins he gave when he was about to smash something up.

Oh, great, just what I need.

CHAPTER NINE

The events at Hyperion proved once and for all the importance of autonomous robotics. Their ability to operate independently and without biological support constraints made them deadly in space. Loyal, reliable and powerful, it was inevitable that the next logical development in weapons and ship technology would come in the form of the robot. Little did humanity realise that their inspiration would come from the very Devil they sought to eradicate, Echidna herself.

Robots in Space

The journey into orbit was a rarity for Spartan, and one that didn't require him to crash or board a ship under incoming fire. It was almost pleasant, apart from the issue of arriving with the hidden intention of prepping the crew and troops on board for a possible mission to Hyperion. They had split up after their short chat on Terra Nova and only a handful travelled with him to the ship. Next to him were the Major, Khan and Gun. Gun still wore his eye-patch even though Spartan knew he had been fitted out with a replacement back on Prometheus over a year ago. The other Jötnar were travelling with the marines and Terra Nova guards in a transport due to land in the next six hours. The Major had organised it this way so they could discuss the plan en route.

"You'll be pleased to know the Admiral has arranged for several other ships to make their way here under the auspices of conducting a training scenario with the Cruz."

"Good, how many ships?"

"I'm not sure yet, but I know the assault cruisers Royal Oak and Ark Royal are both heading this way from operations at Carthago. A handful of destroyers have been sent from the escort at the Anomaly as well. I'd say three to four days, and we'll have anything up to ten ships including the Cruz."

"Can't we just get underway immediately? Orders be damned!"

"No, Spartan, no chance. There's one thing high command loves more than trouble and that's somebody that break the rules, you know that. Most of the captains would refuse to go, especially when they hear that every ship that has been sent there has vanished. Did the Admiral tell you that he persuaded the Senate to send three of the new drone frigates to investigate?"

"No he didn't, that's something at least. Let's hope they tell us something before they can be jammed."

"Agreed," replied the Major who sat back and gazed out of the window at the peaceful skies of Terra Nova below them. "You know, every time I do this run it reminds me of the last attack by the Crusader. What a ship."

"What an Admiral," added Spartan ruefully. "A lot of good people died in those last hours."

Spartan looked down to the planet, but all that he remembered was the landing under fire. It had been violent and deadly before he even set foot on the planet. The ground battle itself had been short and bloody, but it had ended the War. He spotted Gun looking at him and remembered his request in the bar.

"Okay, we're here now. What did you want you say?" asked Spartan.

Gun looked to Khan and back to the two marine officers. The two Jötnar looked strange as they sat in their shuttle seats. They had been equipped with extended straps for the seating of the kind usually used for pregnant women. Their girth was substantial as was their height.

"Since the war, my people have been given areas on Prometheus to live. We don't mind the heat, but we are running out of space. We've used all the space Anderson can afford to give us, but the only area left is the new shipyard, and this is being used on new Alliance ships."

Spartan lifted up his hands.

"Gun, there's no way the Alliance is going to give you full control of the planet. They are building more factories and shipyards, and it's going to be one of the largest manufacturing sites in the entire Alliance."

Gun nodded.

"I know, but isn't enough. Our problem is growing with each new Biomech sent to us. The people on Terra Nova and Prime have forgotten us, and now our space is being used as a dumping ground for any enemies of the Alliance that you find."

"I see. Well, what about Anderson? I thought he had been helping you?" asked the Major.

"Anderson is a true friend of my people. With the room running out, he has been helping us to convert three ships as replacements for the Yorkdale, but it won't be enough, and the Alliance will never grant us permission to manage and run our own ships in their territory."

Major Daniels nodded at the news and looked to Spartan.

"I heard something about a container ship being requisitioned for storage use by Anderson. I didn't know it was going quite this way though. He's a canny operator, I'll give him that."

"Okay, I assume there is a question somewhere, Gun?" he asked, still unclear as to the point that was being made.

"The Senate still have not approved Jötnar as citizens of the Alliance. The agreement between Dr Hamis and us has been thrown away. With our new females and the Biomechs sent to us for..."

"Re-education!" added an angry sounding Khan.

Gun grinned at the word.

"Yes, with them our numbers are growing. We have thousands, and they are getting restless."

Oh great, thousands of bored Jötnar with a grudge. I can see what's coming.

"If something isn't done, and soon, my people will force me to take action. I don't want to do this, so I ask you, Spartan, my friend, to speak with the Senate. We fought for your people, and we still build their ships and clear up their mess."

Spartan reached out and placed his hand on his old friend's shoulder.

"It's alright, Gun. You keep your people in line, and I will make sure they resolve this once and for all."

Major Daniels had been listening to the conversation intently. He knew Gun well, and they had also served together back when the Yorkdale had been an armoured transport used exclusively by the 1st Jötnar Assault Battalion. A unit made up of thousands of battle hardened Jötnar, each equipped with heavy weapons and armour.

"I agree with Spartan. When we get back, I'll throw my support into your cause. I argued against the disbanding of the Jötnar Assault Battalion when it was decided six months ago. I know the public were against the idea of

Jötnar troops but that's only because of prejudice against Biomechs in general. One way or another, your people will have the space and life they deserve."

Gun looked to Khan who barely even considered the plan before agreeing.

"Okay, deal. Now, back to this secret mission. Whose head do you want thumped and when?"

Spartan shook his head with amusement and settled back to watch their approach. The ANS Santa Cruz had just come into view, and it was a sight he never tired of watching. The ship was massive, and the rotating sections moved at quite a rate. Three thunderbolt fighters moved passed in formation as they maintained a permanent Combat Air Patrol around the ship.

Yes, you protect this ship, but it's not like we have many available right now, is it?

* * *

Sergeant Morato's first view of the crashed lifeboat was of the shattered body of the ship's captain. Much like her own craft, this one was shredded with anti-aircraft fire from the descent to the planet. She'd assaulted moons, stations and urban settlements before but never under such concentrated and effective gunfire. She looked briefly at Captain George Cornwall, but the sight of his bloodied and broken body snapped her into action.

"Commander?" she called out on the close-ranged secure channel.

Her ASOG troops had already spread out around the crash site, but apart from a few bodies, there was no sign of the Commander or the rest of the unit.

"Commander Petersburg, please respond?" she asked again but once more was met by the digital coldness of silence. Gone were the days of analogue static.

The two columns of marines arrived, carrying their wounded plus all the equipment they had salvaged. The one good thing about the crash site of the second vessel, however, was that it was near a raised, rocky bank next to a gently flowing river. The woodland was less thick here and gave better visibility.

Corporal Jenkins spoke to some of the marines from his unit and then walked over to the two sergeants. His armour was scratched and muddied from the landing and trudging through the filthy, waterlogged ground they had landed in. As he moved towards them, something caught his attention. Sergeant Lovett turned his head and spotted a dark shape in the trees. The marines might not recognise it but he certainly did.

"Biomechs!" he cried and on cue, the eight ASOG troops dropped to their knees with their carbines raised and ready for battle.

It was in the direction none of them had expected when a dozen Biomechs lifted themselves from the water.

They looked much like the synthetic Jötnar he had seen before. They carried the metal armour often seen worn by the creatures in the service of the Union and their Zealot friends. The first to leave the water pounded forward and towards the crashed lifeboat. Sergeant Morato and two ASOG troopers lay directly in its path. It screamed as it ran forward until silenced by high-power shots from their triple-barrelled L52 Mark II Assault Carbines. As its body slumped to the ground, the other eleven creatures surged forward in a loose line. The marines and troopers opened fire, sending streaks of ammunition from their weapons. Four more were brought down but the rest kept moving forward.

"Take cover!" shouted Sergeant Morato, but it was already too late. The creatures crashed into their positions, moved past, and disappeared into the treeline behind them. One marine was sent to the ground by the impact of the last charging Biomech and was saved from being painfully crushed by two ASOG troopers smashing it away with the butts of their carbines. Then just as quickly as it had started, they were gone.

Teresa lifted herself from her position and scanned the area around where they stood. No more Biomechs appeared to be there, but she stayed where she was to double-check. The thermal imaging showed the shapes of the marines plus subtle changes in the scrub and foliage. She turned to speak to Sergeant Lovett but then detected a small heat bloom to the west.

"Stay down, possible hostiles, two-hundred metres to the west!" she called out.

The small group of kept low and held their weapons ready, expecting yet another Biomech assault.

"Please respond, this is Captain Carlos, 1st Company. I have wounded marines with me."

Teresa breathed a sigh of relief at the sound of the officer. She lifted herself up and walked slowly in the direction of the approaching force. The IFF system on her suit identified the nearest to be friendly, but the others were not yet in range. She turned back to her own forces that were still staying low and expecting trouble.

"Hold your fire, possible friendlies entering the area."

Four marines moved out of the treeline first and behind them came a group of navy crewmen. Teresa didn't recognise them, but they could easily have come from one of the cruisers. She looked at them carefully until recognising the armoured form of Captain Carlos. The rest of his group entered the clearing as he moved directly to Teresa. His armour was almost the same as his men with just subtle differences in insignia and a marking on the side of his helmet.

"Sergeant, is this it? Where is the Captain and the XO?" he asked quickly, wasting no time on pleasantries.

Teresa shook her head and waved her left arm out to her depleted force.

"This is it, Sir, twenty-three marines, including eight ASOGs. We salvaged what we could from our bird and headed here at the request of Commander Petersburg."

He looked at the crashed lifeboat and noted the markings from the Santa Maria.

"What about you, Sir?" she asked, almost dreading the answer.

"My people are spread out. A few were shot down near the source of their signal. The rest are anywhere between here and a radius of nearly three hundred klicks."

"Three hundred?" exclaimed Sergeant Lovett.

The Captain nodded slowly at his comment.

"Yeah, we took a lot of fire on the way down...a lot. I picked up over a dozen of the cruisers' lifeboats and pods heading to the west coast. They'll have to look after themselves for now. They are weeks away from us. I've got two platoons of marines and about the same number of navy crew from the cruisers."

As he continued to explain their situation, the rest of his unit arrived and spread out around the clearing. The navy crew carried a number of containers from their craft with emergency supplies and survival gear. It wasn't much from what Teresa could see but was better than nothing. One of the marine sergeants ran over and saluted.

"Sir, just got word from Lieutenant Eastwood. His platoon is heading this way. They all made it down in one piece, but their boat's a write-off."

"Good...very good," he said, considering their current predicament.

"Okay, what do we know so far?" he asked.

"Well, until your extra platoon arrives we've got, what, about a hundred and fifty people with weapons and gear for just over half of them. Food and supplies from the ships, plus a small amounts of survival gear and two sets of engineering kit," explained Sergeant Lovett.

"Sir, have you seen this?" asked Corporal Jenson, one of Teresa's ASOG troopers.

She turned to look at the man who was pulling at a piece of metal inside the wrecked vessel.

"What is it?" asked Captain Carlos.

With another tug, part of an armoured suit popped out, much to the surprise of everybody there. Teresa instantly recognised the shape.

"It's a CES suit, you know, Combat Engineer kit. Is it operational?"

The Corporal vanished back inside for a few more seconds before lifting his head back out.

"No damage, it looks intact to me, Sir."

The Captain nodded at the news and glanced around the site. It was a large area, several hundred metres in diameter with the treeline on three sides and the gently flowing river to their backs. The crashed boat took up space on the one side near the western treeline. The three of them waited patiently as he examined the situation.

"Okay, this is the way I see it. We're spread out and weak right now. We dig in, establish a defensive position, and then get as many as we can to this location. When we're dug in, we'll send out patrols to look for survivors, and see if we can find out what the hell is going on here."

Sergeant Lovett nodded in agreement, but Teresa looked less sure.

"Sir, what about a rescue attempt? The Alliance will surely send more ships, and when they do, those weapons will do the same. We have to find a way to either disable them or get a signal to the fleet."

"True," replied the Captain. But for some reason, his attention was drawn to the carcasses of the Biomechs littering the open space. In particular, he was interested in the one that had fallen just metres from the boat.

"Did they attack you?" he asked to the surprise of both Sergeants Lovett and Morato.

"Of course, they came right out of the water and rushed our position," Sergeant Lovett answered. Teresa gave the Captain a confused look but saw the last Biomech that had moved past their position and had been heading to the trees.

"They tried to reach the trees? Why?" Captain Carlos asked.

Teresa looked at the body and back to the river. Now she was truly dumbfounded. She walked back to the body and examined it carefully. The shape, the armour, they were all exactly as she had seen before. They were definitely the monsters created by the Zealots to fight in the war that had split the Confederacy. Then she saw it. Their weapons! She turned around and pointed to the creatures' arms.

"Look, no weapons."

Captain Carlos nodded, finally understanding what was going on.

"They weren't attacking your position. They were running through it."

All of them turned and looked back to the water; the barrier that had at first seemed to offer safety now looked as dangerous as the trees around them. Sergeant Lovett walked to the edge of the water and bent down to place his right hand into its depths. The suit protected him from any unusual chemicals or temperature levels, not that it mattered though as the water was perfectly fine. He looked back at them both.

"If they were running this way, then something must have been chasing them."

Sergeant Morato and Captain Carlos looked at each other, neither saying anything for a few seconds.

"Sergeant, bring your people here. We need to construct a strong defensive position and fast. We're also going to need to get power, air and water filtration sorted out. I don't know about you, but I'm already getting to the limit of my air supply down here. If anything else comes this way, we need to be able to spot them. I need your ASOG team to recce the area for any signs of what might have chased them here. Understood?"

She saluted smartly.

"Yes, Sir!"

She walked away but only made it a few metres when the Captain called her again.

"Sergeant, any idea what happened to the XO and his people?"

She shrugged. "No, Sir, he called me and said to get here. Then we heard signs of a firefight, and he was gone. Either they left the area or something took them."

He nodded in agreement and she turned away to move back to her team.

* * *

Spartan was starting to lose his patience. They'd been on the Santa Cruz now for two full days and still no word from the Senate. Three times he had tried to get to the ship's captain to try and persuade him to leave, but Major Daniels always seemed to find him before he could make contact. The only concession that had been made was that the ship had spent most of the time travelling to rendezvous with several other ships in deep space to conduct military manoeuvres. But today was not for planning a rescue, no; today was simple close quarter training for the units stationed aboard. He walked into the training hall to find two lines of marines waiting patiently. In front of them stood a marine drill instructor busy extolling the virtues of the M11 bayonet. As he entered, the man stopped, turned and saluted.

"Officer on deck!" he barked.

Every marine present stood up smartly to attention. As he moved closer, he recognised his old instructor back from when he had been a raw recruit. It seemed like it had been years and years since they'd met.

"Spartan the gladiator!" he said with a glint in his eye.

"Sergeant," replied Spartan, doing his absolute best not to laugh in front of the assembled men and women. Only one platoon on the ship was made up of veterans, the rest were either experienced marines from Carthago or new recruits. Either way, none of them had seen combat of the intensity that Spartan had faced. Spartan nodded to his old instructor to continue and then moved to the side to watch.

"You'll note that unlike the rest of you maggots, the Captain here has been in the trenches, and he's seen the blood and guts. Since the War started, men like the Captain and myself have been in action against rebels, Union soldiers, Zealots and even Biomechs. Hell, the Captain was one of the first people to even see a Biomech during the Siege of the Titan Naval Station."

He turned around and looked towards Spartan.

"Captain, they've all completed their basic training. I understand you and your team are here to pass on your experience with our enemies. Do you have anything to say?"

Spartan looked at the dozens of marines and realised he'd prepared nothing for the training session. Though he had a wealth of knowledge and experience, he'd been so caught up in getting information on Hyperion that he'd done nothing on the ship. As he looked at their faces, he was reminded of those he'd lost in countless battles. It was his duty to ensure as many of them came home. He considered talking about weapons, but a perfect distraction came when Ko'mandor Gun entered the hall. An audible sigh of surprise and excitement spread at the sight of the great creature. Gun ignored procedure and simply marched directly to Spartan. It gave him an idea.

"Yes, I have a few things to say," he said, took a few steps forward towards the marines to cut off Gun. His old friend stopped and tilted his head in confusion and looked back to the marines before moving to Spartan.

"Ah, bad time, Captain?"

"No, you're just in time, actually."

Spartan moved out into the middle of the hall with Gun beside him. He stopped, looking up and down the eager faces of the new marines. About a two-thirds were male, most in their late twenties. The women were of a similar age, but he knew from the paperwork that a good number had come from the troubles on Carthago, the same planet Teresa was from.

"How many of you have seen a Biomech before?" he asked.

About half of them lifted their hands.

"How many of you have seen one in the flesh before?" he asked.

Only one hand stayed up. It was a short, black woman in her mid-thirties with dark hair and muscular frame. Of all those around her, she seemed the calmest and the least excited at the sight of Gun.

"Tell me what you saw."

"Sir! Yes, Sir. I was working at the Tech School at New Carlos, back on Prime when the trouble started. My family paid for my entire class to leave the school and transfer to Terra Nova."

Spartan nodded at the story so far.

"Go on."

"Well, we were leaving orbit and heading for the usual nav-point prior to starting the long trip home when we were hit. It was a corsair raider, one of the Zealots I think. It was over fast, really fast. They boarded our ship and took us prisoner before shipping us away. You see, it wasn't just Zealots. When they took our ship, they sent in Biomechs... like him," she said with her hand pointing out to Gun.

"A month later and half of us were already dead. It wasn't until a tip-off from the Kerberos Underground that led a rescue team to the Rim where we were being held. So yes, I have seen Biomechs before, Sir, and I've seen how they perform in battle. They are tough, merciless and deadly in combat."

Spartan rested his chin in his hand and thought on her words.

"I've heard many stories like this one before, and each one is a tragedy. Biomechs overran Prime and were used on dozens of colonies as shock troops. There are different models and different generations. The earliest and simplest were bastardised creations, combining the body parts of all manner of creatures. These were mindless monsters but deadly nonetheless. Later came the partly, and then finally the fully, synthetic Biomechs. It is critical that you understand the differences between them. Questions?"

He should have known better than to thrown in a statement like that to marines. The Biomechs had a fearsome reputation, and there was probably nothing more contentious in the Alliance than the future of the Biomechs. The first person to raise his hand was a tall, thin looking man with a deep scar marking his cheek.

"Sir, I don't wish to sound rude, but why are they alive? Haven't we suffered enough?"

Gun stepped in front of Spartan and stared at the man. Spartan tried to intervene, but it was useless. Gun wanted to say something, and he already knew from experience that you never tried to put barrier in front of him.

"Biomechs are not evil, marine. They were created just like humans with in vitro. Would you demand the death or destruction of children born in a lab or hospital?"

Spartan was surprised; the words were more complex and eloquent than anything he'd heard from a Jötnar before. Even so, he spotted a chance to intercede and grabbed it before the conversation could start to slip.

"That's a good point. The Jötnar exist and so do the other Biomechs, and we can't change that. The Jötnar have proven their worth and their loyalty time and time again. There are few warriors in the Alliance that can stand toe-to-toe with them, and that's why they are here. Ask any marine that's served with the Jötnar, and they will tell you the same."

He looked at them and could see a great gulf of a difference between their views on Gun. He knew it should make little difference to him, but he still found it painful.

"Okay, who thinks they've got what it takes to bring him down?" he asked, trying to calm the mood. Incredibly, not a single marine lifted their hands.

"Nobody?" he asked in surprise.

"Are you sure these are Alliance marines?" asked Gun, though he was sure he was actually being serious.

The drill instructor walked over to Spartan and leaned in closer.

"Sir, they've heard the rumours about the Jötnar."

Spartan looked to Gun who just shrugged and then

back to the Sergeant.

"What rumours?"

"They kill in training and battle. Why do you think they won't practice?"

Spartan couldn't believe what he was hearing.

No wonder Gun and his people are getting such a hard time.

"I see, so you are marines that will back down when presented with a fight. I can't explain how disappointed this makes me feel. What will happen when you face a Biomech ambush or a full frontal assault? Sure, you can just blast away with your standard issue firearm, but what if it jams, runs out of ammo, or they just happen to smash their way through?"

He walked the entire length of the line of marines to where the crates of training equipment sat. He bent down and lifted the lid to reveal all manner of blunted fighting sticks, knives, bayonets and rubberised rifles and carbines. He looked over to his shoulder to Gun.

"Ko'mandor, what weapon do you prefer for close encounters?" he asked while presenting a variety of simulators.

Gun grinned, knowing full well what was coming next.

"Knives!" he said with a chortle.

Spartan reached in and took out two long training blades, each about a metre in length, and tossed them over to Gun. The Biomech caught them both, one in each hand and twirled them around in a pointless but amusing fashion. Spartan reached in and pulled out an L48 dummy rifle with a rubberised M11 bayonet already moulded into the shape. He then smashed down the lid and walked back into the middle.

"Being as none of you marines will stand for the challenge, I will take it myself."

The embarrassment and humiliation of the group was complete, but that wasn't Spartan's intent. All he wanted to do was to encourage those on the fringes to do something, anything. A woman at the back lifting her hand finally rewarded him.

"Sir, I'll help you," she said.

Spartan smiled. "Good, so there is a marine in here after all."

The instructor laughed at that comment.

The woman moved out from the lines of marines and stood in front of him. He looked up and down at her, examining her poise and physique in detail.

"Your name, marine?" he asked.

"Private Kathy Pezal, Sir!" she barked in reply.

She was tall with short, golden hair and narrow black eyes that gave little away. Like all the marines, she was fit and her body toned in the right places. She reminded him a little of Teresa back when he'd first met her on the way to the Santa Maria.

"You think you can bring him down?" he asked with raised eyebrows.

She looked at Gun who was busy pacing back and forth in the hall. Every few seconds, he would push forward into a mock cut or stab with the weapons. Private Pezal gulped as discretely as she could before looking back to Spartan.

"No, Sir. I will do my best though."

Spartan smiled at her comment, but his face quickly returned to his default grim expression, one he seemed to have worked on for such encounters.

"I see. So you will stand and fight a monster like him even though you know you will lose? What would help you win?"

She looked about the room and pointed to the others.

"More marines, Sir!"

Spartan nodded and indicated for her to return to the line.

"Excellent, and that is what I wanted to hear. Do you know what the very first lesson was that I received from your own drill instructor here? He told me that I worked alone, and that I wasn't part of a team. I might have had the body of a warrior, but this drill instructor told me I might look like a marine, but a marine I was not!"

Spartan looked to his old instructor and saw the man was nodding with agreement at his words.

"A marine is a rifleman, and we all know that, but a marine must work with his brothers and sisters. One marine is deadly, but a squad is almost invincible in battle.

If you're fighting a monster like my loyal friend Gun here, you need friends."

He stepped up to Gun and jabbed with the bayonet fitted to his training rifle. Gun parried it and then stabbed Spartan gently in the chest. Even so, the impact knocked him a little and it took a second to get his breath back.

"Private Kathy Pezal, grab a training rifle and stand here!" he said.

She was fast, and in seconds stood next to him, shoulder to shoulder with their bayoneted rifles.

"Now, if I stab, and Gun responds as before, my fellow marine can then stab him while he is engaged. Like this."

This time, as Gun's counterattack came in, Private Pezal's own bayonet struck Gun in the chest. Spartan turned to the others and placed a hand on the Private's shoulder.

"This is how we take on Biomechs, the same way we take on any threat. We rely on our friends and use of skill, training and determination to overcome the odds."

CHAPTER TEN

Mutation returned to the forefront of discussion, following tests on the final batch of Jötnar at Prometheus. Many opposed their conception, but the ethical arguments were halted by the final agreement between the Confederacy and the Jötnar prior to the former's dissolution. The introduction of minor changes in the software produced a number of unexpected results before the project was shutdown. Variations in size, shape, sex and intelligence were just some of the reported changes and created new strengths and weaknesses in the race.

Lessons on Mutation

Spartan and a group of marines were busy on the target range when the news arrived. It started with the arrival of a private carrying a rubberised datapad of the type usually carried by Spartan. Before he had finished reading the rest of the message, another group of recruits had already arrived at the door to tell him. Each was acutely aware of the missing ships near Hyperion, and most knew of Sergeant Morato's disappearance. Private Kathy Pezal entered the target range and saluted to Spartan.

"Sir, we heard the news," she exclaimed excitedly.

Spartan was only three-quarters through the file but already had run through the critical parts of the report. He tried to read the last bit, but the small group of marines were waiting impatiently. Eventually, he would have to say something. He lowered the device and looked at her.

"Yes, I've heard. ANS Minotaur has just sent out an unencoded distress signal about Hyperion."

"Yes, but have you seen the videocast from Terra Nova? They have footage from the Minotaur in orbit."

"What?" he replied, surprised.

Spartan cleared his weapon and moved to the range officer who took the weapon and his unused ammunition. Two of the marines spotted him get up and moved to follow him.

"What is it, Sir?" asked the elder of the corporals.

"There's video of the trouble at Hyperion. I'm going to the CIC. You carry on with your work."

With that he was gone and out through the door. It took some time to head through the many sections of the vast ship to reach the heart of the vessel. As he walked, he checked the details of the information that was being sent down through the military channels. With one of the reports was a section about enemy jamming and unidentified weapons, but much of the specific information had been redacted. After a few more minutes, he arrived to find most of the senior officers also there to see the Captain. He waited briefly while the marine guards checked those at the door before he could enter the CIC. The security was much more stringent than normal, and he noted one of the lieutenants was even turned away.

"Captain Spartan, here to see the Major," he explained to the sergeant. They both knew each other well, but even so the man checked on his internal communications gear before waving him through. He entered the large room to the sight of Major Daniels, Captain Schaffer, and his executive officer Commander Malone. But what caught his eye was the series of still images of what appeared to be a large battle. Major Daniels spotted his entry and turned from the two naval officers.

"Captain, I was about to call you to join us. I take it you've heard the news?"

"Yes, Sir, the ANS Minotaur has just made contact, something about an attack at Hyperion and some unusual weapons. The news reports are pretty vague, and the military feeds are not much better."

"That's about it, publically. Come and look at this."

Major Daniels beckoned him closer to view the images on the main screen. It was currently frozen on a still of a bright flash, but with a quick nod one of the tech officers moved the feed back to the start. The video was quite shaky and appeared to be from one of the external feeds. It showed the circular shape of a planet.

"That's Hyperion, by the way," explained Captain Schaffer.

Spartan nodded, keeping his attention on the video. The shapes of four other ships were clear to the right, especially the great bulk of the Marine Transport, ANS Santa Maria the sister ship of ANS Santa Cruz. The depth of field changed drastically and distorted the video.

"What's happening?" he asked.

"It's the acceleration. The cruiser is pulling away from the planet, and the camera is trying to maintain the image using optical zooming. It is only enough for fifty-three seconds, and then the camera is at its limit. Watch for the forty-two second mark."

Spartan looked back at the video and kept an eye on the time-code at the bottom left. Although it was running in real-time, the feed seemed to slow down as it reached the mentioned time. Spartan squinted at the distorted shapes of the ships. They jumped and twisted, and then he spotted. The bright colour orbs of light that were rushing up to the taskforce like shells from ground based cannon. The last few seconds showed very little as the ships shrunk to blurred dots along with weapons. He looked back to the Captain.

"I don't understand, what was that?" he asked with a

confused look.

The Captain pressed a button and changed the view to that of a video stream sent directly from the Captain of ANS Minotaur. The Captain looked shaken, and the crease lines on her face easily betraying the pressure and responsibility she must have felt for leaving the other ships behind.

"This is Captain Lewis of the ANS Minotaur. We have just escaped heavy ground fire from Hyperion and are requesting all and any Alliance help. Hostile forces are blockading the planet, and they have erected a wide area signal block. ANS Thunderer has been destroyed with the loss of all crew, and the status of the rest of the Hyperion Taskforce in unknown."

Spartan felt nausea building up at the thought of what had happened to the ships. He'd assumed there had been trouble but nothing the marines and ships couldn't handle. According to this new information, there was a good chance the ships could be damaged or even destroyed. Major Daniels spoke before he could ask any questions.

"So we know one cruiser is down and one escaped, that leaves two more and the Santa Maria unaccounted for. Did Captain Lewis have any more information on what happened?"

The XO shook his head, speaking on behalf of the Captain who had turned to look at the starcharts.

"No, the Minotaur is still suffering periodic power losses.

The last message she sent contained her full log prior to their escape. Seems they were disabled by something from the planet, and there is some kind of base and compound on the surface."

Major Daniels turned back to Spartan.

"I know what you're thinking, and I'm working on it. Good news is the reconnaissance drones should be there vey soon, so I expect we'll be getting our marching orders soon."

Captain Schaffer nodded in agreement.

"Yes, and the rest of the fleet are not far away either. The destroyer group from the Anomaly arrived two hours ago and have already adopted an escort posture around us. Both Assault Cruisers are due to arrive in ten or eleven hours. It's a good-sized force by any measure. I've contact from Admiral Churchill, and he is already en route with three more ships from Terra Nova, including a ship I'm not familiar with. The Tamarisk I think he called it."

Spartan's interest piqued at the name of the ship. It was a small vessel, a Q-Ship by all accounts, and one used by Commander Anderson and a small team to effect a rescue of him and the General back on Prometheus. Captain Schaffer noticed his look of recognition.

"You've heard of her?" he asked.

Spartan nodded but said no more.

"Sir!" called out a science technician from behind his terminal.

"What is it?" replied the XO, his tone implying irritation at the interruption.

"We have an encoded transmission from the reconnaissance drones. One made it to Hyperion and scanned for seven minutes before being destroyed."

"Send it here," said the XO.

It took only a few seconds before the screen filled with detailed information from the drone. It didn't take long for such a vessel to start its analysis, and it had transmitted from the minute it arrived. Detailed information on debris and planetary surface scans indicated there had been a space battle, but there was nothing useful from the planet. What was interesting was the set of long-range images of a group of ships in orbit. The officers examined them in detail, trying to establish which ships they were and what exactly was going on around the planet.

"Is that the Santa Maria?" asked Spartan as he did his best not to sound too desperate.

The technician was already working hard on the imagery and sent over a cleaned up version that clearly showed a crippled cruiser and a badly damaged marine transport. Both were still in orbit, but there were no signs of power or life.

"What the hell is that?" asked the XO as he pointed to three shapes on the port side of the great transport.

Once enlarged, the nearest looked like a vessel the size of a landing craft or naval tug. Though big, it was dwarfed by the size of Santa Maria and the unidentified cruiser. More interesting though, its shape closely resembled that of a large metallic bug. The group of officers squinted as they stared at the bizarre object.

The communications officer interrupted their amazement with critical news.

"Captain, incoming message from Admiral Churchill. He says it is urgent. It's about Hyperion."

Captain Schaffer glanced over to Major Daniels and nodded as if it was a message he expected. Even the XO seemed unsurprised at the news.

"Here we have it," said the XO grimly.

Captain Schaffer nodded to him and then looked to the communications officer.

"Put him on the main screen."

The face of the Admiral appeared almost immediately. He was inside a CIC much like on board ANS Santa Cruz, but none of them recognised the crew in the background.

"I will be there shortly. I have just received orders from Alliance High Command. Video and imagery has leaked to the press about our missing ships and also that we have a potential hostage situation on the planet. Rumours are spreading that the Zealots have captured General Rivers. It's being played as a demonstration of Alliance incompetence. Our orders are simple, recce the system and launch a rescue mission if it is deemed safe enough. The fleet will be assembled in eleven hours, so that's how long you have until we leave this area. It will be a ten-day journey from your current position."

Captain Schaffer rubbed his cheek as he listened to the news. It was hardly unexpected, but he was concerned at the almost total lack of information.

"Admiral, do we have any more news on what happened out there? The last signal from ANS Minotaur was sparse at best. Do we have no intel on the area?"

Admiral Churchill looked behind him as if he expected to be watched and then leaned in as if to whisper.

"I will explain further when aboard your ship, Captain. Needless to say, there are concerns about Hyperion, concerns that go beyond hostages, ships or even the General."

He straightened himself up before continuing.

"Get your ship ready. Once the taskforce is assembled, we will be off at full burn. Check your systems, we cannot afford to make even a single mistake. This isn't as large a fleet as I hoped, but it will have to do. One marine transport, four cruisers, five destroyers and the Tamarisk, make ten vessels in total. It's not like the fleet is back in the War, but it is still a formidable force. Is Major Daniels there?"

The Major moved from the right so that he was in view of the camera, and the Admiral could see him. Spartan stepped in as well, not wanting to be left out of the conversation.

"Ah, good, I see that wherever the Major is, I will also find Captain Spartan. I take it you have heard the same information as the rest of us?"

Major Daniels nodded.

"I thought as much. Make sure your troops are ready for battle. I understand you have been training four companies of ground troops. Check their jungle fighting and survival skills, Major. Something tells me they will need them. I have also arranged for a company of Terra Novan soldiers to join us. They are green but well trained. That should give us around five hundred ground troops plus your experienced officers and Gun's unit of Jötnar. There are also a number of technical specialists along to assist. I have several intelligence specialists from Kerberos, as well as a Navy weapons research team to provide scientific and technical support."

"Sir," replied Major Daniels.

Admiral Churchill checked something on one of his screens and looked back at the camera. In the short delay, Spartan leaned close to Major Daniels and whispered as quietly as he could.

"Do you get the impression the Admiral has spent the last few days assembling a lot of people for this mission?"

The Major didn't have time to answer, and all he could do was gently nod as the Admiral continued his short briefing.

"I therefore confirm that by order of Defence Secretary

Howalt Sones, and on behalf of the Senate of the Centauri Alliance, I have been placed in supreme command of this force. From seventeen hundred hours today, Operation Sol Invictus is a go. Hyperion is our destination. The eyes of the Alliance are on us, and that is why I must bring you one additional detail. It isn't what I wanted, but we have been asked to bring a media crew along with us to document the mission. It's a three-man unit, and they have been vetted by Alliance Intelligence."

With that final statement, his video communication ended, and the screen changed back to a wide-angled view of the small fleet of destroyers stationed around ANS Santa Cruz. Captain Schaffer took in a long breath before speaking.

"The press, on our ships?" he muttered, evidently unimpressed with the news.

"Well, this is it then, gentlemen. To your stations and prepare your forces. We might only be a day out from Terra Nova, but that will at least cut some of our journey time. I need everything ready, so when the second the fleet is assembled, and the Admiral on board, we can leave. A lot can happen in ten days. I just hope that if anybody is still alive on Hyperion, they can hold out for another ten days."

The officers saluted, and Major Daniels and Captain Spartan left the CIC to enter the main corridor. They walked in silence back towards the main marine habitation areas before the Major spoke with a clam but concerned voice.

"I know Teresa is out there. But she's not on her own. She's with friends, and if the General is still alive, I can promise you he will be working on a plan. If anybody can survive for weeks in the wilderness and surrounded by Zealots, it's Teresa."

Spartan did his best to smile in agreement, but deep down he was worried, very worried.

* * *

General Rivers woke up to the feeling of the worst headache he'd ever experienced. There was something strapped to his face, and his first instinct was to rip it off. As it came off, he could smell the rich air of Hyperion, thick with hints of vegetation and dampness. The humidity felt like a warm fog in his throat. He inhaled, but the air seemed thin and stretched out. His vision started to blur, but he heard somebody's voice, and the mask was replaced on his head.

"Keep it on, Sir. The air isn't great around here. You'll get used to it."

His eyesight started to return, and he could see trees moving past him and up into the air. It took a few more seconds before he realised he was lying prone on a makeshift sled and being dragged through the woodland.

"Soldier," he called out weakly, "what happened? Where

is Pontus?"

The soldier, a man in his filthy PDS armoured suit, leaned closer to speak.

"General, we were forced to abandon ship because of the ground fire. I think one cruiser escaped. We tracked your beacon on the way down and ditched some twenty klicks from here. We found you and three Zealot bodies over a kilometre from the crash site. There were some Biomechs in the area but we moved them on fast, Sir."

General Rivers shook his head, desperately trying to remember what had happened. Brief images of the struggle in the craft and a fight in a swamp came to him but no specifics. Pain behind his eyes returned and he slumped back and took several more breaths before speaking again.

"Where are we going?"

"Well, Sir, we're heading for the rendezvous point under Captain Carlos. They've established a fortified compound until rescue gets here."

Compound? He was now totally confused as to where he was.

"Where are we?" he asked.

"Sir? Hyperion. The boats and pods are scattered all over. We ditched four days ago, and it's taken us this long to cover the ground."

"We?" he asked.

"Yes, Sir, we crashed with thirty-one crew from Santa

Maria. Your guards made it as well. They are up ahead with the designated scouts."

His mind was starting to clear. Something must have happened on their journey through the atmosphere because he didn't recall ever setting foot on Hyperion.

"What happened to me?"

"Not sure, Sir. We were hit coming through the atmosphere. Luckily, we didn't burn up coming down. We lost half the crew when we ditched. So far, we know Captain Carlos, Sergeant Morato of the ASOGs and about two hundred marines and crew are heading for the compound."

A high-pitched scream came from the woodland as if somebody or something wanted to speak to them. He noted the posture of the people about him as the crewmen with their masks and the small number of marines levelled their weapons to the mist clouded trees.

"What's happening?" he demanded.

"It's the jungle, Sir. There are Biomechs out there, but they haven't attacked us. They are watching and following though. We managed to kill one, and they are definitely Zealot controlled. They even have the Echidna markings on their armour."

General Rivers slumped back onto his crude sled and tried to understand exactly what was going on. The dispersed landing was one thing, but he still didn't understand why they were all travelling so far when commonsense dictated they stayed near the landing sites and waited for help.

"Okay, ten minutes break. Send out pickets, watch yourselves out there!" called out an unfamiliar voice. The tone shifted, but it could just as easily have been his hearing as it was to being their voice.

The group stopped, and he found his sled was being rested against a fallen tree. He could see the others moving about now and was surprised to see a few working without their respirators or PDS suits. Most slumped to the ground where they stood, but at least three or four slung their weapons and moved out to the perimeter to check for signs of the enemy. He looked about to try and find a friendly face, but they all looked like faceless crewmen. One person appeared to be in charge of the group but was too far away to be seen. He lifted his hand out and touched his face. He could feel the thin plastic mask, but there was no other armour or obvious wound. He pulled his hand back and spotted the officer in charge move passed him.

"You, Sir!" he called out. The louder he spoke the more his head hurt, and he winced at the pain.

"General, how are you feeling?" asked the officer. The tone of voice had already dropped in volume but also changed in pitch. He was as surprised to see it was a woman as he was to see the firm voice wasn't a marine, but in fact Lieutenant Nilsson from the Santa Maria. The ship's communications officer looked as though she had taken charge of the survivors.

"Lieutenant Nilsson?" he asked in surprise.

"Yes, Sir. I'm the next more senior here. The rest of the officers were killed at the next crash site. We're heading for the compound to the south. It's the designated rally point."

She moved much closer now, and he easily recognised her face. He remembered her from back on the Crusader, the old battlecruiser that he and Admiral Jarvis had shared for so many months in the War. His head was hurting, but already his mind was racing ahead and trying to collate all the information that he had heard so far. Lieutenant Nilsson sat next to him and reached out to check the dressing on his head.

"How is it?" he asked.

"You'll be fine, Sir, just a bad case of concussion to deal with now."

He noticed she wasn't wearing a respirator and seemed to be managing fine.

"What is the problem with the air?" he asked.

"It's the air mix, not quite what we're used to. It takes a few days for your body to adapt. You've been on the oxygen since we found you. I couldn't afford to lose you, Sir. Your mixture is already cut down to half, and by tomorrow you should be able to breathe normally. It's still not easy, a bit like breathing at high altitude back on Prime. Takes a while for your blood to oxygenate and lungs to catch up."

General Rivers nodded; he was finally starting to get a picture as to what was going on. He had no doubt in the officer's ability to lead the party or even with her survival skills. But what she lacked was the big picture, that of the mission. Deep down he knew there was something on this planet, and as the General in command of the operation it was his job, no, his duty, to ensure the mission succeeded.

"The mission?" he asked.

A whistle interrupted them both. It was low tech but instantly gained the attention of the small group. The young Lieutenant signalled for the General to keep his head down, and then she took cover. There was a rustling sound in the woods and he could see a group of dark shapes moving towards them. Half a dozen L48 carbines clicked quietly as those carrying them removed the safeties and prepared for a bloody battle.

"Lieutenant Eastwood, Alliance Marine Corps," said a nervous but slightly optimistic voice from the shadows.

Lieutenant Nilsson stood up, indicating with her left hand for the others to stay down. She pointed her carbine at the shape and spoke quietly.

"Lieutenant Nilsson, Communications Officer, ANS Santa Maria."

The foliage ruffled once more, and from the darkness emerged the armoured shapes of six marines, each carrying their weapons at the ready. In front of them stood their commander who opened his visor to show his face.

"Good to meet you, Lieutenant, you made it then? You've made quicker progress than we anticipated."

Lieutenant Nilsson gave a hand signal to her own people to let them know it was safe to move. Her small band emerged from the undergrowth and foliage, and for the first time General Rivers could get a good look at them all. The guards were his personal protectors, and it was clear they were the only fully training warriors in the group. One moved over to check on him.

"Sir, good to see you awake. You had us worried," he said with a grim expression.

"How far away is the compound?" asked Lieutenant Nilsson.

"Less than an hour. Like I said, you made good progress."

He turned and waved to his team before looking back to her.

"You've done your people proud, Lieutenant Nilsson. Let us help you to the base. We've got supplies, power and weapons. You might also want..." he stopped when he spotted the sled and the shape of General Rivers.

"General?" he asked in surprise.

Without checking with Lieutenant Nilsson, he walked passed her and directly to the commander. He stood smartly to attention.

"General Rivers, Sir. We were under the impression

you'd been taken hostage."

The General returned the salute and shook his head.

"No, rumours of my demise have been exaggerated. Get me to your compound as quickly as possible. We have business to attend to if we want to get out of here, and more importantly, we have people to help on this forsaken planet."

* * *

It took the rest of the afternoon for the group of crew and marines to make the journey to the compound. Although the distance could have been no more than seven kilometres, the sodden ground, frequent marsh and swampland and over a dozen Biomech sightings compounded it. By the time they arrived at the site itself it was getting dark. Even General Rivers was on his feet when they reached the improved compound. They made it within thirty metres of the palisade wall before a marine called down to them.

"Who goes there?" he shouted.

From down on the ground, it wasn't east to see the man. He was calling from what looked like a control tower. A flaming torch burned quietly away at the rear, and the dark shape of a large firearm protruded from the front and towards them. Below the tower was the outer defence of the compound. It was like something from Earth's ancient history. The outer wall was nearly five metres tall and built entirely from wood. Partially sharpened stakes stuck out and away from the wall at regular intervals. Along the top of the wall burned dozens of simple torches. Four guards popped their heads up from the barricade to look down at those outside. It was primitive but effective.

"Lieutenant Eastwood, back from patrol. I have survivors from the fleet, including General Rivers."

The man in the tower said no more but did swing an electrically powered lamp around to inspect the group. The light bumped between several of them before it was switched off, and the man called down to somebody inside the compound.

"Impressive, how long did this all take?" asked General Rivers as he waited to be let in.

"You'd be surprised how quickly people can build something like this in an emergency. The outer wall was up in just over a day. The rest took a little longer. We didn't have much of a choice. It can get pretty unfriendly at night around here."

General Rivers looked confused.

"Biomechs?"

The Marine Lieutenant shook his head.

"No, Sir, we've had the occasional Zealot patrol out here. But with the secure compound, we can make sure they don't get in amongst us, and we can send out teams to stop them reporting back."

"Back?" asked the General. "Have you tried following them to see where they are coming from?"

A large wooden door that had been reinforced with sections from the outer skin of a landing craft was dragged open to reveal a bustling camp with scores of people moving about preparing food, checking weapons and working on damaged equipment.

"Not yet, Sir. Right now, we've been searching for survivors and making sure no Biomechs or Zealots get away alive from here. Once they find us, they will certainly be back and in force."

The General nodded but didn't look convinced. They moved inside and quickly spotted the crashed vessel off to one side. More than twenty temporary shelters had been built, and three watchtowers constructed of just wood marked the three corners of the triangular site.

"Who is in charge here?" asked the General.

A small party appeared from one of the shelters and moved towards him. They were all Marine Corps personnel, and although they wore their PDS armour, none were wearing helmets. He recognised Captain Carlos immediately.

"Captain, I should have known it would be you," he said happily.

"General, it's not much, but it will do for now."

He looked to the left and to the smiling Teresa. They knew each other after she and a small team had rescued

Spartan and him from the Zealots and their allies on Prometheus. It had been a bloody fight that ended in a full-scale revolt against their control.

"Sergeant Morato, it appears we are in trouble in foreign lands once more!"

The General turned around and looked at his new home, nodding with satisfaction. There was easily enough space for up to five or six hundred people plus a clearing for anything up to the size of a shuttle and landing craft. He turned back to the Captain.

"Okay, I can see you've set up a defensible position. Give me a full sitrep. I need to know our numbers, reconnaissance, supplies, and combat effectiveness. Even more importantly, have you been able to make contact off-world or with any more survivors?"

Captain Carlos saluted and then gestured towards one of the shelters.

"We've set up that one as a temporary command centre. We have produced rough maps of the area and established four small sentry outposts a kilometre away in each direction.

"Excellent work. Show me. Oh, and where are Captain Cornwall and Commander Petersburg?"

They moved off to the shelter while a number of crew and civilians from the ships came over to assist the new arrivals. Lieutenant Nilsson approached Teresa with a worried look on her face.

"Sergeant?" she asked.

"Yes."

"Have you noticed something strange with the wildlife here?"

Teresa nodded in agreement and looked about for somewhere to sit down. She spotted a few empty ammo crates and indicated for the Lieutenant to sit down with her.

"Yes, you could say that. They don't seem to want to attack us, but they are very interested for some reason."

Lieutenant Nilsson looked out to the wooden walls and the dark shapes of the trees that lay much further away. She felt as if she was barricaded inside a castle of ancient times.

"We thought they were hunting us, so we killed a few of them. They have the armour and markings of the Zealots, but they only fought us when we attacked them. Is it their programming, or is something else going on?"

Teresa shrugged.

"I don't know. Spartan keeps telling me that with the Core destroyed all the Biomechs lost their central control and reverted to their core memories and experiences. Maybe these escaped from the Zealots and have been living in the wild?"

Wild Biomechs? Thought Lieutenant Nilsson. *Is that better or worse that Echidna Zealots?*

CHAPTER ELEVEN

The Anomaly and its secrets were never fully understood during the War. Apart from a fully functioning Spacebridge, the derelict structures seemed unnecessary complications for a natural phenomenon. The discovery of computer equipment over three centuries old started a series of philosophical and scientific arguments that raged for months until the discoveries on Hyperion.

Computational Methods Vol. IV

Captain Spartan, Major Daniels and Admiral Churchill looked at the planetary scans from the drones once more. They'd been looking over the information for days now as they tried to formulate a plan, based on the limited knowledge of the area. Admiral Churchill walked away from the table for a moment, his forehead in his hand as he thought.

"We've only got three more days left, and I'm still not happy about this. When we get there, we will have to be fast. You saw the reports from ANS Minotaur."

Major Daniels moved several units on the map of the planet and then stood up straight to look over to the Admiral.

"We're not going to have to take chances with this one, Sir. We have a rough idea of the range of their weapons as well as the electronics and communication jamming gear that they have access to."

"True, but what about the lack of control on the ships? How did they disable our vessels so effectively?"

There was a short pause as they considered the question. Spartan was the last to speak, but he was sure the two men were looking at the problem in the wrong way.

"Look. They either used technology based on or around Hyperion, or they had inside help. Minotaur suffered the same problems, but when she reached a safe distance not all of her systems were back to normal. It can't be a signal, so they must have got something aboard."

Admiral Churchill nodded.

"Like those damned AI Hubs we found on our ships before?"

Spartan lifted his eyebrows at the idea and nodded in agreement.

"Could be, how though? That would mean there are still traitors in our ranks and with access to the command and control systems in our ships. We've checked our people time and time again."

Admiral Churchill walked back to the board and brought up the schematics of the ships involved in the original taskforce. There was little in common with each ship, not even their host planets or configuration. Alongside each of them were the captains and their senior officers. He ran his finger along them all but could find nothing of note, until he reached the XO of ANS Santa Maria.

"Ah," he said, almost to himself.

Spartan walked up and looked where he was pointing.

"What is it?"

"Commander Petersburg. He's the weakest link in the entire fleet. He's second in command of the flagship and has a history that is well known in the Navy. Experienced, skilled, and rated at the top of his class in the Academy, yet he's managed to avoid open battle every single time."

Major Daniels rubbed his cheek as he considered the comments.

"I've known good men, good officers that by a stroke of luck managed to avoid combat. Sometimes it's intentional, but most of the time it isn't. How does this help us? We still don't know what they did or how they stopped so many systems from working?"

Admiral Churchill didn't seem particular impressed with their thoughts even though they were perfectly justified. He brought back the map of the planet. With the press of two buttons, it zoomed into one particular part of the world.

"We know this was the source of the ground fire. I suspect there is a base or site of some kind being used by the enemy. Controlling Hyperion requires total domination of the space around the planet. Our priority is to disable the weapons on the planet. Once this is done, we can send in one ship at a time to establish what power or strength the enemy has."

Major Daniels seemed a little happier at this first suggestion.

"My ground troops have been training for days now, and Spartan and his Jötnar have practiced over a dozen scenarios from frontal assault and hostage rescue through to hand-to-hand with Biomechs. They are ready for whatever you want them to do. We're packing five companies plus change."

"How about your Vanguards?" asked Admiral Churchill.

Major Daniels nodded at the question.

"Just half a platoon, I'm afraid. There wasn't time to transfer the gear from Terra Nova. Also, most of the men trained up on the gear are training other units. Still, sixteen is better than none, and they are all experienced."

All three looked at the map and the flashing zones around the suspected weapon emplacements. He then brought up an additional monitor that showed the ANS Tamarisk. Admiral Churchill waited a little while longer as he examined the details before him. As the senior officer, he was responsible for commanding the Taskforce but had also been given tactical command of the ground operation.

"My plan is simple. The fleet will move in to a position not far from where ANS Minotaur made first contact. We know this location is clear from both weapons fire and communication blocking. This is our operating zone, and no vessel will leave it unless it meets our agreed criteria."

He placed his finger on the display and drew a circle around the point in space he had selected. He pointed back to ANS Tamarisk.

"When in position, ANS Tamarisk will advance into medium orbit and drop a strike team down to a position near the ground batteries. It will be small and include the most experienced Special Forces and technical crew to the surface."

Major Daniels shook his head in disapproval.

"Admiral, I appreciate the need to disable their systems, but dropping troops directly onto their weapon position? That would be suicide, Sir. They will detect the ship in orbit and probably destroy it before it can launch shuttles. We'll be dead before we get through the atmosphere."

The Admiral shook his head, and Spartan watched as he pointed out several of the more unusual features of the ship.

"No, not quite. The Tamarisk is the most advanced

special operations vessel we have. It's taken over a year to fix the damage she sustained during combat at Prometheus. She has the best computers, including an active intelligence countermeasures suite that should help if they attempt to take control. Even better though, she carries a complement of three black ops shuttles. After her last mission, she was enlarged to carry more troops and equipment. You know the shuttles; they were developed for dropping teams into combat undetected. Each one can carry eight fully armoured marines into battle. After re-entry, you should be able to land before their systems can lock on and track you. Unless they are looking in the exact spot, you should be able to land undetected."

Spartan liked the resources available, but the intelligence from the surface suggested a site that could contain thousands of warriors and unknown weapons and counter-measures.

"Admiral, twenty-four marines against their entire operation?" he said incredulously.

Even Major Daniels looked less than inspired at the idea. He looked at the Tamarisk and her layout with interest. He'd heard rumours of the ship, but following the fighting at Prometheus, most had been classified.

"This ship, what's so special about her? Won't they just attack as before?"

At that comment the Admiral smiled.

"No, she is our trump card. The Tamarisk is a heavily

modified transport. She matches the specification and configuration of a light transport that is still registered. Even a close scan at fifty metres won't reveal her extra armour, computer equipment or weapons."

"She's armed?" asked the Major.

The Admiral simply raised one amused looking eyebrow at his question. He tapped a key that altered the schematic to show the cargo containers spread around the hull. Inside each one were batteries of weapons. She might look like a civilian transport, but she had been heavily modified into what was known by the military as a 'Q' ship. Hinged plates covered the weapons that were hidden in the containers, and additional armour had also been installed. In reality, she had the firepower to take on a ship of the same size, possibly even larger; even more importantly, she had surprise on her side when moving into hostile areas of space.

"Nice," explained Spartan as he read the details. He was very familiar with the ship but had no idea she was quite as tough as the information revealed. Admiral Churchill turned away from the displays and looked at each of them.

"I will leave the operation of the ground phase of the battle to Major Daniels. Just understand that until the ground-based weapons are disabled, I will not be able to commit Santa Cruz and the five companies of marines and Terra Novan Guards. I suggest you pick the best force you can for the operation. Reinforcements will be waiting for instant insertion onto the battlefield. The cavalry will be ready, but when they come in will depend on you."

* * *

"Contact!" came the radio message on Teresa's internal communications unit. Although her visor was up, she was still finding it tough to get used to the air on the planet. Those with breathing conditions, especially three of the crew with asthma, were forced to reply on the oxygen scrubbers and masks all the time.

"Watch for reinforcements. We don't move in until we know this is the lot of them."

The rest of her ASOG troop kept low, training their weapons on the small party of people moving towards them. As they came into view, she instantly recognised the robes of the Zealots. She's seen them enough times before, and it took a great deal of self control to not squeeze off a few rounds there and then. Their level of indoctrination always amazed her, and as they moved closer, she again wondered what could possibly drive them to do the terrible things they did.

"Something else is coming, a machine," said Sergeant Lovett who was position thirty metres off to her right and protecting their flank. Teresa turned her head slowly to check that direction and spotted the machine as it came within ten metres of their position.

What the hell is that?

It was unlike anything she had ever seen before. Standing almost five metres tall, it had the shape of a four-legged beast, yet was obviously mechanical. It moved with subtlety and poise that was nothing like the autonomous drones used by the marines for resupply and fire-support. On its flanks was a pair of pintle-mounted firearms of an unknown configuration. Its head was shaped into a metallic wedge with cameras and antennae facing in multiple directions.

Don't come any closer!

A shout from behind the scout party drew the attention of the machine. It twisted around with lightning speed. The cameras on its head swivelled like an insects eyes, and the weapon mounts tracked in the direction the sound. Two of the Zealots ran back to pursue whatever it was, but the machine was faster. Without hesitation, or offering a warning, it fire a quick burst of gunfire into the jungle. An inhuman scream of pain was silenced by yet another burst. The Zealots ran off into the darkness, and behind them followed the hellish machine. After they had moved away, she lifted her body up but only by enough so that she could see the direction they had head in.

"Follow them but stay back. I don't want to have to fight that thing, not yet!" she said in a firm but measured tone.

The ASOG unit of eight men and women moved out

in a loose line to follow the Zealots and their mechanical ally. Teresa was positioned in the centre of the unit. One of her experienced corporals pushed further to the front to take the point position. It was slow work, made difficult both by the thick foliage and also the need to stay hidden and undetected. A quick look at her map showed they were now over six hours from the compound and still moving.

They'd better take us somewhere useful, she thought optimistically. The last thing she wanted was to spend days instead of hours traipsing through the jungle while following a deadly beast.

* * *

The compound was almost in pitch darkness, save the odd light from burning torches that ran around the perimeter or at the entrances of most of the shelters. A decision had been made early on to keep the lighting to a minimum, so as to avoid unwanted attention. Even so, the place was still busy with two more six-man units preparing their gear to continue to map out the area around them. Captain Carlos stood outside the entrance to the designated command shelter and saluted at the approach of General Rivers.

"Any news from the scout teams?" asked the General.

"Just one," he answered, indicating the General to step inside.

Inside the dark interior, the setting transformed from

one of spartan surroundings, woodland and nature to one of electronics, mapping equipment and stored weapons. Two Navy crewmen were busy monitoring the communications equipment while supervised by Lieutenant Nilsson. She saluted the approach of the two senior officers.

"I've just received another message from Sergeant Morato. She says her unit is tracking a Zealot scout party plus a machine."

"Machine?" asked General Rivers.

Lieutenant Nilsson handed over a military grade datapad device that showed a grainy but detailed image of the four-legged contraption. He looked at it for a few seconds before handing it to the Captain.

"Any information on what exactly it is? Something like our autonomous resupply mules?"

"Not likely, General, look at the sensors on its front and the weapon mounts. I'd say this is some kind of scout machine, possibly a sentry."

General Rivers looked unimpressed.

"Autonomous?"

"Unknown, General."

"I see," added General Rivers. He then moved over to the scruffy looking map that contained as many revisions as it did actually information. Their compound was clearly marked in the centre, and a number of blocks were positioned to represent each of the scouting parties.

Sergeant Morato's ASOG unit was the furthest out by a considerable distance.

"How far out are they now?"

"Uh, about six kilometres so far, and the enemy force is apparently still moving."

The room flickered slightly as if a strobe light had just been flashed outside. It was followed by another half a dozen before the sound of loud, rolling thunder rippled through the compound.

"Great, that's all we need," said Captain Carlos.

Almost immediately, a torrential downpour of hailstones hitting the roof greeted his words. General Rivers shook his head at the arrival of the bad weather.

"Lieutenant Nilsson. I want to know the minute you hear anything new." He turned to the Captain of the marines.

"Captain Carlos. Get a team out and double-check this site for rain protection, especially the walls. We don't want flooding. I need our supplies and gear dry and ready for combat. We don't know how much longer we are going to be here."

* * *

To Teresa it seemed as though they had been following the machine and its Zealot companions for weeks, but it had barely been a whole day. Slogging through the dense foliage was only made bearable by the fact that the machine itself had created a loose trail for them to work through. The weather had finally turned against them with over seven hours of torrential rain. Luckily, it had now has eased off for a few hours, but with dawn just breaking, the trickle of rain had returned and storms threatening to follow. It was proving to be an exhausting and miserable patrol.

"Sergeant, clearing up ahead," said Corporal Dalton Nylund as discreetly as he could.

The unit dropped to their knees once more as they waited for the enemy to move a little further away. They had already stopped in almost a dozen similar places, and the lack of cover was a major concern. If the machine turned around, or the Zealots retraced their steps, they could catch the troopers in the vulnerable open. This time, however, something was different. Corporal Benedict Alessandro, the unit's resident paramedic, confirmed Teresa's suspicions.

"Anybody else hearing that?" he asked.

Teresa nodded in his direction. Even though she wore her helmet, the sound of machinery was unmistakable. With a subtle change in reception strength, she amplified the internal speakers of her suit. The sound level increased, and she could make out the sound of heavy equipment and even voices.

About damned time!

"Okay, two teams move out into flanking positions but stay in the tree line. Stay down and record everything you see. Do not engage, I repeat, do not engage."

The two squads, led by Sergeant Lovett and Sergeant Morato moved the short distance to the edge of the jungle canopy and waited for the swirling mist to clear. The strong wind created gaps in the cover every few minutes, but for now the visibility had been reduced to no more than twenty metres. With every additional second, Teresa worried. Anything could be in the mist, and they would have no time to withdraw if spotted.

"It's clearing, stay low," said Sergeant Lovett from his position off to the left of the ASOG troopers.

It took a few more seconds before the mist started to clear, and then as quickly as it had arrived, it drifted away to the trees, giving them a perfect view for at least several hundred metres. The sight that greeted them all almost made Teresa involuntarily gasp. It took all her self-control to stay down and quiet.

Gods, what have we found?

In front of them, at a distance of at least eight metres from the tree line, was the base of a small, rocky mountain. In the centre of it was a wide-open space that must have been carved out over a long period of time. Stone structures, including vast columns, supported the roof. A dozen long curved steps led inside. They were almost fifty metres wide, and easily big enough for a small vessel to land directly inside. Inside the structure, she could make out multiple sources of blue pulsing energy, much like what she had seen at the AI Core back on Terra Nova. But there was something different about this place. The design and architecture was unlike anything she had ever seen before and was surrounded by hundreds, if not thousands, of people who seemed to be working on it.

"Are you seeing this?" asked Sergeant Lovett.

"Uh, yes. Are you recording it all?" she replied slowly.

"Oh yeah."

As well as the massive artificial structure, there were plumes of black smoke rising from dozens of vents cut directly into the mountain. The smoke mixed with the dense air and fog to create a swirling cloud that covered the entire site in low light. It gave the impression of it approaching night even though it was actually in the early hours of the morning.

This place is incredible. Artificially constructed into a mountain, or is it a volcano?

Teresa turned her gaze to the right of the structure and followed a party of about fifty people. They were poorly clothed and dragging sleds full of cut rock behind them. Other parties moved metal girders while small teams used welders and cut directly on the exposed parts of the temple. Patrol parties of up to a dozen Zealots marched about the site, but none seemed particularly interested in looking for signs of them. Teresa looked carefully at the centre of the mountain, but something seemed to be moving out into the open. It had the same smooth gait of the four-legged machine they had tracked, but this one looked larger. As it moved into the low light, something was clicking in her mind, and she fell back in pain.

"Sarge!" called out Corporal Alessandro as Sergeant Lovett dragged him back into the undergrowth.

A terrible screaming sound erupted from inside the structure and buzzed in Teresa's head. It then reverberated in her skull like a terrible wail. She ducked down and fell to the floor. She tried to touch her head, but the helmet blocked her hands. Corporal Alessandro held her down and hit the connecting strips on the helmet to remove her helmet. Sergeant Lovett moved over to check her, shaking his head as the loud screaming sound penetrated his helmet. The effect was almost like that of a high –pressure drill being powered up inside the helmet.

"Sergeant Morato, can you hear me?" he asked as he looked down at his fallen comrade. Teresa looked back at him, but already the sound level had dropped, and the pain had fallen to a more reasonable level.

"Sergeant, looks like the workers are feeling it too!" said Corporal Nylund.

He looked up and to the site to see a large number of the workers covering their ears as the large mechanical machine moved out from the safety of the mountain and moved off to the right. It was followed by an escort of six of the four-legged machines of a design identical to the one they had been tracking.

"What's going on?" asked Teresa as she remembered she'd left the internal volume on her helmet at almost maximum so she could track the mechanical sounds. It was no wonder the shrill scream from the machines had caused her so much pain.

"Uh, you need to see this," said Sergeant Lovett.

Teresa shook her head and did her best to clear her mind. The mist was continuing to clear, and as it pulled away from the mountain, the rest of the unit fell silent. Teresa lifted herself up a little from the damp ground and looked in the same direction as the others. Her head still pounded, but she was able to forget all of it when she saw the ring of four more mountains, each much like the one they had discovered, and each of them positioned around a central structure shaped like a large stone dome. Streaks of blue energy crackled and flashed from pylons attached to the mountains that ran down like the legs of a spider to the central dome. The entire site, including the dome and the myriad of buildings around it, was more like a tiny city, but it looked ancient and mostly derelict and deserted. It was massive, probably two hundred metres tall and beautifully carved and designed. It reminded her of some of the ancient churches she had seen in images of Old Earth.

"Those mountain structures look like they are sending

power of some type directly into that central structure," explained Corporal Dalton Nylund, their technical specialist.

"Yeah, but power to what?" replied Sergeant Lovett.

As they watched, the dome started to lift itself, supported by dozens of thick pillars. The mechanical machines assembled nearby along with more of their kind until almost thirty of them waited. They all faced the dome and stood completely still. As the dome moved up, she could make out a purple orb pulsing and rotating inside it. The orb itself was many metres in diameter and seemed to flash and spin, suspended in mid-air. Sergeant Lovett turned to look at her with a look of astonishment on his face.

"What the hell is this place?"

Teresa looked carefully at the site and at her sensor package in her helmet.

"I don't know, but I'll tell you this. We aren't leaving until we know more. What are they building? What are those machines? And lastly, what is going on in that dome?"

They all looked back to the dome that lay between each of the mountains. It was surrounded by a dozen large towers, atop of which were mounted what looked like multi-barrelled weapon systems. Thousands of workers toiled around the dome, and it was then that Teresa spotted something odd. She pulled her helmet back on and accessed the optical sensors built into the system. The stabilised telephoto lens gave her a close look at the dome.

"Cracks," she said quietly. "Whatever is happening, this place is needing a lot of repair work."

As if to answer her comment, the roof of the dome stopped moving with a loud thud. The reverberation of the massive structure shook the ground around them, and she saw small chunks of dirt and rock tumbled from its flanks. The trees around their position also trembled at whatever was happening. She looked back to the dome and noticed even more power seemed to be surging towards the dome itself. The orb grew in intensity, and the people working nearby ran for cover or hid as the surge increased.

"Sarge, do we want to be hanging around for this?" asked Corporal Alessandro.

"Just stay down and watch. Anything we learn here could save lives. Just keep recording anything of interest."

As she looked about, she could see that between the site they were near and the next mountain, lay a large patch of broken ground. Close examination showed that it was ruined buildings or structures of some kind. They were not new. In fact, they looked to her more like buildings with a history of hundreds of years, maybe older. But even better, they seemed of little interest to the workers, the Zealots or the machines. Teresa slid back into the thick undergrowth and signalled for the others to come closer.

"Okay, here's the plan. We need intel, and I have a plan on how to get it. See that site to the right, about two hundred metres in from of the dome," she said while pointing.

The ASOG troopers glanced quickly and returned their attention to her.

"Right, I will take my squad to the ruins and set up a monitoring package to overlook the dome. If we time it right, we can get it positioned and then move back into the jungle. We can use the package to send a navigation pulse when the General decides its time to attack."

"Attack?" asked Sergeant Lovett. "You're not serious are you? This place is teeming with Zealots."

"Don't forget those machines as well."

Teresa shook her head.

"No, I am quite well aware of that. Aren't you curious to know where all the Biomechs are? Trust me, the General will want this place shut down."

"He will do when he sees this," explained Corporal Nylund, holding out his scanning tool. The others looked at the data but little of it made sense to them. Teresa raised an eyebrow in confusion.

"See those towers around the dome?" he asked.

Teresa nodded.

"Yes, the ones with the weapon batteries fitted?"

"Okay. They aren't just weapon mounts. They are sending a strong blanketing signal out into space. According to my instruments, it's the same signal that blocked communications with our ships, and it's still blocking long-range comms on the ground."

Teresa understood that part perfectly.

"So if we can disable them, we'll have planet-wide communications and be able to reach anybody in orbit?"

He nodded, and the eight ASOG troopers turned their gaze back the series of artificial mounts, towers and buildings that covered the open space in front of them. Teresa's excitement at the news on the towers quickly dissipated as she realised the enormity of what they had discovered.

What would I give for a unit of Vanguards and a few hundred Jötnar right now!

Her thoughts of the Alliance Biomechs instantly brought back her memories of Spartan. She could only imagine what he was up to right now.

"Right, you know the plan. Sergeant Lovett, your squad will provide overwatch, my squad will plant the gear and signal you when we're ready to leave. Be careful, we can do without having to fight all of that!"

With that short message, she moved off along the tree line but always staying low and in the cover of the foliage. It took almost four minutes to cover the jungle until they reached the point directly opposite the ruined buildings. From there, she could see the small mountain to her left but no sight of the overwatch squad.

Good, she thought. If they were visible, they would be instantly compromised. If they were discovered this close to the enemy compound, they could expect to lose their unit and probably be tracked back to their own base. She turned to her right. There was another similar mountain, along with its own array of many pylons and scores of thick pipes and cabling running down to the central dome, hundreds of metres away in the depression to her front. All that stood before her and the home of the glowing orb, were scores of ruined structures and buildings. The nearest was only twenty metres from the tree line where she waited.

"No signs of movement in the ruins...wait, I've got one contact..." said Corporal Nylund nervously.

"Zealot?" asked Teresa.

"Negative, looks like one of our crew. They're still wearing their uniform. I recognise the insignia from Santa Maria. Dammit, he's coming this way."

"What?" Teresa exclaimed.

They kept low and watched as the figure emerged from the rubble and did his best to scale one of the smaller walls. Off in the distance, two Zealots shouted and pointed in the escapee's direction. One lifted a weapon and fire ineffectually at the man. Corporal Nylund lifted his L52 Mark II carbine, but Teresa placed her hand on the barrel and shook her head.

"No, we can't give away out position."

"But Sarge!" exclaimed Private Hughes, the youngest of the squad.

More shots hit near the crewman, and a couple even struck close to the marines. Teresa almost laughed at the ineffective shooting, but the movement of the machines near the dome instantly killed her mood. Only two stepped away and faced their direction. For a second, she had a dreadful feeling they might detect the marines. She pulled herself lower to the ground, and the other three did the same. The same high-pitched scream as before blasted across the open space, but this time the filters of her helmet managed to reduce it to a painful but manageable level. The energy blast from the machines pintle mounted weapon was much like the coil system used by her carbine, but it seemed vastly more powerful. With a loud thud, a great column of dust and debris blasted into the air.

"Stay down!" she called out on the suit's intercom unit. It was short ranged but could easily manage about a hundred metres with line of sight before the ground-based jammers could have much of an effect. Teresa kept her head to the ground, but even with her acoustic dampers on maximum, she could hear and feel the approach of one of the machines. Her head told her to move and to get far away, but she knew that any movement and they were dead. Then just as soon as it had started, the machine moved away. She lifted her head just a few centimetres, so she could see to top of the machine as it stomped away and rejoined its comrades near the dome.

"We're clear."

The four-man unit resumed their positions and checked for signs of the enemy. The column of dust continued upwards, but nothing remained of the unfortunate crewman that had tried to escape from whatever was taking place at the site. A few of the Zealots seemed to take the escape attempt as an opportunity to attack more of the prisoners, but luckily none were actually hurt in any serious way. Teresa checked the horizon, but it looked as clear as it was ever likely to be.

"Come on, I don't want to stay here any longer than we have to," she said.

The small group moved out from the tree line and down into the remains of whatever had been built in the past. As they moved through the outskirts of the first buildings, it was clear that a number of the structures were actually parts of an old temple. In the centre was a square based pyramid with many steps leading to the top. They weaved around it, continuing onwards to the ruined base of a circular structure. There was nothing but mud and broken rock in the middle, but along the inner wall of the building were the carved shapes of buildings, people and machines.

"Sergeant, what's this?" asked Corporal Alessandro.

She stopped but only for a few seconds.

"No idea. Record everything you can see and then join us."

She continued forward with Corporal Nylund and took up position along the final section of ruins that faced the dome while the other two stayed back to record as much of the markings, images and information as they could in the limited time they had. Once in cover, the Corporal removed a monitoring package from his pack on his back and placed it on the ground. While he configured the unit, Teresa placed dust and small rocks around it to camouflage it from a cursory glance.

CHAPTER TWELVE

With the end of the War that had torn the old Confederacy apart came a new attitude to the military. Gone were the distinctions between Army, Marines and Navy and instead all were combined into a smaller but more professional elite arm. With this change came a requirement for more flexible ships, ones that could operate fighters and landing craft just as often as they carried marines and their heavy equipment. The old days of ships of the line and separate transports, died with birth of the Alliance.

Naval Cadet's Handbook

The arrival of Sergeant Morato's ASOG team caught almost every one by surprise. General Rivers had assumed the worst and mobilised everybody available, including the Navy crewmen, to defend the compound against the expected attack. When they had emerged on the river, moving slowly on an improvised raft, they'd almost been shot to ribbons. Only the quick thinking of Captain Carlos had averted possible disaster. Sergeant Morato walked into the camp with the seven troopers to cheers from those inside. General Rivers was already out of his shelter and waiting near the marine fireteam as she moved inside.

"Sergeant, I see the rumours of your demise were much exaggerated."

Teresa saluted, though it was slower and more ragged than usual.

"Sir, it's good to be back."

"We were expecting contact from your team nearly two days ago. Can I assume you found something?"

Teresa grinned through the open visor of her helmet. Her armour was filthy and not one part of it seemed to be the same colour. Mud slid down her legs, and thick scratches ran from her ankles to her armpits. The others looked no better. It was as if they had been dredging the river for the last week.

"You could say that, General."

She turned to her unit and nodded to Corporal Nylund.

"Get the recording gear into the field command post." She looked back to General Rivers. "This is pretty big, Sir. I think you'll want all the officers to see this."

"Is it something we can use?" he asked optimistically.

"It's more than that, Sir. I think it might be the key to this planet and possibly the entire War."

At that last point his eyebrows lifted in interest.

* * *

The first view of Hyperion sent a shudder up Spartan's spine as he watched from the bridge of ANS Tamarisk. Spartan hadn't spent much time on the ship before. In fact, the last time he'd seen the craft had been when it was salvaged following the rescue at Prometheus. There were few reminders of that bloody struggle, and to all intents and purposes, she seemed to have been improved in almost every way. The rest of the Taskforce had already made rendezvous with ANS Minotaur and were keeping at least ten hours away from the planet to avoid weapon fire or equipment jamming. Spartan pulled himself away from the bridge and out through to hatch that led to the small CIC. Inside waited the small team he had selected specifically for the mission.

I hope to God I've chosen the right people.

He'd assembled an odd mixture of forces, including marines, Vanguards, soldiers and Jötnar. From the limited information they had discovered, he knew he had several basic tasks to perform. He had the best marines and scouts in the Taskforce to help locate the enemy dispositions and resources; and a mixture of Vanguards and Jötnar to provide combat muscle. What worried him was that they might simply be unable to disable the weapon systems before they were overwhelmed. It would take up to six hours for the Taskforce to be able to move into position and start landing the rest of the ground troops. He moved into the middle of the CIC and glanced at the status monitors.

"Captain, all systems are fully operational. Passive jammers are on, and our weapon systems are primed and ready," said Sergeant Kowalski.

Spartan looked at the small crew with confidence. Most of them had been at the summit on Terra Nova, but a few he had only met prior to their introductions in the Taskforce. Kowalski was a highly experienced marine and a computer tech expert with a somewhat shady past. As well as having served on Tamarisk at Prometheus, he was also one of the top specialists on the Prometheus colony under Commander Anderson. Sat next to him, and monitoring the remote feeds, was the gruff Agent Johnson from the Kerberos Intelligence Unit. His experience had been in working with the Kerberos Underground during the War. Spartan knew his knowledge and experience of fighting unconventional operations would be critical in the fight. His only real experience with most of this team was with the Jötnar and a handful of the Vanguards. Khan watched over them both with a look of bemused interest and boredom. It was an odd mix, but Spartan was very familiar with the attitudes of his Jötnar friends.

"How is the assault team?" he asked.

Khan nodded slowly.

"Not bad. Could do with a few more, twenty-four isn't much for a ground assault."

"We don't need to win this thing. We just need to disable their systems, so we can bring in the large ships to coordinate a full-scale operation."

Khan tilted his head slightly.

"Perhaps, but we don't have much to go on yet, do we?"

Spartan couldn't disagree with that. All they knew was that ships had been crippled or destroyed, and that large numbers of pods and lifeboats had made their way to the surface. Deep down, Spartan worried that the entire planet could be teeming with Union soldiers or Biomechs. What if it was another of the horrific plants like the one he had seen on Prometheus?

"Uh, you're gonna want to see this," said Kowalski in a tone that bordered on excitement.

Spartan leaned in to look at his screen. It showed a topographical map of the surface. Most of the land mass was rocky, and there were several mountain ranges. The quality of the imagery was poor, probably due to the thick atmosphere and frequent mist at low level. The most obvious thing was the amount of trees. The bulk of the planet looked like a giant forest.

"I don't see it, just lots of trees, so?"

Kowalski pointed to three points on the display.

"There, three," he explained to Spartan, but the icons

and data told him nothing of much use.

Kowalski shook his head, once more annoyed that he was going to have to explain the obvious. It was both a gift and a curse that he was forced to endure. At least that was how he rationalised it to himself.

"Well, it seems that so far we have approached without being detected. Our passive system gives off little to no detectable signature, and our radar systems are off. Unless they happen to be looking right here, they will not find us."

Spartan nodded but still looked confused.

"Yes, I read the tech notes on her. An impressive ship, no doubt."

He then pointed to the screen.

"But what about those points?" he added.

"Oh...right," replied Kowalski sheepishly. "Well, first of all, I am picking up massive, and I mean massive, energy levels in this mountainous region. The really weird thing is that the power build-up matches the exact same signature of the Anomaly."

Spartan leaned back at the news.

"What does that mean?"

Kowalski shook his head.

"Uh...no idea, but it is interesting. The other thing is these points."

He tapped three more locations; one of which was quite close to the mountainous region.

"Each of these areas is transmitting a very weak Alliance distress pulse. They are coded to the new frequencies and are shifting based on the new algorithms. I suspect that's the only reason they haven't been detected yet.

"Alliance? From the lifeboats?"

Kowalski nodded.

"Yes, Sir. Even more interesting though, is the site closest to the mountains. It has the strongest signal and is positioned near this river. I can't look any closer. We'd need satellite coverage at lower altitude and with advanced optics. The mists and weather conditions down there are cutting visibility down to just a few kilometres."

"Okay, so we have a few lifeboats. What's so special about that one?" asked Spartan, still no closer to understanding the point Kowalski was trying to make.

At that last comment, Kowalski grinned so widely his teeth almost seemed to gleam at him.

"It's a full tactical assessment of the area, along with identity codes for a number of NCOs and officers. Looks like the General is there with Captain Carlos, and at least a dozen more people of note."

Spartan was about to speak, but Kowalski knew exactly what he was going to say.

"Yes, one of those on the list is Sergeant Morato."

The mention of her name gave him renewed hope. Although the senior officers kept trying to tell him how likely it was that they would have survived, he knew from experience that ships attacked or destroyed in orbit had a poor chance at performing a full evacuation before breaking up. The mere possibility that Teresa was there sent a jolt through his body. Nothing could have motivated him more.

"Can you get a signal down there?" he asked.

Kowalski shook his head.

"No way, Sir. The minute we send any kind of signal, they will know we're here. All we have is the element of surprise."

Captain William Lockley pulled himself into the CIC from the bridge. He had been monitoring the feeds and was already up to speed on the situation. A short, slightly overweight man, he had been responsible for defending one of the landing zones on Euryale. His combat experience, both on the ground and in space, was unmatched in the fleet.

"We can't stay here long, Spartan. We have a big enough window to launch all three shuttles in one go. As soon as you're out of the ship, I will withdraw to the minimum safe distance and await your go transmission."

Kowalski looked up at him.

"We can spread the shuttles out or land in one place, Sir."

Spartan looked at the displays and the proposed landing sites. It seemed pretty straightforward to him. Either they landed at one of the crash sites and linked up with any survivors, or they moved directly to the source of the massive power levels. In either case, he had no idea what to expect. He was tempted to strike the power source, but his experienced strategic side begged him to not throw away their one chance on such a gamble. He took a quick breath and pointed at the landing site.

"Put us there. We need numbers and intel on the possible enemy site. If the General is down there, I can promise you he is probably already halfway through retaking that place."

"Understood, Captain Spartan. How long until you are ready to leave?"

Spartan looked to the others in the narrow CIC and grinned at them.

"Ten minutes. Just let me get to the shuttles."

With that, he was already pulling himself along to the grab rails and to the hangar part of the ship. Agent Johnson, Sergeant Kowalski and Captain Lockley returned to their stations and started the release procedures required to launch the shuttles. Spartan made quick progress and was at the first airlock before he activated his intercom.

"Khan, load them up, we are leaving."

"Yes!" roared the Jötnar with approval.

Even Spartan was unable to hide a smile at the Jötnar's evident excitement. He closed the airlock behind him and continued to move through the gravity-free part of the ship.

One way or another, we finish this, today.

* * *

General Rivers was as speechless as the rest of the officers as they watched the video feeds recorded by Sergeant Morato and her ASOG troop. The quality of the footage was shaky, but the site of the massive structures, machines, workers and the great glowing orb left little to the imagination. The General examined the information in detail before turning to Teresa.

"What the hell is this place?"

Corporal Dalton Nylund, the ASOG's technician lifted his hand and stepped forward. He handed over a heavily modified datapad to him.

"This might help. We found engravings at what looked like a ruined temple of some kind. We didn't have time to examine it, but we did photograph as much as possible. Our equipment estimated most of the ruins are up to two-hundred years old."

General Rivers examined the first few images before waving over Captain Carlos and two of the Navy officers. The first images showed what looked like an orb, very similar to the one under the dome. This one was in space and surrounded by gantries and structures.

"Looks like the Spacebridge at the Anomaly," one of them said.

"Yes, but look at the sequence. The first one shows this machine with people stood around it. The next is showing more of those dome buildings being constructed. Is this showing what happened in the past?" asked Captain Carlos.

Teresa shook her head as she relooked at the images.

"I don't know, but the shape of the site is very odd with the mountains and the dome in the centre."

An engineer from the Santa Maria examined the imagery and scratched his chin.

"I'll tell you one thing. That isn't a mountain range. It's one mountain that's had the centre excavated. That's why it looks more like a crater surrounded by mountains."

General Rivers nodded in agreement.

"Yes, makes sense. So if that's right, then this orb must have been buried. They must be here to unearth it for some reason."

"Maybe," replied Captain Carlos, but he didn't sound convinced. "We've only had colonies in this region of space for just over three centuries. Why haven't we come across anything like this before? It also doesn't explain what the Biomechs or the Zealots or doing down here."

"General, there is more," explained Teresa.

She pressed a button on the video unit they were using, and it flicked instantly to a live feed of the dome at the heart of the enemy base. Unexpectedly, it was still glowing, and flashes of what looked like electricity crackled around it. Hundreds of people hid and cowered around the place as the flashes continued. The room fell silent as those present looked on in surprise. General Rivers spoke quietly but continued watching the feed.

"Good work, Sergeant, this is exactly what we need. Do you have any idea what this thing is designed for, though?"

"No, Sir. We discussed it on the return here. Our thoughts are it could be anything from a massive signal generator to some kind of artificial intelligence hub."

"Like the one on Terra Nova?" he asked rhetorically.

"Maybe," Teresa replied. "But one thing I do know, I've never seen machines like that before, apart from those that came aboard the Santa Maria. They seem unique to this planet."

She pointed to the dome.

"My gut instinct tells me this area, the machines, the Zealots and the Biomechs are all linked. Maybe the survivors from the Great War five decades ago hid down here and found the site?"

General Rivers seemed intrigued at the idea.

"Interesting. The Zealots have always been the right hand of somebody else. We thought it was Typhon and his brothers, but to do the things they've done they must have had help."

He turned and looked to the other officers assembled in the cramped room.

"This changes things considerably. Not only is it our

duty to fight and survive, but we also need to understand what is happening here. Our mission must change to the capture and study of this site, no matter the cost. I want anybody with historical, engineering and scientific knowledge to go over the data recovered by Sergeant Morato's team, and see what you can piece together. In the meantime, the rest of us need to find a way to get a signal away from this planet. We need help, now more than ever."

There was no more time for discussion as the compound's klaxons blared. It was loud and painful to hear, filling each of them with dread. They had been installed for emergency use only, as the noise was bound to draw the unwelcome attention of the hostile inhabitants of the jungle. The makeshift command centre emptied quickly as they all rushed to their allotted positions. As some of the crew, left General Rivers grabbed two of them.

"No, you both stay. I need answers from this information, and fast."

He then took one last glance at the feed and moved to Teresa who was already at the doorway and checking her weapon.

"Sergeant, did they follow you back here?" he asked.

Heavy gunfire ripped through the base, and before she had time to answer, the two were out and moving into firing positions along the perimeter. Teresa was still in her filthy PDS suit, whereas the General wore just the chest part of his armour.

"No way, Sir, we covered our tracks and followed a zigzag course. They must have tracked electronic signatures or something else. He nodded in agreement but was well aware that even the ASOG troopers were not ghosts.

"Get your people to the walls, Sergeant. We have need of your skills once more."

She saluted and moved out, indicating for her comrades to follow her to the barricades. Light was already starting to fade in the camp, and with the never-moving mist, it was hard to see what was happening before the enemy reached point-blank range. Teresa climbed the crudely constructed ladder and rested her carbine on top of the wall facing the direction of the enemy.

"Gods! she exclaimed.

The terrifying image of scores of Zealots running foolhardily towards their wooden defences almost made her stagger and fall from the crude raised position. She checked the safety on her weapon and joined in with the rest of the defenders. Concentrated rifle and carbine gunfire tore them apart before they made it even halfway from the tree line to the fences. But the Zealots weren't the problem, and even as she helped in gunning them down, she wondered if they were being driven to the barricades rather than choosing to attack. Out of the mist, and behind the Zealots, appeared the great metallic machines. The mere sight of them froze her in mid movement. It was hard to make out their exact shape, but the size and moving limbs confirmed to her they were the same or certainly very similar to the large four-legged machines at the dome. They made slow progress but inched towards the base like a pair of armoured beetles, their powered metal limbs ripping foliage and woodland apart. From deep within their bodies came that terrible screaming sound, and she spotted at least three crewmen fall from the wall in terror at the noise.

They must have found our trail. We spent hours covering it. It just doesn't make sense.

A long burst of gunfire from the machine to the right quickly snapped her out of her daze, however, especially when the blast ripped open a hole in the barricade and cut down two marines in a burst of blood and metal.

"Kill them!" she screamed, and with one deft movement selected the full-power setting on her carbine. She'd rarely used the weapon on that setting before, but something about those alien-looking machines told her she'd need every ounce of firepower at her disposal. She took aim at the nearest and hit it with a single triple-round blast. Unlike the rounds fired from the other firearms, the carbine's massive advantage in muzzle-velocity, combined with the armour-penetrating slug, tore fist-sized holes from the machine. The battle for the compound had begun.

* * *

Threat alarms blasted through the interior of the shuttle as ground-based sensors tried to identify the three craft. Their rapid descent through the atmosphere would have been relatively easy to detect, but the craft had been specially designed to give off no obvious signatures. Spartan just hoped they would be picked up as meteors or even better, missed completely. Either way, they were almost past this stage of their descent, and the design and build of the shuttles would make them all but impossible to detect as they dropped down to their selected landing zones.

"Lieutenant, what's our safe distance with these shuttles?" he asked the pilot through his Vanguard armour's comms unit.

The man turned back briefly to answer.

"About forty to fifty klicks in a straight line. Once we're down to the surface, we can stay below most active scanners to nearly ten kilometres. After that..." he shrugged.

Spartan nodded and looked to the other seven occupants of the shuttle. He'd split up the expertise on each craft so that there was a degree of redundancy in the landing. There was no sense having all the tech experts in one shuttle and all the assault troops in the other. He'd taken Khan, Kowalski, two Vanguards from his old unit and three of the most experienced marines on the Santa Cruz. The Vanguards were of a similar size and build to Khan, but it was the mechanics, power systems and armour that provided the muscle for the marines as opposed to Khan's physique and brute strength. Unlike the PDS armour worn by the marines, this much larger suit was a development of the much older and more primitive Combat Engineer Suits. It was powered and included thickened protection, integral blades and firearms. The Vanguards had proved themselves on multiple occasions during the heavy close quarter combat on a multitude of colonies.

"Khan, you ready for this?" he called over to his friend.

The Jötnar simply grinned in response. One thing Spartan could always count on was the brutality and enjoyment of combat by him and his people. The Jötnar were easily the equal of the Vanguards and capable of taking on multiple Zealots or even another Biomech one-on-one.

"Sir, my scanners are picking up the coded signal from the target. It is phasing out as expected."

"Good," he replied.

The pilot returned to his own screen but continued speaking as he made adjustments. His co-pilot checked the ground below them with advanced passive imaging gear, but even this low, the thick atmosphere and mist made it very difficult.

"We'll be under their radar in just over a minute, and then it's the quick burn to the landing site."

Spartan hoped beyond hope they weren't too late. He was well aware that just surviving on a foreign world was hard enough without potential enemies to account for.

"Any sign of survivors yet?"

"Nothing yet, I am picking up a tracking station near the suspected weapon sites. It's good gear but not likely to pick us up now at this height. There's something else as well."

Spartan swallowed, expecting the worst.

"What?"

"It's the power levels. They are off the charts. There's no way they need this level of energy to power up their tracking or weapon systems. There's something else down there, Sir."

"Yes, I don't doubt it. Just get us near the signal source as quickly and quietly as you can."

The man nodded and carried on with the low-level flight procedures. From the small windows, Spartan could see very little except the thick haze and water droplets covering the toughened glass. He turned and looked back to his team.

"Don't forget the air. Initial assessments show a higher than normal level of nitrogen. It's breathable, but only just. Use the rebreather on your suits as much as possible."

Khan laughed.

"What?" Spartan asked.

"Where's my rebreather?" he asked.

Spartan looked at his friend and realised he'd completely forgotten to ensure the Jötnar were equipped for the atmospheric conditions below.

Damn it! He thought angrily.

"Don't worry, we'll manage," he said without a second's doubt.

The craft bumped and jostled as they settled into a low-level course over the treetops. Both the craft and the pilots were the best the Alliance had to offer, and even Khan seemed impressed at their skill. It didn't take long for them to cover the distance to the landing zone. Spartan spotted the dark grey shapes of the two craft following behind them.

"Twenty seconds, we're coming in over the river. I'll put her down in that clearing." said the pilot.

No sooner had they started the landing procedure than the starboard side windows lit up bright yellow. A light patter like rain ran along the body, and then they were within a hundred metres.

"Sensors picking up signs of movement, heat signature... what the!"

The shuttle shook as the pilot tried to manoeuvre, but it was much too late. Something heavy struck one of the movable engine pods, and the shuttle was heading down. It was a testament to the skill of the pilots that they managed to bring it down in one piece. They struck the riverbank hard and came to a stop in the mud. The doors hissed open, and as per usual, Spartan was up and out. Instead of stepping into a crash site, he found himself in the middle of a battle.

What have they gotten themselves into?

Directly in front of him was a very basic wooden fortification that must have been about the size of a sports field. Three of its sides faced the thick jungle while a much lower palisade protected the water edge. Inside were stacks of boxes, tents, shelters and the stripped remains of what looked like an escape shuttle or lifeboat. Scores of people were positioned on or near the high wooden walls and were blasting away with Alliance issue firearms. Khan stepped beside him, and the other five spread out into a firing line, scanning for signs of hostiles. Sergeant Kowalski moved to the cockpit to check on the status of the pilots. Khan looked briefly at the sounds of battle then back to Spartan.

"Looks like we came to the right place!" said a happy sounding Khan.

"Yeah, come on, we need to find out what the hell is going on here."

They sprinted further into the compound and skirted off to the left where a group of Navy crew were carrying a box of ammunition to the fence. One of them spotted him and stopped.

"Sir? Lieutenant Spartan?" he asked incredulously.

Spartan had no idea who he was, but they were obviously friendly. The uniform was of the old Confederate Navy pattern but that meant little. He was only too familiar with the problems of units, uniforms and logistics since the end of the War and the forming of the Alliance. He reached out and grabbed the shaken looking man by the shoulder.

"Who is in charge here?" he asked.

The man looked up to the barricade and the silhouetted shapes above them. Flashes of orange and yellow light lit them from behind. As Spartan watched, a stream of bullets rip through the wood and cut down a marine who tumbled back and to the floor.

"The General...General Rivers," he stuttered.

Rivers!

"To me!" he shouted and ran to a pile of crates and boxes that gave access to the fighting platform. He couldn't make it all the way to the top, as his bulk in the Vanguard armour and the weak construction of the platform and the barrier, would have easily tossed him back to the ground. He reached a high enough vantage point so that he could see out and towards the commotion outside the compound. Hordes of people were rushing to the defences but being cut to ribbons by accurate rifle fire. It was the sight of the mechanical beasts that shook him.

"What the hell is that?" he shouted while simultaneously lifting his right arm. Built into his suit was a pair of linked L48 rifles, the standard weapon used by most marines. It fired a standard 12.7mm round equipped with an integral proximity mode on the bullets. The rifle normally carried a magazine of twenty rounds of variable operation ammunition. These state of the art bullets could be set to explode at a certain distance or when they reached the proximity of their target. He aimed at the nearest of the machines and opened fire. Both barrel flashes away and the gyrostalisied mount gave him near perfect sustained fire accuracy. The rounds embedded into the metal frame and then exploded. Each of the rounds tore chunks of metal and wiring away, yet still the machines pushed onwards.

"Spartan?" shouted a familiar voice.

He fired a few more shots before spotting a dark shape rushing along the parapet towards him. His gut reaction was self-defence, and he swung out his left arm and activated the dual weapons. Luckily Khan grabbed the metal of his arm and pushed it up, so the rounds fired away harmlessly and avoided cutting the now visible shape of Teresa into a bloodied corpse.

"Watch your aim!" he growled and then joined the others on the firing line.

"Teresa?" replied Spartan in surprise. He'd hoped, even prayed she had been there, but it had never occurred to him he would find her so fast and in such a violent and dangerous situation. She leapt forward and landed just a metre away. They were both in armoured suits, and all she could do was open her visor and smile at him.

"I knew you'd come."

Spartan nodded grimly.

"Yeah, our timing is always great, isn't it? What's

happening?"

Teresa looked back to where she had been stood. The armoured shape of General Rivers and a handful of marines fired away into the enemy forces. Alongside them was the bullet-ridden form of an improvised Alliance flag. The General looked over and saw Khan and then Spartan below him. He turned and lifted his visor.

"About damned time you got here! Tell me you brought friends?"

As if in answer to his question, the two additional shuttles flew overhead. Each performed a quick circle while the now extended pintle mounted coilguns blazed away at the enemy machines. The nearest came in to land while the final shuttle performed a final strafing run before setting down in a space being hastily cleared by Navy crewmen.

"We have a ten-ship taskforce in orbit. Once the guns are down, we can have five companies on the ground. Gun is up there, and he's itching to land."

General Rivers clenched his fist with pleasure and jumped down from his fighting position to grasp the armoured fist of Spartan's Vanguard armour. In his battered PDS armour, he looked half the size of Spartan.

"Dammed glad to see you again. Tell me everything."

CHAPTER THIRTEEN

The great battle for the Titan Naval Station has been considered one of the most audacious battles in the Corps' history. Outnumbered and attacked on all sides, the men and women of the Marine Corps recaptured the heavily defended base in the middle of a bloody and costly space battle. It was the first great victory in the War but also provided a much-needed base from which to coordinate the war effort. The victories of the Proxima system, and the eventual fall of Terra Nova, could never have happened without this first heroic success.

Great Battles of the Confederate Marine Corps

Spartan and Teresa stood opposite General Rivers who was busy pulling up the detailed maps the scouts had formed in the last week. It had been weeks they'd been apart, prior to Spartan heading for Terra Nova. Even so, their personal lives came second right now with the sound of battle ever present on the hostile world of Hyperion. Since the arrival of the last two shuttles, the fighting had died down, but there were still sporadic bursts of gunfire. Captain Carlos emerged from the entrance. He stopped in front of the General and saluted.

"Sir, the enemy forces are withdrawing."

General Rivers nodded grimly.

"Good, what about those machines?"

Captain Carlos shook his head.

"One is still in action. We damaged it. By all accounts it should be on the ground in pieces. It is leading the retreat. We calculate they must have around a hundred troops still left, and most of those must be injured."

He turned to Spartan and reached out to shake his hand.

"So glad you arrived when you did. Your Jötnar Khan led a counter-assault at the breached wall. I've never seen one in action before. Sure changed my opinion of them, just wish we had a few more."

Spartan nodded ever so slightly.

"Yeah, that's usually the way. We have five companies up there, including Gun and a small force of Jötnar."

"We need them down here, so what's the plan General?"

General Rivers looked at the three of them and back to his maps for a few more seconds. He lifted his right hand and scratched his eyebrow as he thought. Spartan could see he was conflicted, and the frailty of their position was clear for all of them to see. Even when he had landed, the enemy were pressing the walls and had forced a number of breaches with heavy weapons. Another similar sized assault might succeed. If they attacked in greater numbers, it would be over...and fast. General Rivers understood this, and Spartan suspected this was where his reticence rested.

"You haven't seen the intelligence Sergeant Morato and her team recovered. You don't have time to study it, so I'll give you the short version. From what we can ascertain, there is a structure here that has been in position for up to the last two hundred years. Apart from a large number of ruins, there are a series of power sources, each connected to a central hub that is heavily guarded."

He handed Spartan a datapad containing a series of images of the site. It had been annotated by the engineers in the compound; along with estimated power signatures and enemy strength.

"Who are these people?" asked Spartan, pointing at the dark shapes around the structures.

"Workers, prisoners...maybe slaves. We don't know, other than they are subservient to both the Zealots we can see and those machines. The central dome appears to be protected by magnetic shielding. At least that's what the readings suggest."

Spartan looked less than impressed with the information.

"Okay. But what is this site being used for? Apart from

the danger of them attacking here, what is the time critical problem here?"

General Rivers brought up the images from the ruins that Teresa had returned.

"Recognise this?" he asked.

Spartan looked carefully at the images, each one showed an object or series of objects, some of which appeared very familiar. He stopped at the fourth one.

"The Spacebridge?"

General Rivers shrugged and showed him a shattered stone with what looked like a diagram; lines connected a number of circles. It meant nothing to him. He looked back to General Rivers and lifted his eyebrows.

"It's a map, Captain. The Navy techs picked it up right away. It is partially damaged, but according to them, it marks a number of the planets in this star system, including Terra Nova, Proxima Prime and here."

Spartan straightened up a little before speaking.

"I still don't get it. We have a site full of Zealots and a number of machines that could easily be Biomech variants. Images and maps from the last few hundred years of our star systems, and a lot of people being forced to work on this dome location."

General Rivers stepped closer as if he was about to share some great secret.

"My people believe there are only a few solutions to this problem. What we do know is that the machines come from that dome. Sergeant Morato established a comms surveillance post in the ruins, and over a period of an hour, we have monitored four more machines move from the dome."

"I see, so it could be a fabrication plant of some kind?" suggested Teresa.

"Perhaps. There is one other thing, and it is something I can't get my head around."

"What is it?" asked Captain Carlos.

"The dome itself, it shares readings with the Anomaly. That, plus the images on the ruins, suggests an old link between the orb and the Anomaly."

As they spoke, there was a bright flash on one of the displays. Captain Carlos pointed it out, and all four turned to watch yet another of the four-legged machines move from out of the bright light. Flashes and sparks ran from the hills surrounding it, and dust and debris ran down the sides of the structures as though a minor earthquake was occurring. Spartan watched in fascination as the machine moved away from the dome, but it was the columns of shapes moving behind it that shocked him the most.

"What the hell is that?" he demanded.

Teresa shook her head.

"I've seen those before. Three came aboard the Santa Maria with their Zealot commander, Pontus. They are vicious, like nothing I've seen before. From what I could tell, they were fully autonomous but carried out his orders, to the letter."

The orb dulled, and part of the dome's structure snapped and dropped down nearby two workers. In seconds, a team of people were being pushed towards the debris while another team used ropes to climb the dome and start repairs.

"So now they have another thirty of these things. Is it me, or does it seem a bit of a coincidence that reinforcements arrive the minute they confirm the location of your base?" asked Spartan.

General Rivers and Captain Carlos looked at each other.

"We need this place shut down. Whatever it is, it is a clear and present danger to the Alliance and us. These reinforcements could be the start of a Union fight back."

He looked to Spartan and Teresa.

"I suggest you check your troops and get them ready for our next task. Meet me back here in fifteen minutes. Whatever we decide to do its going to have to be done fast, or those things will be down on us like a ton of bricks."

"Sir!" barked Spartan, followed quickly by a smart salute.

He stepped out of the place along with Teresa, leaving the Marine Captain and the General to discuss strategy. Once outside it was clear the battle was over, for now at least. Dozens of wounded were being dragged back from where they had been fighting so that the medics could get to work on them. Khan walked towards them with a carbine totting Kowalski stood beside him.

"Kowalski?" asked a surprised Teresa.

She lurched forwards and grabbed him almost as eagerly as she had Spartan. The two went back to the Prometheus operation and had worked and fought beside each other for weeks. When she finally stepped back, there was a temporary uncomfortable silence before Khan spoke.

"So, what next?"

A growl, much like that of Khan, came from near the damaged shuttle on the riverbank. The lower barricades were still intact but only lightly defended on that side. From out of the water emerged the heads and shoulders of four Biomechs. Kowalski aimed his carbine, but Spartan knocked his weapon upwards as Khan was rushing towards them. It was a foolhardy charge, but by moving into their line-of-sight, the crazed Jötnar stopped them firing.

"What the hell is he doing?" asked Kowalski.

The first Biomech emerged from the water, and Khan intercepted it on the muddy bank. They crashed together with a thud, and Khan expertly flipped and threw the creature onto its back. The other three emerged from the water and moved closer. There was something strange going on though, as they stopped a short distance away.

"Hold your fire!" called out Captain Carlos who had just arrived on the scene.

Khan roared with an almost animalistic growl at the Biomechs and helped the fallen creature to its feet.

It looked similar to Khan, but its body was less well-developed and covered in scratches and marks. A rough bandage was attached across its left shoulder from some previously inflicted wound. It straightened its back and to the surprise of them all, it spoke.

"Who?" it asked in a rough voice with its head tilted slightly to the left.

Khan stood up tall and looked back to the marines and others in the compound to ensure they didn't shoot, before looking back.

"My name is Khan, I am a Captain in the Jötnar."

"Jötnar?" asked the Biomech.

"Yes, that is what we call ourselves. We are free from the Zealots."

The Biomech seemed to understand this and nodded towards Khan.

"We fight them. The machines kill us now."

Noise from the riverbank announced the arrival of two-dozen more Zealots. They were dressed in the familiar dress and robes all the marines were used to. Most carried looted Confederate weapons and all attacked with the savagery and ferocity that only their kind resorted to. Half of them made it to the wooden stakes before rifle fire struck them. Some ran for Khan, and the others pushed past to get inside the compound.

"Kill them!" roared Khan.

The Biomech nearest to him turned around and rushed

at the Zealots. With strength and incredible agility, it dodged the first burst of gunfire and struck its right arm into the man's face. A second strike followed, and then the enemy overwhelmed it. Khan and the others waded in to help, but in doing so, they stopped most of the defending marines from helping out of fear of hitting Khan. They watched in awe as the four Biomechs and Khan smashed and hacked their way like harvesters working through a field. In less than a minute, the enemy were routed, leaving a single man badly wounded and screaming on the ground.

"Leave him!" called out Captain Carlos and waved over two medics who ran over to attend to the wounded man.

Spartan moved closer to the Biomechs and tried to assess what was happening, but more sporadic gunfire flashed around the base. He looked back to Teresa who was slightly behind and to the left.

"This isn't going to stop, is it?"

She shook her head. He took a deep breath and shouted over to his Jötnar friend.

"Khan! What's happening over there?"

He turned around from the group of Biomechs and looked directly towards Spartan. His armour was bloody from the short fight with the Zealots, and Spartan recognised the rage on his face.

"They are telling me about the Zealots. Looks like they've been hunted down here since you sent out the signal on Terra Nova. They want revenge more than we do!"

Spartan nodded in surprise.

"Uh...okay. Are they a danger to us?"

Khan shook his head.

"Only if we attack them first."

Teresa tapped Spartan's shoulder and moved closer to the group. She stopped next to Khan and opened her visor to reveal her face to both him and the Biomechs. With the air supply assistance gone, she found it harder to breathe and did her best to alter her breaths to make then slower and deeper. Khan nodded at her approach and looked to the confused Biomechs. Each of them towered almost three metres tall, yet she looked unconcerned.

"This is Sergeant Morato, an Alliance Marine, and one of the people responsible for saving the Jötnar."

The four Biomechs looked at each other before the one that had been talking with Khan moved towards her. He looked at her for a moment and then reached out and struck her in the shoulder. The blow was hard, and she stumbled and fell to the floor. Kowalski shouted out and rushed forward, but Spartan grabbed him.

"No, just wait..." he said quietly.

Teresa lifted herself up and moved back to the Biomech who waited patiently. She straightened her shoulder and barged into its lower chest while striking her armoured fist into its torso. It barely moved, yet when she stepped back and looked up, it was grinning at her. Spartan released

Kowalski but slowly, so as not to draw attention.

"That is a Biomech introduction. Be glad they aren't doing the usual fight to the blood or loss of limb."

Kowalski looked back at him.

"You're telling me we have a truce?"

Khan heard his voice and looked back at the marines.

"Better than that. We might have an alliance."

* * *

Admiral Churchill paced back and forth inside the spacious CIC of ANS Santa Cruz. It seemed like it had been weeks since he'd heard from Captain Spartan and his ground combat team. In reality, they'd been gone no more than a day, but he was becoming impatient. The fleet was ready, but the more information he received from the Captain of ANS Minotaur, the more he worried about moving any closer. Captain Lewis' engineers had discovered dormant code in their computer systems, but all the timestamps had been removed. The good news was that in theory the fleet could move into orbit without fear of losing systems and power. That didn't mean the ground batteries were nullified. The new footage shown to him by the Captain had been truly shocking. The surface weapons had destroyed an entire cruiser with a single blast.

"I know what you're thinking," suggested Captain Schaffer as he watched the Admiral examine the video feeds of the attack on the small force, previously commanded by General Rivers.

"What? Oh, yes," said a slightly confused sounding Admiral Churchill.

He turned around to the grim faced Captain.

"My real concern is what happens when Spartan contacts us? It will take us hours to get people on the surface to help, and by then it could be too late."

The Captain looked worried at the implication.

"I understand that, Sir, but what happens if we sit in orbit and stay too long. Putting it bluntly, he has twenty-four people down there. We have thousands in our ships. Can we risk our vessels for a small group?"

Ko'mandor Gun heard his comments from where he stood waiting near the tactical station. At the mention of Spartan, he snorted in derision.

"Gun, you have something to add?" asked Admiral Churchill.

Gun looked up to them and nodded slowly.

"Yeah. It's not just Spartan down there. It could be all the men and women taken hostage or hiding out. We abandon them, and we risk thousands."

The Admiral looked back at the video feed one last time and froze the image on the first weapon impact. His engineers suggested it was a combination atomic device mixed with something else. They were vague, but he understood why, they simply had no idea. The weapon was fast, guided and capable of tactical nuclear levels of power.

"Look, I don't like any of the options, but we aren't here to run this mission based on possibilities. Spartan will get the guns offline. He's never failed before. According to my calculations, if he landed safely, he should be at the enemy compound by now. I want this taskforce in orbit and scanning the surface. All ships will have their crew and systems ready for immediate withdrawal from the area if there are signs of danger."

"But, Sir!" pleaded Captain Schaffer.

Admiral Churchill shook his head.

"No. We will do all we can to mitigate any dangers from the surface. Recheck our systems and post extra crew at the key part of each ship. Any signs of failure, and they can take manual control of lost systems. Upon arrival, I want all reconnaissance drones and fighter cover to move into lower orbit and run missile decoy duty."

Commander Malone, the ship's XO, sighed at the news, but he seemed less appalled at the plan than his Captain.

"Move to it, people, I intend on starting the engines in the next twenty minutes."

* * *

Teresa and Spartan waited inside the cover of the tree line and checked area of rocks one last time. It was the first clear area and section of sky they had seen in the seven hours since leaving the compound, and Spartan was getting desperate about sending a signal. The longer they waited, the more worried he became about receiving help from the fleet.

"Looks clear," said Teresa through their intercoms.

Spartan nodded, and the rest of the ASOG unit moved forward and past the rocks to secure the woodland beyond. Spartan clanked forward in his Vanguard armour and took up position on the rocks themselves. On his left leg was a sealed hatch, usually used to carry spare ammunition or fuel. He pressed the release button and withdrew the coded transmitter gear given to him by the Admiral prior to leaving. He'd already set the coding system but still checked his actual message he was about to send one last time. It was short but detailed and gave Admiral Churchill all the information they had on the enemy disposition, capabilities and the timing of their attack. The transmitter device was about the size of a small rucksack and featured a built-in automated tracker and encoded laser unit. The power source would expend all of its energy to send just a handful of messages, but the signal strength would be very powerful, and strong enough even to burn through the thick haze and out into space, providing he could locate a line of sight to the fleet. He, Teresa and three more of their team, were on a batch of rocks near the river while they waited.

"Are you sure about this?" asked Teresa.

He looked at her in her battered and partially damaged PSD suit. He looked like an armoured gorilla next to her, yet he made no more noise than her, primarily down to the outstanding level of engineering and resources laboured on the armour.

"I know it's a risk, but we need their help."

"What if we are too late? Or we fail?" she added.

"Then a lot of good people down here and up there will die."

He checked the setting one final time and hit the release button. It took a few seconds while the unit updated its positioning. Provided the fleet was still waiting at the assembly area, the signal would reach them. Though it was wideband, the accuracy was critical, as the system was line of sight. A slight trajectory change of a single degree would miss the ships by kilometres. Even with the increasing arc, it would still need the level of accuracy only possible with an automated tracking head. He'd already be given clearance by General Rivers to do so, especially since seeing the video of the enemy reinforcements entering the camp. There were two main proposals concerning what the Orb was. Most considered it was the exit point for some kind of manufacturing planet, whereas a smaller group were convinced it was a shielded entry point for an underground fortress or rallying point.

"There, it's done," he said calmly.

He was about to step down when the red failure light blinked three times.

"What?" he muttered in confusion.

"What is it?" asked Teresa.

Spartan bent down and pressed the button to open up his thickly armoured helm. The thick, musky air rushed inside, and he felt as though he was inhaling soup. He kept calm and examined the unit and its log screen.

"I don't understand. There is no signal lock at the rendezvous location."

Teresa bent down and examined it as well before looking up to Spartan.

"Why?"

Sergeant Lovett spotted the commotion and moved closer to hear the end of their conversation.

"Either they are unable to respond, or unwilling," he suggested.

Spartan nodded in agreement.

"True. The signal lock has to be confirmed by a return transmission. I bet the Admiral has banned all outgoing signals in case they are detected down here. Come on, all we can do is assume it worked. Once we have the guns down, we can do a wide area scan and see if we can spot the ships."

Teresa looked at him oddly.

"Spartan, you're serious? We can't detect vessels that far away. The gear can only pick up ships in orbit that are broadcasting friendly IFF signals."

Spartan smiled at her.

"Let's hope they are there when we need them, then."

He nodded to Sergeant Kowalski who packed the unit back up it its rugged mounting and slung it on his back. He and the rest of them moved back from the rocks and into the jungle. They had already pushed ahead of the main force to carry out this task and quickly returned to their previous course. Spartan and his small force of reinforcements mixed in with Teresa's ASOG unit to form a motley vanguard unit to move ahead of the rest of the force. It hadn't taken much persuasion to encourage General Rivers to organise a counterattack on the enemy compound. What had surprised Spartan was that the General had made them abandon their own base in its entirety. It reminded him of the old saying of' burning your own ships', and he just hoped they wouldn't be forced to retreat back to a base that no longer existed.

"Still, if we lose here, what will a few wooden barriers do for us?"

The marines, soldiers, Vanguards and Jötnar moved in a loose line on a trail that ran parallel with the direction of the retreating Zealots. From where they were now, Spartan could just about make out the heat signature of three men, each still running to catch-up with the last of the four-legged machine that clambered its way back. The mission was a simple one. They would identify the weakest part of the enemy base, and under the cover of an all out assault, Spartan and a select team would infiltrate the site and disable or destroy the tracking system and weapons. Once the guns were down, the fleet could move into position and deploy five companies of ground troops plus provide air cover.

"General, we have the enemy in sight. According to your maps, we're two kilometres from the nearest mound in their compound."

There was a short delay before the General responded.

"Good work, keep moving forward. Any sign of them bringing in reinforcements yet?"

"Negative, Sir, but I am picking up increasing power levels ahead. It must be the dome and its power sources."

They continued onwards with the General and Captain Carlos bringing up the bulk of the forces in three columns, comprising of nearly a hundred men and women each. Only half were trained combatants, but today each of them carried whatever weapons they'd been able to recover from the bodies of the Zealots. It was one of the rare occasions where Alliance personnel could reclaim old Confederate weapons from those taken by the enemy.

* * *

Teresa reached the tree line before the rest of the ASOG team and kept her head down while scanning for enemy forces. Sergeant Lovett was with her, and Spartan brought up the rest of the mixed vanguard of units.

"What do you think?" asked Lovett.

Teresa continued checking the enemy position with multiple optical modes. The thermal imaging worked fine for the Zealots and the workers but picked up almost nothing from the machines.

"I don't like it. They are still working on the dome, but look over there." She pointed off to the right where the dome was located.

Sergeant Lovett turned his head and spotted the light glinting off a large number of the multi-legged machines and at least a hundred Biomechs. Through the magnified optics on his PDS armour, he could see these Biomechs were substantially different to those like the Jötnar. They were more heavily armoured, and each group stayed close to one of the larger machines.

"Is it me, or the machines look like they are in charge here?" he suggested.

"Yeah, looks that way."

Agent Johnson, the man from the Kerberos Underground that had joined their small unit, checked the base with his binoculars. Unlike the others, he wore a much lighter suit that was often used by paramilitary forces and police tactical units. The armour was lighter and rather than a fully fitted helm, he instead wore a low-profile ventilator and helmet.

"Yeah, I've seen these defensive deployments before on Kerberos. A few of the facilities we hit were guarded by Union troops. They don't rotate the guards like we would. Instead, they move one at a time. Makes them damned difficult to attack."

Spartan nodded while watching the enemy. Agent Johnson appeared to be correct, as he watched a single Zealot move away to be quickly replaced by a similarly equipped man. The Zealots seemed agitated about something, and that was when he spotted the surviving machine that had attacked their compound in the jungle.

"Crap, look!" he said.

The machine was stood next to a trio of other similar machines. They were moving their limbs as if discussing something important. That was when Spartan saw the form of a tall man wearing armour and a long flowing robe.

"That's him!" said Teresa excitedly.

A group of Zealots, all carrying rifles, ran up to the robed figure, bowed and then ran off towards the large group of machines at the dome.

"That's who?"

"Pontus," she replied. "I think he might be their leader. If not, he's pretty high up."

Agent Johnson pointed off to the right-hand side of the identified man.

"Have you seen the machines over there? Look!"

The larger of the machines was herding a group of the prisoners into a loose line and moving them around the entrance to one of the small mountains.

"No, they must be onto us. Look, they are positioning prisoners around their key installations. Get yourselves ready, we need to get this operation moving."

A short distance behind them was the rustling of leaves that marked the approach of General Rivers and the first of the three columns of troops from their own compound. Spartan checked the horizon and paid specific attention to the nearest of the small mountains surrounding the dome. He turned back and looked at their small group before connecting to the secure channel being used by the commanders of the Alliance ground forces.

"General, are you receiving me?" he asked.

"Affirmative, loud and clear," came back the quick response.

Spartan nodded and looked at the enemy compound once more before continuing.

"The dome is being well protected by Biomechs, troops and those machines. It looks like they are preparing for something, maybe our attack. I suggest you start the assault against the most remote hill position. I will move my team into the ruins in front of the dome. When we have the chance, we'll storm it and set out thermite charges."

"Understood. I'm moving 1st Company into the tree line to protect our left flank, 2nd Company will initiate the attack, and 3rd Company will be held in reserve. Good luck."

"You too, Sir."

He looked to Teresa and the motley group of marines, technicians, Vanguards and Khan, who always stood out compared to the rest.

"This is it then, let's get into position before the General lights the place up."

He moved off with Khan, Teresa and Sergeant Lovett. The remainder followed along with the extra equipment plus several crates of charges. They reached the point where Teresa had set up the monitoring point in the rubble and ruins in front of the dome when the crackle of gunfire came from behind them. As one, the entire group threw themselves down and crawled behind any cover they could find. Spartan looked back and could see in the far distance the dark shapes of scores of marines and crew storming the hillside. They seemed to be covering ground very quickly. He almost smiled until the grinding sound of machines nearby indicated a large group of the multi-legged beasts and their Biomech and Zealots warriors were relocating to meet the attack.

"Do we attack?" asked Khan.

Spartan shook his head, lifting himself slightly to look at the orb. They were still a good distance away, and a number of ruined buildings blocked their path. More worrying was the sight of four of the machines still waiting outside and at least thirty gun toting Zealots.

Where are the Biomechs?

That was when he spotted the armoured creatures inching their way through the ruins and towards his hidden unit. Most of them must have gone to assist in the battle, but he could see five, possibly six of the great beasts. They moved differently to the ones he had seen before, and it was clear they were fitted with more equipment and armour. His gut instinct told him these were the next iteration of the Biomechs; stronger, better protected and presumably indoctrinated by the machines or the Zealots to fight. Since he had sent the signal from Terra Nova, every single connected Biomech to the AI Hub had lost it's programming and reverted to its natural state. More than that, the signal had permanently destroyed the programmable section of their minds, making it impossible for them to be enslaved in such a way again. As he watched them, one stopped and stared directly at him.

Oh, great!

He flicked the switch inside his Vanguard armour to activate the arm-mounted L48 rifles.

"On my command," he whispered quietly through the comms unit.

CHAPTER FOURTEEN

With the fall of Terra Nova, it was assumed the Church of Echidna had been destroyed. The collapse of the Union, the freeing of the Biomechs, and finally the systematic slaughter of those Zealots still fighting should have marked the end. Instead, the events at Hyperion showed the reverse was true. Echidna was much more than a symbol, and the leaked reports on the incident there described something truly unexpected.

Holy Icons

General Rivers watched from the tree line as the first two platoons rushed across the open ground and reached the entrance to the mountain structure. The remaining marines fired at any enemy that dared to try and halt their progress. In the first minute, it looked as if they had achieved total surprise, until the troops from closer to the dome turned and counterattacked. Just a few more minutes, and both sides were bogged down in a firefight across a strip of land between the two landmarks. Captain Carlo stood nearby and was busy coordinating the snipers and sustained fire that would keep the advance party alive.

"General, 1st Platoon have control of the entrance, should they move inside?"

The General shook his head.

"No, we just need to keep them busy enough for Spartan to do his job. Tell them to secure access to the place. Send in the next platoon to move inside. We have to keep this area clear and ready for withdrawal."

Captain Carlos moved back a few metres and organised the next wave of thirty people. This group were a fifty-fifty mix of Navy crew and marines. All were armed, but the selection of weapons was variable. One thing he was aware of was the almost complete lack of heavy weapons. With just a few words, they moved out from the cover of the trees and ran the gauntlet of the Zealots' gunfire. Two were cut down, but the rest made it to the great entrance to the mountain. They slipped inside and vanished from view. The ground between the trees and the mountain was a mixture of flat terrain, rocks and low ruins from distant buildings.

"Captain, get bodies out there. We need to stop them reinforcing the mountain."

As the marines moved out, a great trembling motion shook the ground. He looked to his left and watched two of the mechanical machines move from the dome and start their inexorable course towards their position. He almost froze as the first opened fire with pintle mounted heavy weapons. They struck with the same degree of firepower as the coilguns being used by the ASOG troopers. Part of one of the buildings ripped apart and smashed a fully armoured marine to the ground.

* * *

The Biomech had been watching Spartan for almost a minute; at least he assumed that was what it was doing. The others in the group continued to pick their way through the rubble as if they were looking for something. Teresa watched from her position behind a low, badly smashed wall when she noticed where the nearest Biomech was stood.

"Oh...great! It's the package I left behind. They must have picked up its signal."

It took Spartan a few seconds before he realised what she had actually been talking about.

Right, the camera she left.

He looked to his left and out into the distance where another group of Zealots and one machine was heading in their direction. Off to the right, the firefight had now expanded from the hillside and down to the tree line as General Rivers used his troops as best as possible to demonstrate against their forces. A crackle of energy rippled down the hills and to the dome just as he'd seen on the video feed.

"Damn, that means another one of those machines is coming through," he said quietly to the rest of his team. "We need to get in there now and stop them, or they'll keep bringing in reinforcements."

He selected the channel to speak with General Rivers and was immediately greeted by the sound of gunfire and explosions.

"Spartan, what's happening there? Have you disabled the guns?"

"Not yet, Sir, it's the dome. They are bringing in more troops. If we don't stop them, they'll overrun our positions before we can finish our mission."

There was a short pause before the General came back.

"I have a platoon inside, along with a tech team, and they think it's possible to isolate the tracking system by knocking out one of the power generators near the base of the mountain. They have already hit resistance inside, but they think it's possible."

"How?" Spartan asked.

"The tracking station is on the other side of this hill. When they take out the targeting unit, they will only be able to manually attack the guns, so it will make them all but useless. If I do this, it means I'll need to keep this area clear of the enemy while they do their job."

"They are already moving in on you, Sir. Don't forget, you're already carrying out the diversion."

Teresa crawled over to him and tapped him on the helmet.

"If we hit the orb, I bet they will turn back to fight us."

Spartan looked at her, but he already knew she was right. The orb was clearly the single most important part of this compound, and when they initiated an attack, the enemy would surely throw everything they had at them.

Damn, we've done this the wrong way around!

"Okay, General. We will assault the orb and draw as many of them onto us as possible. If you can spare any troops, send them through the woods to reinforce us."

There was a short crackle but no response from the General. Spartan wanted to wait, but the Biomechs were still there, and one had found Teresa's equipment. With one quick movement, it ripped the unit from the ground and held it aloft.

"Now!" he shouted and lifted himself from the rubble. Khan was up already, and without even bothering to shoot, he rushed the nearest of the enemy. The two creatures collided with a loud crunch. Spartan took a step forward and blasted the Biomech to the left with a burst from each of his arms. The L48 rifles tore chunks from the creature's armour and flesh, but it still took nearly twenty of them to bring it down. The rest of the unit spread out but kept low, firing short bursts from their weapons and made short work of the last two. Khan straightened his back and roared at the sight of his defeated foe. He ripped the large firearm from its arms and pushed on to the orb.

"Get to the dome and secure it, fast!" shouted Spartan.

It was an incredibly risky stratagem, as the dome was situated in the heart of the compound. The only good thing was that most of the machines, zealots and Biomechs had already left to do battle with the forces of General Rivers. But two machines remained as well as nearly thirty Zealots. Spartan ran forward and was amongst them while they tried to organise themselves. Bullets rained down on his armour, but he did his best to ignore them and smashed through three of them to reach the first machine. Two of his Vanguards came with him, taking full advantage of the thick armour and heavy weapons to clear a path to the orb.

"Spartan!" shouted Khan, and instinctively, he turned to spot a Biomech swinging a glaive at his head. He lurched to the side, but the blade still scraped down his armour and embedded in a shoulder joint, luckily causing no damage. He lifted his left arm, only to find it grabbed by the four–legged machine. It was at least twice his height, and the side-mounted guns were already tracking towards him. Khan leapt onto the Biomech and dragged it down, finally freeing him to twist one of them into the line of fire.

"Bring it down!" he shouted.

The other two Vanguards moved around the machine and fired and stabbed with their razor sharp blades fitted to their arms. The machine was tough, and it took a dozen high-power rounds from the ASOG troopers to finally bring it down. The last machine forced itself on the group and managed to crush two of its own Zealots, and it made for Spartan. He lifted up his arms to fire, but it was then that he spotted more than thirty of the smaller eight-legged spider-like machines Teresa had described. They must have been hidden in the rubble behind the dome, and they threw themselves into the small group with savage abandon, hacking down marines and Zealots at will.

"Captain, the guns!" called out Kowalski on the intercom.

Spartan looked up to see one of the massive gun batteries turning on its raised platform and start tracking something up in the sky. His attention was pulled away as one of the smaller machines appeared next to the even larger machine and stabbed at him, managing to embed one of its razor sharp blades into his visor. As the sensors flashed with warnings, he looked to his right to see Khan down on one knee but still hacking and shooting with his looted Biomech weapon. The marines were putting up a hell of a fight, but already they were outnumbered and still thirty metres from their objective. He lurched to the side and fired a long burst of gunfire at the smaller machine, watching two of its arms ripped off.

"Yeah!" he shouted and lifted his arm to fire at the gun battery. He was only able to let loose four ineffectual shots before he was forced to duck and avoid another strike.

Damn it! Guns won't bring down those things.

* * *

Admiral Churchill waited with the patience of a saint as the crew ran through a detailed scan of the surface. It was risky, but the warning signs had been there the second they arrived in orbit. Scrambled radio signals and heat blooms flashed around a small mountainous area on the ground. His gut instinct told him it was a fight of some kind, and if Spartan was alive, he was convinced the man would be right in the middle of it.

"Well, what have we got?" he asked impatiently.

His XO was stood near the tactical officer, double-checking all the information that was coming in.

"Sir, you're right. It's definitely a ground battle."

The warning alarms started up inside the ship. It was the vessel's automated countermeasures system.

"Incoming fire, it's the ground batteries," called out the tactical officer.

Admiral Churchill pulled the intercom from its mount and took a short breath before speaking. He knew this was the fight every single one of them was dreading. All he could do was promise himself that this time it would be different.

"This is Admiral Churchill. Commence ground

operations. All ships prepare for bombardments. I want every gun, missile, decoy and fighter between us, and those weapons. We will lose no ships today!"

It was a short order, but the words galvanised the fleet into action. Every man and woman was ready, and it took just seconds for the first of the shuttles and landing craft to launch from the hull of the Santa Cruz and begin their descent to the ground battle. Even as the first two projectiles hurtled up from the ground, a dozen drones and fighters were moving in on an intercept course. Every single railgun and missile system in the fleet trained in on the approaching projectiles and waited to fire.

* * *

Somehow Spartan and just over half of his team had survived and beaten back the bloody assault around the orb. It was already starting to glow, however, and more and more enemy troops were appearing from the bases of the other hills and from inside the many ruined buildings. A quick glance told him they faced seven of the large machines, up to fifty of the smaller ones, and an untold number of the Biomechs and Zealots. He was starting to think the attack on the dome was perhaps not his most tactically astute of ideas in the last few years.

"Everybody get to the dome, and find any cover you can!" he barked.

The small group covered the ground quickly and placed their wounded behind whatever shattered walls and rubble they could find. At this distance, it was clear the dome was much bigger than any of them had suspected. He moved inside and lifted his visor so that he could see past the four large cracks now obscuring his vision. Teresa took up cover behind one of the largest columns and turned around to watch the approach of the enemy reinforcements. Spartan tried to contact the General, but once more he was greeted with static. He looked inside the dome and was surprised to see banks of computer panels. Two men, both Zealots, completely ignored him and tapped a series of buttons in a separate rush. Spartan wasn't sure what they were doing, but he was sure it wasn't good.

"Get back!" he roared.

Both ignored him, and Khan staggered towards them, leaving a trail of blood from a vicious looking leg wound. He grabbed the first man around the throat and hurled him at the wall. The second tried to run, but he lifted his Biomech firearm and sent a single deadly shot into the man's back. Whatever technology lay behind the weapon was uncertain, but the Zealot was smashed to the floor in a pool of blood. Khan turned back and grinned at Spartan. He respirator was off and blood ran down his cheek.

"You crazy bastard!" laughed Spartan. "You can breathe okay down here?"

Khan nodded, evidently amused that Spartan found it

difficult. Kowalski had already moved inside, along with one of the techs from the Santa Cruz. They examined the displays and started to work through the screen of data.

"I can't believe this," said Kowalski as he brought up a map of dots.

Spartan leaned in to look, but Sergeant Lovett was waving off to the right. He moved to the gap where he was kneeling and looked out. There were now hundreds of the enemy, and all of them assembling around the dome, but so far none of them had attacked them directly. He looked over to his left and could see the firefight still going on around the hill.

What are they waiting for?

"They're mobilising for a push, I think," said the Sergeant.

Spartan wasn't so sure. It was obvious to him that half of their number would be enough to stop them. There was simply no logical reason for them to just wait around and watch them disable the dome.

"Watch your zones, they will attack soon. Hit the fastest ones first, buy us all the time you can."

He then turned back to Kowalski who was still working through screen of data.

"Well, what is it, and can you stop more of them coming through?" he asked.

"I can't tell you what it is, but I can tell you it is an entrance to somewhere. This map is a list of destinations."

"Like an elevator?" suggested Spartan.

"Maybe. Anyway, I can't shut it down from here. Those two bastards have already locked us out. It has to be configured from the other side."

Spartan looked less than impressed.

"You're kidding?"

Kowalski looked back to him.

"With enough time, I might be able to hack this."

A loud mechanical scream came from the horde of Zealots, machines and Biomechs that were waiting outside. The Zealots began chanting. It was something Spartan hadn't heard before, but there had been rumours of something similar in the fighting on Euryale prior to the arrival of the relief marines. Spartan checked his ammunition counters and was mortified to see he was down to only a quarter of what he had started with.

"Wait for it!" he called, now expecting the worst. Instead, the sound of General Rivers greeted him on his suit's intercom.

"Spartan, the guns are going down any second!" His voice was muffled, and it sounded as if he must be inside the hill, as well as Captain Carlos. A loud bang came from the side of the dome, and he leaned out to spot streaks of blue electricity flashing at different points along the side of the hill. They were quickly followed by ripples from a dozen small explosions coming from inside.

"What's that?" shouted Teresa.

"The guns, they should be down!" replied Spartan.

"Like it's going to make much difference. Look," said Khan with an arm extended out and to the open space around them. The mass of hostile forces had broken into a run, and it would be just seconds before they crashed into the small band of defenders.

Gods, we'll never hold this place!

Spartan lifted both of his arms and opened fire, along with the rest of the unit. The skill, accuracy and combined firepower of the unit were impressive. At the front were the smaller machines, and it took a good number of rounds to bring each one down. Every few seconds a substantial blast from the ASOG's coilguns ripped holes through their lines. Even so, scores of them continued forward.

"If we get out of this, I'm gonna push for artillery support!" shouted Sergeant Lovett.

Yeah, do that!

"Why aren't they firing?" asked Teresa.

Spartan didn't have time to respond, but he suspected they were loath to damage the structure. The nearest machine made it to one of the many openings at the base of the dome and pushed inside. Spartan blocked its way and slammed the tip of his left fist into the centre of its torso. With a flash, it shuddered and dropped to the ground. Two Zealots came in from behind and hit his legs with rifle fire, setting off more internal alarms. A quick burst of fire from Teresa dealt with them, but it wouldn't be enough.

"What's the plan, Captain? We're going to get overrun down here!" cried Kowalski.

Spartan hacked and stabbed as he did his best to stop anything coming in through the gap between the pillars. The other Vanguards did the same, using their bulk and armour to shore up the ways in while the ASOG troopers and marines filled in the gaps. For a second, Spartan was hopeful, but the movement on the other hills brought him back to earth. He could see swarms of the machines coming out like bugs leaving a nest. Behind him the orb started to glow, and a high intensity buzzing sound rippled through the dome. Spartan turned for a second and caught Kowalski's gaze.

"Spartan! We need to go through and shut it down on the other side!" he screamed.

He took a step backwards, but two Biomechs forced their way up to him and reached in to strike him. Khan leapt in and attacked them with a glaive from one of the fallen creatures. Spartan wanted to stay and help his friend, but he knew the orb would allow even more of them to arrive. He spun around and moved to the light. Kowalski grabbed one of the rucksacks and jumped inside. With a white flash, he vanished from view.

"Kowalski, can you read me?" he called out, but the intercom was silent apart from the continuing garbled messages running through the battle. He looked back one last time to see the sight of his tiny unit fighting off the overwhelming sea of machines and flesh. Gunfire, grenades and blades flashed, yet somehow they were holding. The larger and slower four-legged machines were still clanking forward, and he knew just one of those would be able to crush them. He turned back to the orb and stepped closer, only to see the shape of a group of Zealots facing him in what looked like a mirror. He jumped at them, but instead fell through the orb and into a dark, grimly lit cavern. He staggered, and only the quick thinking Kowalski stopped him from crashing into the floor.

"Where the hell are we?" he asked.

Kowalski shook his head.

"No idea, but the gravity is slightly higher, and the air composition is different."

Spartan was confused, but he quickly remembered the Zealots. He spun around, but there was nothing behind him except the glowing orb.

"Yeah, they jumped through as we came in. They'll be fighting our people already, so we don't have much time."

Spartan looked inside the place they had just arrived in. It was a wide cavern, easily large enough to fit a small ship inside of. It felt slightly damp, and the temperature was colder than the place he had just left. Kowalski was already checking a series of computer displays, but Spartan wanted information. He stepped further away from the orb and looked out into the depths of the cavern. He could see lines and lines of shapes, and each of them at equal distances apart and lined up like soldiers on parade. Every hundred metres or so was a much larger shape that reminded him of something. Then one of them moved, and he instantly recognised it as one of the four-legged machines.

"What?" he muttered inside his suit.

Kowalski heard him and turned around to see the great horde of thousands of machines moving as if they had just awoken. On a ledge, perhaps two hundred metres away, were a group of figures that were animated and pointing back down to him and Spartan.

"Uh, I think we should get going!" he said and then moved back to the computers.

Spartan continued watching the shapes and tapped the mission recorder on his suit to collect a record of everything he could see. Out in the middle of the hall, hundreds of metres away was an even larger shape; like that of a Biomech, but slowly lifting to a height of incredible proportions. It started off as just a few metres but then increased to more than ten and continued upwards. It stretched out its arms like some kind of foul metal demon.

"Uh, Kowalski. Can you shut it down?" he asked nervously.

"I need a few more minutes. The security on this thing is insane. I think it is locked down on our location back on the surface."

Spartan shook his head at the shape of the monstrous machine as it finished taking shape. It reminded him of some sickening combination of a Biomech, machine and the half woman, half serpent icon of Echidna he had seen on so many Zealots before. Around its feet ran scores of people, all of them hooded and chanting.

No way, it can't be?

He looked back to Kowalski.

"Forget it, we need to shut this thing down. Help me set the charges, then we get the hell out of this place!"

* * *

The first two assaults had been driven back with heavy casualties. General Rivers had now deployed all of his reserves to the ground around the entrance of the hill. Those inside were already working their way back out but were being harassed by an almost limitless number of the enemy. He and his small squad of marine guards moved from the tree line and into the cover offered by the ruins. Off into the distance, he could make out the hundreds of enemies that appeared to be besieging the dome.

Spartan surely cannot succeed amongst all that?

Another wave of Zealots and machines moved to attack his own position, and the dozens of defenders did their best to hold them off with gunfire. He couldn't fail to notice the horde of enemy forces moving from the others hill. They could be no more than a few minutes away, and deep down he knew he couldn't hold them back.

Should we fall back to the jungle?

His thoughts were interrupted by a familiar voice from the entrance to the hill. It instantly grabbed his attention, and he twisted his head to see Captain Carlos and two of the Terra Nova soldiers appear. All three were covered in filth and blood, but at least they had managed to shutdown the tracking hardware. They leapt from the cover and ran the short distance to where he and his forces were dug in. From the hill emerged more of their unit.

"Some of you made it back, then?" he asked grudgingly.

"Sir. Oh, and General, we've brought friends!" said the Captain, and he slumped down near the General and lifted his rifle.

From out of the hill emerged the remainder of the Captain's unit, but behind them followed small groups of people. Some wore civilian clothing, others rags. But the majority wore old military uniforms. He recognised a few as Alliance Navy, but a large group were Confederate militia from Avagana, the colony back on Prime. Most were carrying captured weapons, and every one of them was out for revenge. They poured out into the ruins and rubble around the mountain's base and joined the defenders in the battle.

"Excellent work, son, damn fine piece of soldiering."

He looked back to the enemy, and his smile vanished

at the sight of three of the four-legged machines plus hundreds of smaller ones and a similar number of Biomechs. They'd regrouped and were rushing across the open ground.

So the Zealots are the junior partners here.

A volley of rockets from near the rear of their formation whistled overhead and exploded in the tree line.

"Hold them back! Don't let them break through!" he shouted.

Two bright lights flashed from the nearest of the huge machines, and streams of heavy cannon rounds smashed around the General and his entourage. Two marines were shredded by the firepower, and the blast itself blew him out from his cover and against a low wall.

"General!" cried out of his surviving guards, but he was also cut to ribbons by repeated gunfire from the approaching enemy.

Flashes ripped through General Rivers' PDS suit as the incendiary rounds fired by the enemy tore into the plating. His helmet and visor were badly scorched and cracked but not enough to stop him spotting the movement in the jungle. Another round struck him in the shoulder and pinned him to the wall. The suit pumped drugs directly into his bloodstream as well as flooding the interior with a gas based clotting agent. With a supreme effort, he lifted himself up to a seating position and drew the secondary sidearm from the mounting on his leg. It was nothing more than the marine issue pistol, but it kept him in the fight.

"Stop them!" shouted an unseen marine before four Biomechs stormed through the frontline and into their defences. He took aim at the closest and squeezed the trigger. In a blur, a shape leapt from the jungle and smashed into the flank of the Biomech. He shook his head, but his vision was already fading out from blood loss. He strained his eyes once more but couldn't believe what he was seeing.

Biomechs...on our side?

* * *

Kowalski was almost finished setting the thermite charges around the supporting pillars and walls surrounding the orb. Spartan had wanted to destroy the computers, but Kowalski's suggestion was to try and barricade the entire area off while causing more substantial damage. The charges themselves were highly powerful and capable of burning through even the toughest armour or structures. He had taken up position behind one of the pillars in the hope of avoiding being spotted, but it was pointless. They must have been seen on their way in, and the group on the higher ledge were still busy talking. From down below, the legions of the enemy were moving towards where he and Kowalski waited.

"Come on, man, they'll be here in half a minute!"

Kowalski connected one last part to the bomb and hit the timer sequence. It started counting down as soon as he released his finger.

"Okay, done, let's get out of here!"

The two moved to the orb and not a moment too soon. A great roar like that of a screaming banshee echoed through the chamber, and each of the creatures and machines paused as the large mechanical monster lifted itself out from the lower level and towards the orb. Simultaneously, the power surging into the glowing ball increased, and the size of the orb doubled in an instant.

"Stop them!" screamed the man up on the ledge.

"Pontus, you asshole!" shouted Spartan, and he loosed off a short burst at the man before Kowalski pushed him into the orb. His last view was of the rounds smashing around the men, but he had no idea what was going on, or if he had hit any of them. As quickly as they had arrived, and he was back in the moist, blood soaked interior of the dome. It was like a scene from hell itself as marines, Biomechs, Vanguards and even unarmed civilians fought at close range. Bodies littered the site, and he had barely any idea who was friend or foe.

"Watch it!" shouted Kowalski as a blade slammed into Spartan's helmet and added yet another large crack in the thickened glass. He lifted up his armoured arms just like a boxer that was covering up in a fight and deflected as many blows as he possibly could.

"This is Captain Spartan to all Alliance forces. The dome is about to blow. Fall back to the tree line. I repeat, all Alliance forces withdrawal, now!"

He charged at the nearest group of machines, and the small number of survivors inside joined him in one desperate charge from out of the complex. He spotted Khan and a group of a dozen Biomechs hacking and stabbing at one of the four-legged machines they had somehow tipped onto its side while marines fired at a distant group of Zealots who were falling back to the cover of the ruins. A small group of marines were pinned down near the outside of the dome by the gunfire of the last remaining upright machine. Its heavy pintle mounted guns blasted at them and kept them down. One of them was Teresa.

"Everybody out! It's going to blow!" screamed Spartan through both his intercom and the fitted loudhailers on his Vanguard suit. Most of those that could move were already falling back, but the vicious melee made coordinated action almost impossible. He turned back and hacked his way through anybody or any thing that stood in his path. That was when the roof of the dome stated to lift, and the enemy reinforcements rushed out like water falling over a cliff. Even as the stream of machines and Biomechs turned the tide against them, a much more terrifying threat appeared. The great mechanical beast, the very essence and form of Echidna herself filled the light with its darkened silhouette.

CHAPTER FIFTEEN

*The new colonies of Epsilon Eridani, Gliese 876 and Procyon
became part of the first wave of colonial expansion following
the end of the War. With the resources of the newly founded
Alliance, and the technological leaps brought about from that
war, these new colonies would increase the wealth, population
and importance of the more remote parts of the Alliance.
The five star systems would become the core of humanity's
greatest empire in history.*

The New Colonies

Spartan reached the pinned down marines at the same time
as a large calibre projectile slammed into his armoured leg
and jammed the knee joint. He twisted and fell, landing
just three metres from Teresa and the handful of their
team still remaining. He tried to call out to her, but most
of his systems were now failing. With the electronics gone,

he lost the ability to use the communications or mechanics of the suit. He punched the eject button, and with a hiss the suit opened up like a clam. He stumbled forward and dropped to the floor. Without the protection of the suit, he was left with his Alliance overalls and thin body armour as used by most crew. His only weapon was his pistol, which he pulled out and raised to face the machine.

"Fall back!" shouted Captain Carlos as he broke from cover and led a party of about a dozen marines towards the jungle tree line. Lines of yellow and white tracers hit around them, and at least three rounds struck the Captain before an explosion threw him through the air and to the ground. His team tried to pull him to safety, but two more casualties forced them to break and run.

"Spartan!" called out a bloodied and wounded Teresa.

A line of bullet impacts marked the armour on her right leg, and blood covered her chest and left arm. He took careful aim at the machine, pulled the trigger, only for the entire machine to explode and spread shards of debris across the battlefield. A flight of Alliance Lightning MKII fighters passed overhead and split up to circle over the battlefield. Right behind them came six shuttles, and behind them another two landing craft, and all of them heading for the open ground near the wounded General Rivers.

"Keep your head down, Spartan!" shouted Kowalski even though he couldn't see the marine anywhere near him.

He threw himself as low as he could and put his arm over his face to protect himself from flying debris. A massive blast ripped the ground behind them, and he twisted around to see the bright flash around the orb and the huge mechanical machine moving through. Flames and blue flashes ripped from all directions, and then as quickly as it started, the dome structure vanished below a heap of dust and rubble. Another shuttle swept down and landed a little closer, but a rocket struck it as it landed. Luckily, the impact did little more than blow a metre-wide hole in its wing. The doors opened and out jumped a full squad of heavily armed and armoured Jötnar troopers.

Two more Thunderbolts strafed the ground and created a path of destruction in the enemy ranks so that one of the large landing craft could land. Even as it moved in, the many door gunner mounts fired at anybody foolish enough to stay near. The loading ramps dropped down and scores of Alliance marines charged out, and each keen for action, itching to bring down the enemy as fast as possible.

As the battle raged, Spartan pulled himself closer to Teresa and pulled open her visor. Her face was anguished, but she was conscious and her face still had colour.

"How are you?" he asked, trying his best to not sound too worried.

Another landing craft came down and disgorged scores

more troops into the fray. With the dome destroyed, the surviving machines slowed and shutdown one at a time until the only enemy forces remaining were the Biomechs and the Zealots. A small group of Zealots broke from the battle and charged at the fallen ASOG troopers. Spartan turned his handgun onto the first, but it took all of his remaining ammunition to bring him to the ground. Six more almost made it before Ko'mandor Gun and his retinue of Jötnar cut them apart with a long burst of gunfire. The leader of the creatures nodded to Spartan and then moved over to Khan who was busy hacking down a large group of enemy Biomechs who refused to retreat.

"I need a rest," muttered Spartan as he pulled himself up next to Teresa and watched Major Daniels' reinforcements mop up the last survivors. It was short and bloody, but in just a few minutes, the enemy were in full retreat and rushing to the hills or the jungle to escape.

* * *

"Are you ready?" asked Major Daniels as he looked at Teresa and Spartan. Both of them wore their off-duty fatigues as well as a number of low profile bandages over their numerous light wounds. It was a far cry from the battered and smashed armour they had been wearing a week earlier. She looked at him and smiled. Stood beside them was Kowalski, who somehow had managed to avoid any serious injury.

"Come on, then," he said and then stepped inside the main briefing room of ANS Santa Cruz. Scores of Alliance crew and civilians were packed inside and waiting patiently for them to enter. At the far end, he spotted General Rivers, as well as Major Daniels and a small group of Jötnar. They moved down the narrow strip and were followed by a small band of the other injured as they made their way down the podium. Spartan saw Sergeant Lovett to his right where he waited with his fiancée. Other faces he recognised, but there were many from colonies and ships he'd never taken a step aboard before. The audience brought their hands together as they reached the halfway mark. It was the first such ceremony Spartan had attended, and even after all his battles, it seemed odd to be there.

"I introduce to you the leaders of our newly formed Alliance Special Operations Group under the command of Major Daniels. These elite teams have been at the forefront of our continuing battle against those that seek to destroy our way of life."

Major Daniels reached the podium first and moved up the steps to stand next to the assembled senior commanders. Admiral Churchill was present, along with a number of the ship commanders from the rest of the Taskforce. Admiral Churchill and General Rivers both shook his hand before indicating for him to take up his spot. Spartan and Teresa, on the other hand, were moved to the side where everybody could see them. General Rivers nodded to them both and then looked to the crowd.

"Captain Spartan and Sergeant Morato epitomise the skill, bravery and sacrifice of all those that have fought for our freedoms in the last years. They both joined the Marine Corps under unusual circumstances, and yet have become masters in their own right. After scores of battles and combat on a dozen worlds, they made it here and working in different fleets. Their actions on Hyperion, and those of the men and women that worked alongside them, have brought honour to the Alliance. He stepped forward and pinned a star shaped medal on the chest of each of them.

"These medals were the last of the Confederate Marine Corps medals to be cast before the start of the War, and I am proud to award them to two of our most important marines."

He waited for a little while longer before adding one last point.

"I know both of you will argue, but this comes right from the top. The two of you will be taking a much-needed break from the military. You are granted a month's leave, and the requirement to continue your enlistment is hereby revoked. If you stay, it will be as volunteers."

While the crowd cheered, he saluted them both and indicated for Ko'mandor Gun to step closer. The Jötnar leader looked a little uncertain at the attention.

"Commander," he started. "I was going to inform you of this news in private, but I think everybody here would like to hear it. I have received word from the Senate back on Terra Nova, regarding the status of Biomechs and Jötnar in the Alliance."

He pulled out a datapad and held it in front of him to speak.

"As of eighteen-hundred hours today, Terra Nova Time, the Jötnar have been granted full and equal citizenship in the Alliance."

The hall burst into shouts and applause, much to the surprise of the officers waiting around the podium. Gun himself seemed staggered by the announcement and took several seconds before lifting his right arm in the air and shouting to the ceiling.

"It would appear that videofeeds of the battle at the dome have been distributed throughout the Alliance by sources unknown in our fleet."

He looked about, but it was clear he favoured the leak.

I bet it was you. Spartan thought wryly as he watched the General.

"Oh, and there is one other thing. The world of Hyperion is not an easy place to live. It is dangerous, has a painful environment for most of us, and is still the home to a large number of escaped Zealots and indoctrinated Biomechs. You have been offered the world as a homeland, if you wish it. This is being offered to you partly in recognition of your great achievements, but also your great sacrifices on behalf of the Alliance."

The cheering started again, and Spartan stepped up to his old friend and grabbed his arm. The two looked out to the assembled troops and civilians, and for the first time there were joyous faces on those looking into the eyes of the synthetic creatures, assembled and training on the fire world of Prometheus. Spartan smiled at the good news but deep down he felt uneasy.

Why do I think the Jötnar are being given Hyperion to act as sentries in case those things manage to find a way back to that orb?

Teresa looked to him while the others continued to celebrate. She leaned over a few inches and spoke into his ear.

"Vacation? Where do you want to go?"

Spartan looked at her and smiled. It seemed like it had been years, perhaps decades, since he'd had free time where had absolutely nothing to do. For the first time he looked ahead to the future, and there was nothing in front of him that had to be done. For others that might have sounded wonderful, to Spartan though it was the exact opposite. Teresa looked at him and recognised the confusion and wanderlust she'd seen in his eyes many times before. He could see she was waiting patiently for an answer.

"Well, I suppose we could spend some time on Terra Nova. It's supposed to be the oldest and most refined place in the Alliance."

Teresa cocked her head slightly in amusement.

"You, sightseeing on Terra Nova? I was thinking of something a little more adventurous, but I would like to spend some time with our son and my family. I've already spoken to Major Daniels about that, and he says he will do his best to arrange for them to visit us as soon as possible."

Gun heard their conversation and stepped towards them, placing his bulk in the way of their conversation. He looked at each of them.

"I'm planning on setting up hunting parties back on Hyperion. There are still a few religious maniacs and wild Biomechs that need taming. Interested?"

Spartan's face seemed to light up at the news, and Teresa new instantly that their vacation was going to consist of hiding out in a mud-infested jungle filled with things that wanted to kill them. She smiled back at him.

"I wouldn't have it any other way!"

* * *

Agent Johnson and two of his fellow interrogators from Kerberos looked back at the prisoner strapped to the table. The room was darkly lit, and on one side was a glossy wall that hid a two-way mirror behind which sat a dozen intelligence officers. He looked back to the man on the table and glanced at the scars on his cheek.

"I've already told you we know who you are, Chraige

Attez. Your brother Typhon died on this very world, and your other brother, Pontus, is dead on Hyperion. Now tell me, why did we find workers from the Bone Mill amongst the dead at your compound on Hyperion?"

The man looked back at him with nothing but hate and contempt on his face.

"I see, you think that look scares me?"

Chraige Attez coughed and then smiled at Agent Johnson.

"You think you've won? This is nothing. Echidna has woken, and she will return. Nothing can stop her."

Agent Johnson moved away and tapped a button to bring up a large image of the ruins on Hyperion, specifically the crater that was all that remained of the dome and the orb. Unexpectedly, there was no chamber of elevator around it. Next to the image he brought up the shape of the Anomaly, the great Spacebridge discovered towards the end of the War. Lastly, he brought up the devastated underground facility on Prime that had marked the start of the War. He looked at it for a short while before turning back to Chraige Attez.

"Your great saviour, the mechanical beast that tried to come through that dome, is gone. What I want to know is what links the now ruined sites on these colonies and the Spacebridge here?"

Chraige Attez laughed at him, enjoying the man's apparent confusion.

"They are nothing!" he spat out, "Echidna can travel wherever she wants, in space or on the ground, and when she returns, you will all pay, every single one of you!"

Agent Johnson looked at the reflective mirror surface and raised an eyebrow before looking back to the prisoner. He walked back and continued his discussion. On the other side of the glass, the assembled men and women checked the information Agent Johnson and a dozen other intelligence assets had pooled together so far. Each of them wore dark, non-descript uniforms, and the classic mark of the military intelligence division. One woman, a tall, pale skinned woman nodded and tapped a button that brought up a live feed. It was Commander Anderson, the man in charge of Prometheus. The world housed factories, research labs and shipyards that had been reclaimed from the defeated enemy.

"Commander. We have confirmed the materials used at the three sites match the configuration of the artefact you have uncovered on Prometheus. Continue your excavation."

There was a pause of several minutes while the group waited for the signal to be sent through the Spacebridge and then to Prometheus and back again. Commander Anderson looked as though he had heard nothing before finally speaking back to them.

"Understood. Based on my research, it would appear these sites are designed to operate as rifts much like the

Anomaly itself. If we can get them working, my scientists believe they can recreate a small rift between two fixed points."

The intelligence operative looked to her comrades who nodded in agreement.

"Agreed. Continue with your work, Commander, we will be in touch."